# ELIZABETH
## CEC

Lady Germaine Elizabeth Olive Eliot was born in London on 13 April 1911, the daughter of Montague Charles Eliot, the 8th Earl of St Germans, and Helen Agnes Post.

She twice married—first to Major Thomas James in 1932, then to Captain Hon. Kenneth George Kinnaird, the 12th Baron Kinnaird, in 1950. Both marriages ended in divorce. She apparently applied for American citizenship in 1971. She published five novels, the first of which, *Alice* (1949), was a Book Society Choice. Her non-fiction *Heiresses and Coronets* (1960, aka *They All Married Well*), about prominent marriages between wealthy Americans and titled Europeans in the late Victorian and Edwardian period, was a success on both sides of the Atlantic.

Elizabeth Eliot died in New York in 1991.

# WORKS BY ELIZABETH ELIOT

## Fiction

*Alice* (1949)*
*Henry* (1950)*
*Mrs Martell* (1953)*
*Starter's Orders* (1955)
*Cecil* (1962)*

## Non-fiction

*Portrait of a Sport: A History of Steeplechasing* (1957)
*Heiresses and Coronets* (1960, aka *They All Married Well*)

*available from Furrowed Middlebrow/Dean Street Press*

# ELIZABETH ELIOT

## CECIL

With an introduction by
Elizabeth Crawford

DEAN STREET PRESS

*A Furrowed Middlebrow Book*
FM29

Published by Dean Street Press 2019

Copyright © 1962 Elizabeth Eliot

Introduction © 2019 Elizabeth Crawford

All Rights Reserved

Published by licence, issued under the UK Orphan Works Licensing Scheme.

First published in 1962 by Cassell & Co.

Cover by DSP

ISBN 978 1 912574 65 0

www.deanstreetpress.co.uk

For my Mother

# INTRODUCTION

REVIEWING Elizabeth Eliot's debut novel, *Alice*, for the *Sunday Times*, C.P. Snow noted in the author 'an astringent sympathy, a knowledge from bitter experience that life is not easy' while the *Times Literary Supplement* review of her second novel, *Henry*, mentioned her 'light-heartedness, delicious wit and humanity lurking beneath the surface'. Comparisons were drawn with the work of Nancy Mitford and Elizabeth von Arnim, although Snow observed that 'Alice was set in the world of the high aristocracy, loftier, though less smart, than the world of Miss Mitford's "Hons"'. This 'high aristocracy' was, indeed, the world into which, on 13 April 1911, Germaine Elizabeth Olive Eliot was born, her birth registered only as 'Female Eliot'. Time was obviously required to select her full complement of names, but by the time she was christened decisions had been made. 'Germaine' does not appear to have been a family name, although it echoes that of the earldom – St Germans – of which, at that time, her great uncle, Henry Cornwallis Eliot, the 5th earl, was the holder. 'Elizabeth' was the name of her maternal grandmother, Elizabeth Wadsworth, whose grandfather, General James Wadsworth, had been military governor of Washington during the American Civil War. Transatlantic connections were to prove important to this 'Female Eliot'. No hint of an 'Olive' appears in either her paternal or maternal line, so that may have been a mere parental indulgence. Of these three forenames 'Elizabeth' was the one by which the future author was known.

At the time of Elizabeth's birth her parents were living in Marylebone, London, the census, taken just ten days previously, giving us a glimpse into the household. At its head was her 40-year-old father, Montague Charles Eliot, who, with a script replete with flourishes, completed the form, listing also her 26-year-old American mother, Helen Agnes; a butler; a lady's maid; a cook; two housemaids; and a hall boy. Doubtless a few days later a nursemaid would have taken up her position in the nursery. Montague (1870-1960) and Helen (c.1885-1962) had married the previous June. Helen (or 'Nellie' as she was known), although American-born and of American parentage, had, in fact, spent most of her life in the United Kingdom. Her father had died when she was four-years-old and her mother had then married Arthur Smith-Barry, later Baron Barrymore of Fota House, near Cork, Ireland. As Elizabeth Eliot's novels reveal a knowledge of Irish estates and relations, she probably had on occasion visited Fota.

In the newspaper reports of his marriage no mention was made of Montague Eliot's connection to the St Germans earldom, so far was he at that time from inheriting. However, tragedy has long hovered around the St Germans family and in 1922 the death in a riding accident of the 6th Earl meant the title and estate passed to Montague Eliot's elder, unmarried and childless brother. On his death in 1942 Montague Eliot became the 8th Earl of St Germans and his daughter Elizabeth acquired the title of 'Lady'. Montague Eliot had joined King Edward VII's household in 1901 and at the time of Elizabeth's birth was Gentleman Usher to George V, later becoming Groom of the Robes. He held the latter unpaid position until 1936 and from 1952 until his death was Extra Groom-in-Waiting to Elizabeth II.

The 8th Earl's heir was Elizabeth's brother, Nicholas (1914-88) and the family was completed after a long interval with the birth of another son, Montague Robert Vere Eliot (1923-94). Around this time Elizabeth and her family moved to 111 Gloucester Place, a tall house, one of a long terrace on a canyon of a road that runs north-south through Marylebone.

While it is on record that her brothers were sent to Eton, we know nothing of Elizabeth's education. Was she taught at home by a governess; or did she attend a London day school, or an establishment such as 'Groom Place', where we first meet the two young women in *Alice*, or 'Mrs Martell's 'inexpensive but good school on the south coast of England'? Elizabeth's mother, certainly, had had a governess, 70-year-old Miss Dinah Thoreau, who took rat poison in December 1934 and killed herself in her room in Paddington. Lack of money was not a problem for the Eliots, unlike the Pallisers, whose daughter, Anne, narrator of *Henry*, remarks that her family had been 'too poor for my sister or me to be properly educated (although Henry, of course, had been sent to Harrow)'. Naturally boys had to go to school in order 'to have a good answer when people asked where they had been at school. That was why Henry had been sent to Harrow.' The fact that the young women in her novels invariably received an education inferior to their brothers may indicate that Elizabeth did indeed feel that she had not been 'properly educated'. Whatever the reality, a review of the US edition of *Alice* revealed that Elizabeth 'Like many authors, has been writing since she was 10'.

Nor do we know anything of Elizabeth's relationship with her parents. What is one to make of the fact she dedicated *Cecil*, the story of a loathsome, manipulative mother, to her own mother? What is one to make of the tantalising information contained in the publisher's blurb for *Cecil* that the book is 'based on fact'? Which strand of *Cecil*'s plot might have been developed from a factual base? For the novel, quite apart from placing a 'veritable ogress' of a mother centre stage, also deals with drug-taking, murder, and impotency. *Cecil* was published in November 1962, a couple of months after Nellie Eliot, Dowager Countess of St Germans, committed suicide in a hotel room in Gibraltar, having arrived the day before from Tangier where she had been visiting her son Vere. Whatever their real-life relationship it is fair to say that in Elizabeth Eliot's novels mothers tend to be seen in a somewhat negative light, while fathers are noticeable by their absence.

In 1922 the elevation to the earldom of St Germans of her unmarried uncle brought significant changes to Elizabeth Eliot and her family, with visits to Port Eliot becoming more frequent. In 1926 Elizabeth had the honour of opening the St Germans parish fête, held in the grounds of Port Eliot, and made, according to the *Western Morning News*, 'an effective and amusing speech'. Port Eliot, an ancient house, shaped and reshaped over the centuries, is so extensive that, its guidebook confesses, not once in living memory has the roof been completely watertight. If not so ancient, similarly large houses, often in the west-country and sometimes decaying, certainly play their part in Elizabeth Eliot's novels. When Margaret, the narrator of *Alice*, visits 'Platon', Alice's Devonshire family home, she sat in 'one of the drawing rooms. There was no fire, it was bitterly cold, and everything in the room, including the chairs and sofa on which we sat, was covered with dust sheets.' 'Trelynt', the west-country home of Anne Palliser is, post-Second World War, similarly large, damp, and servantless.

Naturally Elizabeth Eliot's position in society meant that in due course she 'did the Season' as a debutante, her presence recorded at hunt and charity balls and even in a photograph on the front of *Tatler*. In *Alice*, Margaret admits that 'The basic idea was rational enough. When a girl reached marriageable age, she was introduced by her parents into adult society, where it was hoped she would meet her future husband. There are many examples of such practices in *The Golden Bough*. Only somehow by the nineteen-thirties it had all got rather silly.' Margaret is presented at court, her Uncle Henry, like Montague Eliot, being a member of the royal household, and observes that this connection 'meant that we had seats in the Throne Room, which was fun, as there was always the chance that someone would fall down. Not that one would wish it for them, but should it happen, it would be nice to see it.'

Elizabeth's 'Season' produced the desired result and in January 1932 her engagement to Thomas James (1906-76) was announced in the press on both sides of the Atlantic. The wedding took place barely two months later in St George's Hanover Square. Thomas James' father, a former MP for Bromley, was dead and his mother too ill to attend. The bishop of Norwich gave a particularly didactic address, much reproduced in press reports, stressing the seriousness of marriage. Were the words of the cleric tailored specifically for this flighty young couple?

After a honeymoon in Rio and Madeira in early 1933, delayed perhaps until after the death of Thomas James' mother, the young couple settled down to married life. Tended by five servants, they occupied the whole of 4 Montague Square, a five-storey house, five minutes' walk from the Eliot family home. In the years after the Second World War Thomas James was employed by BP, but it is not clear what his occupation was during the years he was married to Elizabeth. On the ship's manifest for their 1933 trip he is described as a 'Representative'. Was fiction imitating life when, in *Alice*, Alice and her new husband Cassius sailed to Rio where he was 'to represent a firm of motor-car engineers'? Despite both Elizabeth and dashing, Eton-educated Thomas James having family money, rumour has it that during their marriage they ran up considerable gambling debts, a contributory factor to their divorce in 1940.

On the outbreak of war in 1939 Lady Elizabeth James, now living alone in a flat in St John's Wood, was registered as an ambulance driver with the London County Council. However, nothing is known of her life during and immediately after the war until the publication of *Alice* in 1949. A few months later, in March 1950, she married the Hon. George Kinnaird at Brighton registry office. When asked by the *Daily Mail* why they had married 'in strict secrecy', Kinnaird replied 'We are both too engrossed in our work'. The *Daily Mail* then explained that 'Lady Elizabeth is authoress of Book Society choice *Alice*. Mr Kinnaird is a literary adviser.' Kinnaird was at this time attached in some capacity to the publishing firm of John Murray. This marriage ended in divorce in 1962.

For some years in the 1950s Elizabeth Eliot lived in Lambourn in Berkshire, a town renowned for its association with horse racing. This was clearly a sport close to her heart for during this period, apart from *Henry* (1950) and *Mrs. Martell* (1953), she produced two books devoted to horse racing, one, *Starter's Orders*, fiction, and the other, *Portrait of a Sport*, non-fiction. In *Henry* the narrator's much-loved but feckless brother, the eponymous Henry, is a haunter of the race track. As he observes, 'I can always reckon to make quite a bit racing, and then there's backgammon. Backgammon can be terribly paying if you go the right way about it.' Of Elizabeth's brother, thrice-married Nicholas, *The Times*'s obituarist wrote, with some circumspection, that he was 'a supporter of the Turf in his day, as owner, trainer and bookmaker'. On inheriting the title and estate on the death of his father in 1960, Nicholas Eliot, 9th Earl of St Germans, made the estate over to his young son and went into tax exile.

After her second divorce Elizabeth seems to have spent a good deal of time in New York, mingling in literary circles, and in June 1971, while living in Greenwich Village, at 290 Sixth Avenue, applied for US citizenship. Thereafter she disappears from sight until *The Times* carried a notice of her death in New York on 3 November 1991. For whatever reason, detailed facts of Elizabeth Eliot's life have become so obfuscated that even members of her own extended family have been unable to supply information. Fortunately for us, her mordant wit and powers of social observation survive, amply revealed in the four novels now reissued by Dean Street Press.

Elizabeth Crawford

## Chapter One

'But my dear Anne,' Lady Guthrie announced with all the conviction of authority, 'you must never believe anything a poltergeist tells you.'

I was perfectly prepared not to and nodded my agreement. Even if I had wished to protest I knew from experience the uselessness of trying to interrupt my husband's stepmother when in full spate on any new subject.

She and I had met for the first time twelve years before, in the summer of 1875. I had just become engaged to Charlie and in consequence she had invited me to stay. How well I remember that visit and my trepidation at the prospect of meeting Sir David and Lady Guthrie. How dreadful it would be if they didn't like me, and Charlie's description of his stepmother—very beautiful with golden hair and still in her early thirties—had not somehow been reassuring. I was to be submitted to the harsh judgment of a near-contemporary. I remember thinking, I'm afraid entirely selfishly, how unfortunate it was that Charlie's mother, by dying when he was only a few days old, had given Sir David Guthrie the opportunity—of which he availed himself eleven years later—of marrying for the second time.

The second Lady Guthrie, like her predecessor, became the mother of an only son—whom she adored. Many years after this story ends she had a collection of his letters, together with extracts from various diaries, privately printed, a proceeding which annoyed my husband exceedingly. Personally, if the thing were to be done at all, I should have made a different selection and at the very least left in some of the more candid expressions of opinion. As for instance the diary entry for 5th June 1875:

> 'North Lodge, Stanmore. Lady Anne Marsh who is going to marry Charlie arrived yesterday. She is five foot five inches tall, has fair hair and is not so pretty as Charlie said. At least that is what I think but Mama says one should not criticize.'

So that was how I appeared to the nine-year-old Cecil Guthrie.

My great joy at being reunited with Charlie after a month's separation, together with my general nervousness, contrived to put all thought of Cecil, who did not appear at luncheon on that first day, completely out of my head. Indeed I even forgot to inquire after him of Lady Guthrie, a dereliction of duty which if my mother had known of it would have made her extremely cross.

The first luncheon, at which Sir David, greatly to my relief, failed to live up to the forbidding picture painted of him by Mama, was safely negotiated. I was then granted an interval of reprieve which took the form of a solitary walk with Charlie. On our return and after I had changed I presented myself—by a kind of implied appointment—for tea in Lady Guthrie's boudoir. She and I were alone together and I had the impression that she had arranged matters in this way in order that she might look me over at her leisure.

The arrangement, of course, gave *me* ample opportunity to observe *her*. I decided that she was a good deal less worldly and also more intelligent than Mama had supposed. She was, as Charlie had said, very beautiful with a radiant complexion and her slight plumpness was decidedly becoming. Such a tendency, of course, was more admired in the seventies than—I am writing in the year 1917—it is today. She was wearing black but for whom I do not recall. No one very near to her at any rate or who had died very recently, for Charlie and I were to be married within a few weeks and there was no idea of postponing the wedding. Not that my own family could be said to be very particular as to that sort of thing, for my eldest brother, immediately he succeeded my father, had married within a week of the funeral.

Lady Guthrie and I had been talking for some time without achieving any degree of intimacy. In fact our conversation consisted almost entirely of questions—asked by Lady Guthrie— and answers hesitantly supplied by me. In the end she settled down to tell me about her own family in Ireland. As she spoke I became gradually aware that we were no longer alone in the room. Such a feeling of an unknown or hitherto unnoticed presence, is always disagreeable. I looked behind me and towards the door but from where I sat it was concealed by a screen.

Lady Guthrie, following the direction of my glance, must also have been aware of the presence or perhaps she had been expecting it, for she called out to it in her high clear voice not to be a foolish child but to come into the room properly and, as an afterthought, to shut the door behind it.

For an appreciable second or two there was complete silence, then the door which was a heavy one was shut very quietly and a little boy walked slowly round the side of the screen. The few seconds gave me time in which to imagine what Cecil would be like. I thought he would be wearing a black velvet suit and have long curls reaching to his shoulders. I visualized him as being small and thin and as resembling an infant Charles the First. The child that appeared before us was very different. He was in full Highland dress. His hair of a medium brownish colour was cut short and he was exceedingly handsome. I should have guessed him, on account of the roundness of his cheeks, to have been at least a year younger than his actual age. Having got himself into view Cecil, until prompted by Lady Guthrie, made no attempt to do anything further.

'Darling, come and be introduced to your new sister.' An encircling arm was held out to him and he came and stood in its shelter. His eyes which had never left me did not waver and there was, until he was again prompted, no sign of a smile on the small, rather full, mouth.

The prompting this time took the form of a decided pinch. Cecil started violently, seemed to come out of whatever dream he had been in, said how-do-you-do very politely, took my hand and bowed over it and, at last, smiled. Lady Guthrie remarked that Cecil had been looking forward tremendously to meeting me and had talked of nothing else for the past month. I doubted very much whether this were true but responded by saying that on my part I had been much looking forward to meeting Cecil. He then asked me if both my brothers had been to Eton. I told him that they had and Cecil, Eton being evidently a burning topic with him at the moment, said that so had his father and

Charlie. And he and Mama thought it would be nice if he went there too.

'As to that we will have to wait and see what happens nearer the time.' Lady Guthrie, smiling fondly, ran her fingers through her son's hair. Then turning to me she said that both Dr Granby in London and a doctor whom they had lately consulted in Paris agreed in thinking that it might not be advisable.

I afterwards learned that Cecil was supposed to be highly strung and that Dr Granby thought that he might he tubercular.

'Later on of course he may become stronger . . .' Lady Guthrie's voice trailed away.

'In any case Mama is going to make Papa build a house near Windsor so that if I do go they won't be far away and I shall be able to go home on all the half holidays.'

I said that that sounded very nice and Lady Guthrie said she had already found what she considered would be a perfect situation for the proposed house.

'We never intended to settle permanently at North Lodge and only have it on lease. It was the first thing we could find when my husband retired from Madrid last year. That was his last post as I expect Charlie has told you.'

For the next half hour the conversation was dominated by Cecil. He appeared to be intelligent and I discovered that his main interest was music and that he spoke Spanish, German and French as easily as English.

'Mr Hughes, he's my tutor you know, says that when I go to school they won't like it because I speak with a correct accent.'

'But when you grow up it will be very nice in case you want to be an ambassador like your Papa.'

Cecil explained that there was more to being a diplomat than a mere knowledge of languages. 'What I do when I grow up will depend on how I get on at Eton or with my tutors if I don't go there.'

Lady Guthrie said that that was nonsense and that Cecil would be able to do anything he wanted, provided he worked hard and was always polite to everyone.

'Then I shall be Prime Minister and act in the pantomime every Christmas. And if Lady Anne is very polite too they will make her Queen of England. And Charlie can win the Grand National as often as he wants. And Mr Hughes can have a million pounds and a new suit. I shall be very glad, won't you, Mama, not to see that study old brown one any more?'

'Poor *Monsieur* Hughes *dans son complet marron*—says table in Latin and looks like a *Baron*.'

Evidently, this was a familiar game for Lady Guthrie had no sooner finished speaking than it was taken up by Cecil. 'Mr Hughes's Latin is rather weak—But when he stutters he stutters in Greek.'

They continued with this amidst much giggling from Cecil for some time, becoming increasingly ribald at the tutor's expense. The game ended with the arrival in the room of Sir David and Charlie. On catching sight of his younger son Sir David looked inquiringly at Lady Guthrie. 'I thought he was not to come downstairs until Saturday?'

'I didn't invite him, he came of his own accord.' Lady Guthrie spoke as if this circumstance somehow exonerated Cecil from any blame which he might otherwise be expected to incur for having evaded a punishment.

'And I was so anxious to see my new sister,' Cecil put in, 'that I couldn't wait any longer.'

Sir David did not look pleased but only said that as it was already Cecil's bedtime he had better say good night and go up to the schoolroom.

After I was in bed that night I found myself rather to my surprise thinking not about Charlie who at that time was continually in my thoughts—and still is after more than forty years of being married to him—but about Cecil. I could not get rid, although I knew it was foolish, of the unpleasant impression made on me by his secret entry into his mother's room.

Children, of course, delight in that sort of game. Hadn't I, only a few years before, often hidden behind a laurel hedge by the drive in order to spring out and 'surprise' a usually quite unsurprised adult? But Cecil's trick had had nothing to do with springing out. He had merely waited behind the screen until his mother called to him—and how long, anyhow, had he been there? Lady Guthrie's manner of dealing with the incident had also struck me as strange and somehow disturbing. She had known as soon as I looked in that direction that Cecil was in the room. It seemed probable therefore that she had been aware of his presence before I was, but if so, how odd that she had not said anything about it. But then surely her whole attitude towards him now that I came to think about it was unusual. Here, although she was obviously not at all strict with him, was no conventionally doting mother of a delicate only child. Rather, one would have said, she treated him as an equal. An equal whom she was careful not to offend, of whose temper she was not quite certain.

The passage of twelve years, those between 1875 and 1887, had, so far as I could see, made very little difference to Lady Guthrie's relationship with her son. The young man of twenty-one was as much beloved, as close to her and treated with the same easy *cameraderie* as had been the child of nine.

Many things, but none that touched on tragedy, had happened to all of us during those years. Charlie and I had been married in August 1875 and gone to live in the house in Berkeley Square which we still possess today. Our daughter had been born a year later and our son Alistair in 1878—the same year in which Charlie, having resigned his commission in the Brigade, first stood for Parliament.

Lady Guthrie and Sir David, who after a severe illness in 1879 had been warned that he must never again spend a winter in England, now lived for the greater part of the year in the villa they had bought at Cannes. The rest of their time was spent between Baden and the house at Old Windsor which had been built in order that Cecil, while attending Eton, might continue to enjoy the comforts of home life.

Two years ago Charlie, on the death of a cousin, had come into an estate in Scotland. Lady Guthrie, in spite of having no desire to live anywhere but the South of France, had, I believe, nevertheless been somewhat affronted that Sir David had been passed over in the matter of Kildonan. She seldom failed, when staying with us there as she was now, to make some remark on the subject. Looking at her, as we sat together in the small sitting-room which overlooked the loch, I reflected on how little the years had changed her. A trifle of added plumpness perhaps but there was still no grey apparent in the golden hair and her skin was as fresh and youthful looking as ever. A special cream (in special little china pots decorated with violets) which had been expressly evolved for the Princess of Wales, was, or so Lady Guthrie had told me, the secret. She allowed nothing for her own perfect metabolism but in one whose constant illnesses were the cause of so much anxiety to her husband and son that perhaps was to be expected.

'I said,' Lady Guthrie repeated, 'that poltergeists can be extremely misleading. As Mr Jackson was saying on Tuesday,' and here she leant as close to me as the paraphernalia of the tea table would allow, 'there is no other word for them but teasing.'

Mr Jackson, as Lady Guthrie had told Charlie and me and our house party frequently during the course of the last few days, was a spiritualistic medium who lived in Paddington and didn't *exactly* believe in the divinity of Jesus Christ. In those days of course people didn't much discuss religion at the luncheon table—or at least they did not when it was a question of not believing in something—so Lady Guthrie's disclosures as to the exact details of Mr Jackson's faith had been something of an embarrassment.

'If it hadn't been for the poltergeists,' idly Lady Guthrie picked up the silver trumpet used for blowing out the little spirit lamp under the kettle, 'I am convinced that my private hour with him would not have ended as it did.'

Exactly how the hour had ended she had not told us but apparently she and Mr Jackson had failed to communicate with the spirit of her sister Marion.

I nodded sympathetically, thinking what a pity it was that of all Lady Guthrie's sisters, Marion, the only one who had died, should also be the only one in whose advice, if only it could be obtained, she seemed to place any confidence.

'Perhaps,' I said, 'if you were to try again on your way back through London?'

'I shall certainly attempt it but sometimes with so many wishing to speak to us it can be very difficult. On Sunday at the public meeting there were a great many messages; most of them I'm bound to say rather silly.'

Abruptly Lady Guthrie, without attempting to do anything super-natural with it, which is what I'd been vaguely afraid of, replaced the trumpet on the tea-table. 'Half of them might just as well have been written on the back of picture postcards of Brighton, "All well here, everything very beautiful, don't worry."

At which point, had I known Lady Guthrie less well, I would probably have thought that her enthusiasm for spiritualism was, at best, lukewarm. I would have been wrong. Lady Guthrie never failed to believe completely in anything in which she happened to believe at the moment.

With some curiosity, for I had been waiting for a suitable opportunity to put the question, I asked her what Sir David, inclined to a rather strict evangelism, thought of the poltergeists or at least of Mr Jackson.

Lady Guthrie held up a hand in warning. 'He doesn't . . . as I told you . . . and in anything less serious I would not dream of even *seeming* to go against my dear one's opinion. . . .'

She left the sentence unfinished and I was confirmed in my suspicion that Sir David, occupied with taking the cure at Baden, had not been told anything about either Mr Jackson or her attempted excursions into the spirit world.

'. . . there is nothing you know that goes against our religion; if there were you can rest assured that I would not even contemplate . . . and of course I shall tell him all about it later on.'

She leant back on the sofa. It was evident that she did not wish to pursue this aspect of the subject any further. Her eyes strayed round the room and I wondered if she was comparing it to its disadvantage with her infinitely more feminine rooms at Old Windsor and the Villa Victoria at Cannes.

'In a Scottish castle,' I said, 'one has, don't you think, to be a little austere?'

## 9 | CECIL

'I envy you the view, so romantic to live on the edge of a loch,' and she drew the cashmere shawl she was wearing a little more closely about her shoulders.

I had hoped that she might have come at least a little nearer towards praising the furnishings which Charlie and I had chosen with such care when we moved into Kildonan. But in any case she was saved from having to say anything more by the footman coming into the room with the afternoon post. There were several letters for Lady Guthrie—the one which lay on top of the pile was, as she announced with a cry of joy, from Cecil.

'Forgive me.' But she had already torn open the envelope and was racing through the several closely written pages. Watching her as she read I was touched by her transparent pleasure.

'He is coming, he really will be here tomorrow.'

I said how glad I was that nothing had happened to postpone Cecil's visit.

'I was so afraid you know—although of course I knew that he would *not* disappoint me—that the Marsdens would have made it difficult for him to leave.'

Cecil, before coming on to us, had been staying in Sussex with Colonel and Mrs Marsden, the parents of the girl to whom he was supposed to be more or less engaged.

The engagement, or more exactly perhaps 'the expectation of an engagement', had existed in August 1887 as a tremendous secret for several weeks. The secret was shared quite naturally by Lady Guthrie's mother, Lady Campion, her four surviving sisters and her many correspondents to all of whom she appealed for support and reassurance in the extraordinary circumstance of her son proposing to get married. It was all very worrying, very upsetting and, as she never omitted to add, very wonderful. Undoubtedly it had been on the subject of Lydia Marsden that Lady Guthrie—although she had been a little mysterious about it—had wished to confer with her deceased sister. Marion, being on the 'other side' might so easily have discovered, might she not, that there was something against the girl which was concealed from the rest of us?

'As you know there's nothing I want so much in this world as his happiness, and I do believe and I do hope that he is deeply in love.'

'Oh but I'm sure. . . .'

'Yet even at this juncture in his life he never lets a day go by without writing to me. But then even as a tiny child he was always so devoted, so particularly sensitive. The tenderness of that little boy for a delicate and often suffering mother would only be credited by those who had seen it for themselves. Oh my dear I do hope that your Alistair will one day he as close to you as Cecil has always been to me—but with two children I suppose it can never be exactly the same thing?'

She looked at me inquiringly and I agreed that perhaps it couldn't. Inwardly, I was smiling at the thought that my sturdy nine-year-old son would ever cling to me as closely as Cecil clung to Lady Guthrie. As for my daughter, at eleven years old she was already showing signs of a decided independence. Lady Guthrie would never understand that I preferred them the way they were or that I would even have been rather worried had I thought that there were no schoolroom secrets which the children were not prepared to share with me.

Lady Guthrie folded up Cecil's letter but did not put it away.

'I do not know or rather I cannot quite make out whether he is absolutely committed, and, if he is not perfectly certain in his own mind . . . I think you know that the best thing would be for Charlie to have a serious talk with him.'

'Perhaps, but what exactly is it you want him to say to Cecil?'

As I spoke I knew that my question was over direct. Lady Guthrie did not care for things to be put too plainly. She much preferred all her communications with the world about her to be conducted in half tones and through the media of vague understandings. She considered anything else to be unsuitable to the atmosphere of the perpetual—if not always actual—sickroom in which she lived.

'So much easier I think for a man, and dear Charlie has always been so kind. You remember that time at Eton . . . his father and I so worried and so far away with the Milan doctors absolutely refusing to allow me to travel.'

I remembered only too clearly. The peremptory telegram had arrived in the middle of the Hastings election. Charlie was to proceed immediately to Eton and interview the headmaster: '. . . ask him to explain extraordinary letter received by us this a.m. Edythe deeply distressed and rendered very gravely ill.' The signature that followed was Sir David's but the authorship was unmistakable. Greatly to my relief, for the outcome of the election was by no means a certainty, Charlie had refused to jeopardize his chances of success by cancelling three important meetings which he would have had to do in order to rush off to Eton on the receipt of the telegram.

A leisurely exchange of letters elucidated the fact that the authorities considered that it would be in Cecil's best interests for him to leave the school at the end of the half. He was not, as was carefully explained, to be expelled. The reasons for the decision were that Cecil was thought to be 'not a good influence in his house' and that he worked only at those subjects—French and German—that he knew perfectly already.

In his reply to two hysterical letters from Lady Guthrie Dr Hornby refused to reconsider his decision—at any rate until he could have an opportunity of discussing the situation in person with Sir David. Cecil, as the headmaster freely admitted, had a good brain and was perfectly capable, providing he worked, of taking a respectable degree at Oxford. But at present the boy had no idea whatsoever of discipline, which was possibly to be accounted for by his not having been to a preparatory school and having been much over-indulged at home.

Unfortunately this moderate expression of opinion had a most inflammatory effect on Lady Guthrie. It was not to be tolerated that Cecil should be left for one further hour in the power and under the influence of a man so little capable of understanding him. A further exchange of expensive telegrams resulted in Cecil's leaving Eton several weeks before the beginning of the holidays.

Lady Guthrie, writing the short explanatory preface to Cecil's printed letters, gives no reason for his having left school at the early age of sixteen. She does however quote the headmaster's testimony as to Mr Guthrie's good conduct during the time he was under him at Eton. Dr Hornby continued by saying that Mr Guthrie, in spite of having lost some time in consequence of delicate health, nevertheless distinguished himself highly in the examination for the Prince Consort's prizes in modern languages.

Such a letter, being a necessary passport to a university, is never withheld except in the gravest circumstances. But even when full allowance is made for this fact the 'character' it gives Cecil is not a bad one. Reading it and the private letters about 'lack of discipline' one's heart goes out to the boy who all his life had been hemmed about with tutors and who, until he went to a public school, had passed every night under the same roof as his adoring mother. A mother, moreover, who demanded that he should share with her his every thought! No wonder that when at last allowed the freedom—for so it must have seemed to him—of a public school he should have been guilty, for that in fact was all it amounted to, of an excess of high spirits.

The first Charlie and I knew about the Eton fiasco was when Cecil was ushered on to a platform from which Charlie was speaking. Effecting his entrance after the manner of Sir Henry Irving about to embark upon Macbeth rather than in that of an anonymous person who to his confusion finds himself late for church, Cecil did nothing towards persuading an already unruly audience to compose itself. Afterwards, to give him his due, he was apologetic. It was at his mother's wish rather than his own that he was at Hastings. She had been in no doubt but that his presence during an election campaign would be at the same time useful to Charlie and an interesting experience for her dearest boy. The ungrateful task of consigning the boy on to Milan, without precipitating a family quarrel, was left to me. I managed it by writing a letter to Lady Guthrie in which I said that it was unthinkable when she was so ill that her son should not be at her side.

On that occasion I was able to turn Lady Guthrie's state of near-permanent invalidism to my, rather than her, advantage. Usually it worked the other way round.

'He is of course far too young to marry immediately.' Lady Guthrie was speaking a good deal more loudly than usual which I was afraid denoted that she was making the remark for the second time.

I hurriedly agreed that twenty-one was perhaps rather young for a man, but added that both my brothers had married when they were not much older.

'And with what results!' Lady Guthrie shook her head mournfully but there was triumph in her voice, and I realized now that it was too late that I had presented her with a rod with which Cecil would presently be beaten.

'And your poor dear mother! I think of her so often, to have one's eldest son involved in such a dreadful scandal! It doesn't bear thinking about.'

'My mother,' I said, 'very seldom does.'

'If I believed that anything of the kind could ever touch Cecil . . . so humiliating for your brother with everyone knowing that his wife is not true to him. It was bad enough when it was only the Prince of Wales, but now with the Duke and all this talk about a divorce. And to think that none of it would have happened if your poor brother had waited to choose a wife until he was a mature man.'

'Surely people can choose unfortunately at any age.' I was wondering if it would ever be possible to make her see that almost anything would be better for Cecil than a life passed entirely in the company of an eighty-year-old father and a mother who even now boasted that she shared his every thought.

'And don't you think there is always something rather pathetic about a very young married man; tied down to domesticity and all that it involves before he has had time to see anything of the world?'

I said that as Cecil had already seen more of the world than most men I did not think that in his case being tied down would involve any great hardship.

'In a year or two's time it will be a different thing'—Lady Guthrie continued as if I had not spoken—'and that is why I am anxious for Charlie to talk to him. It will come so much better from a brother and I'm sure Charlie, who's so clever, will manage to make him see how very much better it will be to wait.'

I reminded Lady Guthrie, but with no great hope of its doing much good, that she herself, as she so often remarked, had been married, practically out of the schoolroom.

'But my dear, in what very different circumstances. Dearest David was a man of mature age. I had everything to learn from him.'

She turned once again to Cecil's letter. 'I do not think you know that he *is* completely sure of his own feelings. He writes that I will be both pleased and sorry to hear that he is more in love than ever but later on . . .' she turned over a page and held it out to me, her finger marking the place from which she wished me to start reading: '. . . her absolute ignorance of art is to me a great pity, yet how can one expect perfection? Of one thing I have a very delightful proof, she is joyful with me; and laughs for very pleasure and how happy we are! While you, my darling, are happy, I know, knowing of my pleasure . . .'

At which point Lady Guthrie took the letter back into her own hands.

'The rest is about a novel of Bourget's about which I asked him and he goes on to speak of a novel of his own.'

'I didn't know Cecil was writing a novel.'

'As soon as he has found a plot he will be ready to begin.'

She got up and moved across the room. She was smiling but for what reason I do not know. She stood for a few moments looking out of the window; her arms raised a little above her head and her hands, in one of which she still held her son's letter, pressed lightly against the glass.

## Chapter Two

THE NEXT MORNING Lady Guthrie, as was her custom, breakfasted in bed. Just before ten o'clock I went up to her room. As always when she occupied it, it smelt deliciously of scent. Lying back against the pillows with her hair falling in a shining coil across her neck and shoulders she imparted an air of great luxury to all the objects that surrounded her.

After we had said good morning I told her that Charlie and I had talked for a long time about Cecil the previous evening and that Charlie, after thinking the whole thing over very carefully, thought that by far the best thing to do was to invite Colonel and Mrs Marsden with their daughter to come and stay.

'But my dear,' Lady Guthrie's arm in the billowing lace sleeve went up to her breast. 'I don't think, no, that *cannot* be a good idea. He has been staying with them for the past five days—he went down to Sussex immediately after seeing me off at Euston— it would, as they are not really engaged, be so marked.'

Her reaction was very much what we had expected it would be but I pretended to a moderate disappointment.

'Oh dear, we thought you would be so pleased and that you wanted Charlie to advise Cecil about the future.'

Lady Guthrie repeated that the thing wouldn't do at all, we had meant to be kind but it wouldn't do.

'But Charlie doesn't think he can possibly be of any help to Cecil until he's seen them together. Anyhow,' for I saw that she was beginning to be angry, 'perhaps the Marsdens won't be able to come.'

'You mean the letter has already been sent?' Lady Guthrie looked at me searchingly, 'but the post has not yet gone.'

I told her that I had given the letter to the coachman to post in Dundee when he met Cecil's train.

'Then there is nothing to be done, for the carriage must already have left.'

The blue eyes were coldly furious but it was not her way to show anger openly. She made an ineffective movement towards the bell-rope—which in fact was easily within her reach—and then, sinking back as if the effort had completely exhausted her, asked me if I would be kind enough to ring for her maid.

'Louise is just outside the door.'

'Then please ask her to come in. I want to try and be dressed before Cecil arrives; so sad for him to see his mother always ailing and I try so hard whenever it is in the least possible to *appear* to be in good health.'

It was something of a relief to get out of Lady Guthrie's room. I walked down the wide oak staircase—smelling of beeswax instead of Paris scent, passed through the cool hall and slightly warmer drawing-room and stepped out on to the terrace.

"Well, how did she take it?" Charlie's cousin, Nealie Adair, jumped up from the basket chair in which she had been sitting.

'Exactly as we thought, she wasn't pleased.'

'Poor little Cecil, I do hope that *he's* going to be pleased. Think of having to conduct a courtship with Edythe always at one's elbow!'

Nealie's laugh was gay and utterly without malice. She re-seated herself, picking up the copy of *The Times* which had fallen to the ground.

I sank into the chair next to Nealie's. I was now feeling rather guilty about having invited the Marsdens. The whole idea of getting Lydia up to Kildonan—without Lady Guthrie's consent, which we knew she would never give if she was asked for it, had seemed wildly funny yesterday evening. The suggestion had originated with Nealie and the *coup d'état* planned in the smoking-room amidst roars of, I am afraid, rather ribald laughter.

'Do you think perhaps that we shouldn't have done it? She was so looking forward to having him, except for us, of course, to herself.'

Nealie said that that was nonsense. 'The boy spends much too much time with his parents as it is. He's only been away from them for three months and she'll be taking him with her when she goes to Baden—what more does she want?'

'She is very worried about him.'

'There's absolutely no need to be. Lydia's a nice girl—if rather a goose—and Edythe has known the Marsdens all her life. She ought to think herself lucky.'

'You make it sound so simple.'

'Not at all, it's Edythe who makes it sound difficult, but when, so far as Cecil's concerned, has she ever been anything else? If she'd shown an ounce of tact over that school business and allowed Uncle David to go and talk the matter over with Dr Hornby, the boy would probably have been able to finish his time at Eton. And it was her fault again that he never went to Oxford. Did *you* ever believe in the existence of a doctor who forbade the university—on the score of health—as usual—but saw nothing against a London season? The year Cecil was there I never went out of the house without seeing him and I believe he went to a party every single night.'

'You do hate her, don't you?'

'I think she's selfish, that's all; and I think without meaning to she's ruined his life.'

'How can his life possibly be ruined when he's only twenty-one?'

'As for stopping him going in for the Foreign Office I call that perfectly criminal but what can one do?' And Nealie, remarking that she had been in the middle of a quite fascinating article by the financial editor, returned to the paper.

Fascinating, I reflected, to Nealie if not to many other women but then Nealie was an unusual woman and seemed more so in the days of which I am writing than she does now when women, owing to the war, have become so emancipated.

Almost the entire world involved in a war which has now lasted for more than three years! How impossible such a future would have seemed if it had been foretold to us thirty years ago. How could I possibly have believed then that Charlie, at the age of sixty-seven, would take a regiment to fight in France? Or that I would sit in a room near Sandwich on a winter's evening, as I am now, listening in dread to the sound of German gunfire coming from across the channel? Better not to think of it all or indeed of much else that on that August morning in 1887 still lay in the future. Better to return to myself and Nealie on the terrace at Kildonan to feel once again the warm sun of thirty years ago on my shoulders; to open my parasol and, in delightful idleness, watch Nealie as she reads *The Times*.

In the summer of 1887 Nealie, who had been christened Cornelia, must have been around fifty. I write 'around' for she was always extremely evasive about her age. Charlie used sometimes to tease her by telling a story, which Nealie always insisted he had made up, about her having torn the page on which the date of her birth was recorded out of the family Bible. She was an American and Charlie, through his mother, was her first cousin. Despite the fact of her being some ten or fifteen years his senior she and Charlie had always been great friends and mutually treated each other as contemporaries.

Nealie had been twice married. Her first husband had died in America just after the Civil War when he was still quite young. Nealie had then crossed the Atlantic and settled herself in England. In 1872 she had met and married the redoubtable John Adair, widely known as the Doom of Donegal. Said to have been the only man in Ireland to have taken advantage of the great famine of the forties in order to found a fortune, he was ever afterwards hated, about equally, by his fellow landlords and the peasantry. The Doom, having died two years ago, Nealie was now a widow for the second time. This was no matter for regret to any of her friends for Mr Adair had been thoroughly disliked by nearly all of them. So much so indeed that I never remember meeting anyone—except Nealie herself whom he treated abominably—who had a good word for him. I personally couldn't help thinking of his death, which left Nealie an extremely rich woman, as being a most fortunate event.

Nealie looked up from her paper to ask, inconsequently, for I think it unlikely that there was anything in *The Times*' leading article which would have set off the train of thought, how long we had known Willie MacLaughlin.

'I thought he was so amusing when we were doing all that silly planning last night, and so ingenious, too. I can't think how it was, even when you had the house crammed with people, that I didn't notice him before.'

I said I was glad that she liked Willie for I had been afraid that with the general exodus of our other guests she was going to be bored. 'We've known him since he was practically a schoolboy. His father was the lawyer for this estate for years. Now he's dead and Willie has taken over the job. Charlie says that he's really much too brilliant to be practising up here and ought to go to London.'

'And is he going to?'

'I don't know, you'd better ask Willie.'

'If he wanted me to,' Nealie said consideringly, 'I could perhaps speak to Sir Terrence in the autumn.'

Sir Terrence Lucas, who alas died the year before the war started, was a great personal friend of Nealie's. He had the reputation of being the greatest, some people said the 'trickiest' lawyer of his generation.

'I mean if Mr MacLaughlin is going to join another firm it might as well be the best there is, mightn't it, and then if he has a great deal of Scottish business he can bring them . . .' and Nealie, rattling on, very soon had Willie installed in Lincoln's Inn, making ten thousand a year and on the point of receiving a knighthood.

She only stopped when I interrupted to say how lucky it was we were by ourselves, for if Charlie had been here he would certainly have accused her of meddling. 'What is that thing he is always quoting about your father having had more irons in the fire than there were guns before Sevastapol and you're exactly the same.'

Nealie, intensely proud of her father who had been killed in battle during the American Civil War, said that there was no one whom she would rather be like because he had been a very remarkable as well as a very brave and clever man and his farms in New York had been better run than any she had seen since.

All of which, so Charlie has told me, was quite true and of his six children, Nealie, possessed of enormous moral and physical courage, was the one who most resembled him.

Cecil arrived at Kildonan at about twelve o'clock but whether Lady Guthrie's maid had managed, in the two hours allowed for the operation, to get her mistress dressed in time to receive him I do not know. She chose to be reunited with him in the privacy of her bedroom.

When some time later mother and son joined us on the terrace I was greatly struck, for it had been two or three years since I had last seen him, by Cecil's extraordinary good looks. I thought too that his manner had much improved or perhaps it was just that he had grown into it, as puppies and adolescents do to their feet.

As we went into luncheon I wondered if Nealie had not been guilty of exaggeration when she referred to my brother-in-law as 'poor little Cecil'. The assured man of the world that he had become looked as if he was quite capable of managing Lady Guthrie and dealing with his own love affairs without any assistance from us. At luncheon I was relieved to see that Lady Guthrie had, for the time being anyhow, apparently decided to drop the role, she had threatened to assume earlier, of the always ailing mother. She was now talking away with great animation and some wit. If a role was involved it was clearly that of a sister anxious to appear to advantage in the eyes of a brother whom she greatly admired.

During the next few days I continued to study Lady Guthrie and Cecil with some interest. On his side he was very attentive to her and seemed genuinely to want to spend as much time in her sole company as was consistent with politeness to the rest of us. True, he went out shooting every day which involved leaving her for a good many hours but a great deal was always made by both of them of the fact that he only did so at her express wish.

On Thursday I had a reply from Mrs Marsden. It arrived by the afternoon post which was brought into the morning-room while we were having tea. I finished reading the letter and glanced across at Nealie. I found, for she seldom missed anything, that she was looking in my direction. I nodded and knew by the look of mischief that momentarily appeared in her eyes that she had understood. I wondered what I should do. I didn't want to make a mystery of the thing and thereby give Lady Guthrie what she might consider to be a legitimate excuse for sulking. On the other hand I didn't want to make a solemn announcement of Lydia's imminent arrival, seeming to give it an importance which, except in Lady Guthrie's mind, it didn't possess. Doubtfully, I looked away from Nealie, now tactfully engrossed in her own letters. My eyes passed on to Willie and Cecil, talking together about stags they had shot in the past, to Lady Guthrie delicately finishing a substantial tea and, finally, to Charlie.

'I've just heard from Mrs Marsden. She says she and Lydia will be delighted to come.' I looked at the letter again, 'I think, Monday.'

'What about Marsden?' Charlie made it sound as if his only interest in the news was in knowing whether he was going to have to provide for an extra gun.

'He will be fishing in Invernessshire but they are all invited to the Macdonalds' the following week so they will be able to meet there. It fits in beautifully.'

'Makes rather a lot of women in the house.'

'Never mind, next week we shall have too many men. It's impossible to get it right.'

Charlie said that it would be interesting to see how little Lydia had turned out. 'The last time we were at East Dean she was in short skirts.'

'She's very pretty now, isn't she?' Nealie had turned to Lady Guthrie and we all waited for the answer.

'As to that you will have to address yourself to Cecil.' The gesture with which she accompanied the remark might have been best described as having been taken from the French.

'That's good,' Charlie said heartily and without giving Cecil time to say anything at all, 'always nice to have a pretty girl about the place. What's happened to the children, Anne, surely they're very late coming down this evening?'

In fact our son and daughter's ritual appearance was not due for at least another ten minutes but the discussion, immediately taken up by me and Nealie, as to whether or not this was so and whether, if it were, we ought to send a message up to the schoolroom, made it seem natural for the subject of the Marsdens to be dropped.

Very soon after the children came into the room Lady Guthrie, pleading a headache and urgent letters to be written, announced her intention of going upstairs until dinner time. She rose to her feet, Cecil hurried forward to help her and escorted her from the room. We knew that he wouldn't return, at the very least, until he had ensconced her in the chaise-longue placed in front of the fire which, even in the warmest weather, was kept up in her bedroom.

As soon as the door shut behind them Nealie burst out, 'Four days is too long. She'll find an excuse for them to leave before Monday.'

'What odds would you lay,' Willie asked Charlie, 'against a telegram from Sir David saying that she must come to Baden at once?'

Charlie said that he didn't know if Lady Guthrie would go as far as that but he agreed with Nealie in thinking that she'd probably get away.

I noticed that both the children, thinking that for once their elders were talking about something interesting, were looking at us open-mouthed. The 'downstairs' books' which were supposed to keep them quietly amused while in our company, lay neglected upon their knees.

Turning away from them, I told the others that they didn't have anything to worry about because the Marsdens would be here the next morning.

'Why on earth didn't you say so?' Charlie sounded, for him, quite annoyed.

'Because if I had, Lady Guthrie might easily have arranged to leave tonight. This way she thinks she's got plenty of time.'

'How are you going to explain?' But it was obvious that Nealie was not much interested in that part of it.

'I misread Friday for Monday. It's a thing that could happen to anybody.'

'She'll come down tomorrow morning,' Nealie said, 'and there they'll be. Or at least there will be Mrs Marsden. Lydia we hope will be with Cecil at the very furthest end of the garden.'

'Dearest Mother, You always understand my feelings so perfectly,' the phrase occurs again and again in Cecil's letters to Lady Guthrie. It is like a pattern, sometimes I have thought a sinister one, that coils and uncoils itself, as a line of dancers in a ballet, only to return always to the same form.

'Dearest Mother, How unhappy I am to be away from you. How brave you are, but reading between the lines I cannot be unaware of how much you have suffered.' The letter might as well be dated 1896 or ten years earlier. And how could he bear after he was a grown man to go on signing himself, as he invariably did, your own boy Cecil? The words, as well as the letters themselves, give so little idea of my brother-in-law's character that reading them one has the uneasy impression that they were dictated to him by someone else. Could any mother and son have been so perfectly in accord as the printed correspondence between Cecil and Lady Guthrie would seem to imply? Did Cecil, although to doubt it seems so terrible, ever actually write the letters that are attributed to him? Impossible now ever to know for certain and Nealie, on whose resourcefulness I thought I might have counted to find out the truth, has always pretended to think that there is no mystery at all. Her copy of the letters, if indeed it still exists, is to be found in one or other of her many houses, on a bookshelf reserved for fiction.

As we went up to change for dinner Charlie was still teasing Nealie about her supposed reputation as a match-maker. 'You'd better be careful you know. Somebody was telling me the other day that they thought you took a commission.'

Nealie paused at the head of the staircase which, fortunately, was some way away from the rooms occupied by Lady Guthrie and Cecil. 'That's too silly even to answer and anyhow we're not trying to get Cecil *married*.'

'Really, I thought that was the whole idea?'

'Of course not. All we're trying to do is to see that he has a little fun before he's dragged off to Baden. After all your father *is* over eighty. He can't really be much of a companion for a boy of twenty-one.'

Charlie, who much resented the appearance of selfishness, on his father's part, that Cecil's continual presence at Sir David's side inevitably presented to the world, didn't answer.

'There are always lots of young people at Baden'—I started to move away—'and at Cannes with the sailing and the theatricals and so many people coming and going he always has a wonderful time.'

'He'd have a better one as third secretary in one of those tropical legations they all hate so much.'

Nealie turned into the passage leading to her bedroom and the conversation which threatened to become somewhat indiscreet for so public a place came to an end.

## Chapter Three

CIRCUMSTANCES, how tiresome they can often be, combined to prevent the Marsdens' arrival at Kildonan from taking place in the manner envisaged by Nealie. The charming little scene, in which Lady Guthrie was to come on to the terrace just before luncheon to find Mrs Marsden already installed with Lydia and Cecil nowhere to be seen but clearly understood to be alone together in the romantic setting of the rose garden, was never enacted.

The first intimation we had that things were going to take a different if not actually a wrong turn was when we awoke to a day of steady downpour. No terrace therefore and no rose garden! Next, and this was really unlucky, the London train chose this particular day to be more than an hour late and Lady Guthrie, an almost unprecedented thing for her, was downstairs by eleven o'clock. She found Nealie, Willie and me in the drawing-room—the only room except some of the bedrooms which commands a clear view of the front door. Cecil, whom of course we wanted to have on hand, and Charlie were in the smoking-room and presumed to be discussing business. One hoped that Charlie had been ingenious enough to think of any.

'What a very sad morning!' As we got to our feet and Willie fussed about finding a chair for her, Lady Guthrie advanced into the room.

'And what a sad little fire.' She shivered noticeably as she allowed Willie to install her as near to it as possible.

'I'm so sorry, I'll ring for more coal.' As I pulled the bell-rope I was wondering how I was going to explain the carriage when it arrived filled with obviously anticipated Marsdens.

'I feel so much better today that I had hoped I might finish my sketch, but now . . .' Lady Guthrie looked towards the window.

Following her glance one had the impression that the rain was coming down more heavily and the trees dripping more hopelessly than had been the case a few moments earlier.

'Still, as I *do* feel so much stronger, perhaps this would be a good day for you to drive me over to see dear Antoinette.'

This was Antoinette Lambert, one of our closest neighbours, who had been a childhood friend of Lady Guthrie's.

'If we were to start in half an hour we would be there in plenty of time for luncheon.'

I objected that Mrs Lambert wouldn't be expecting us.

'She doesn't have to be. She said in her letter that I was to come over any day I felt up to it. They always have so many people there that two or three more never makes any difference. I would ask you to send me by myself if she hadn't mentioned that she particularly wanted to see you. She says that you never go there and I'm afraid that her feelings are beginning to be hurt.'

'Why don't we wait for a fine day,' Nealie put in, 'the garden, always so beautiful.'

'It is Antoinette not the garden that I would be going to see, but perhaps,' and here Lady Guthrie turned pointedly away from Nealie and addressed herself expressly to me, 'today will not be convenient?'

She was looking at me so searchingly that it began to dawn on me that 'the Marsden Plot' wasn't quite such a carefully guarded secret as we had thought. All this rigmarole about visiting dearest

Antoinette was therefore arrant nonsense and one had to admit that Lady Guthrie had succeeded in turning the tables on us very neatly. How had she known? The children? Her maid? Yes, that must be it, through the medium of the housekeeper's room.

Caught, although not accused in words, in the ill-bred act of playing tricks on a guest in my house I looked away. Whatever happened now the joke, and it hardly seemed funny any more, had misfired.

The footman came in to put more coal on the fire. Lady Guthrie said that perhaps after all the weather was too bad to allow of us going out even in the carriage. Gloom, always so dangerously close at hand on wet days in the country when the presence of visitors prevents one from following one's own pursuits, descended.

One has to say in Lady Guthrie's favour that when the Marsdens actually arrived she behaved with consummate tact. Receiving her old acquaintance with every appearance of pleasure she thanked Mrs Marsden for the kindness she had shown dearest Cecil during the London season and for inviting him down to Sussex.

'Such a charming party he told me made up entirely of young people. You and Colonel Marsden must have been quite exhausted by the end of it.'

Mrs Marsden, a particularly young-looking forty, did not appear to be especially pleased at having it taken for granted that young people, even in quite large numbers, were bound to be too much for her. She contented herself however with saying how much they had enjoyed Cecil's company and in praising his good looks.

'Not that that is anything new. I shall never forget him as a little boy. One of the most lovely children I ever saw.'

As I placed my guests at dinner that evening I apologized to Mrs Marsden for the lack of men. 'On Monday it will be the other way round but until then we'll have to do the best we can.'

'At least,' Nealie said, 'the three we have got are all extremely talkative and quite fascinating.'

'And an *exclusively* family party can be so restful,' Lady Guthrie said. She turned to Lydia who, as the table had worked out, was sitting beside her. 'Especially nice perhaps for the young. They don't have to make those desperate efforts, as they do during the season, to interest their partners and collect new *beaux* for themselves.'

'My poor Edythe,' Charlie said, 'what a dreadful time you must have had of it when you were a girl.'

'*I* didn't,' Nealie said, 'when I came out I had a most lovely time in Philadelphia and New York and then my dear mother brought me to London and I had another lovely time and went to a ball at Buckingham Palace.'

'Where,' Cecil said, 'you danced the whole evening with the Prince of Wales who finally asked you to marry him.'

'Alas, no.'

The general conversation into which Lydia was quickly drawn continued light-heartedly and a little foolishly but with no jarring undertones. While at the other end of the table Charlie talked to Lady Guthrie who leaned towards him with an air of absorption.

Looking at her I wondered if perhaps all that was needed in order that everyone should be happy was for Lady Guthrie to find some interest that was not connected with her immediate family. As things were everything, her painting, the books she read, the music she played had to be shared as far as possible with her ageing husband and completely with her son.

Sir David had escaped by growing old but what escape from sharing could there ever be for Cecil? Married, whether in fact or fancy, out of the schoolroom she had never learned to 'live to herself'. A new interest, photography or collecting wild flowers? She might easily go in for either of them but never by herself. The new interest would therefore have to be a person, in plain words a lover. Such a simple solution! I looked up to see Charlie turn towards Mrs Marsden and Lady Guthrie glance idly round the table until her eyes came to rest on Cecil. The solution seemed less simple than it had.

The next day was Saturday. The weather had decidedly improved and it was obvious that congenial outdoor occupation must be found for people who had spent the past twenty-four hours cooped up in the house. Charlie offered stalking to the men but neither of them seemed inclined to accept. Cecil it appeared was now much more interested in fishing. Unselfishly eschewing the river, as there were only two beats available, he said that he thought it might be rather jolly to go on the loch. One saw his line of reasoning. As the conversation was taking place at breakfast and therefore out of his mother's presence he didn't have to take any pains to conceal it. Fishing for trout on the loch it was not necessary to have a ghillie, all that was needed was someone to row the boat.

'You'll be back in time for luncheon.' I didn't feel that I could go quite so far as to suggest he and Lydia should take it with them. If anything unforeseen occurred that would keep them out for the whole day that would be another matter.

Meanwhile Charlie was urging Willie to change his mind. It seemed that the day was perfect for stalking and that a perfect stag—which meant that it had more tips to its antlers than most of the other stags—had been sighted on the top moor. But Willie, grateful as he was for the offer of such a thrilling object for a twenty-mile walk, found himself unable to take advantage of it. He had, or so he asserted, woken up that morning with a stiff leg, doubtlessly brought on by the pervading damp of the previous day.

'Nonsense, you'll walk that off in the first half hour.'

It was so unlike Charlie to try and persuade people to do something that they clearly didn't want to do that my attention was caught and, when I saw the expression in his eye, held. He was teasing but with so straight a face that I was certain that no one but myself was aware of it.

I turned back to Mrs Marsden. Would she like a drive and was there anyone in the neighbourhood she wanted to visit? Or I could, if the plan would suit her and Nealie, have a note sent over to Antoinette suggesting that we three with Lady Guthrie, if she felt up to it, should drive over for luncheon.

Mrs Marsden politely agreed that that would be charming. Antoinette Lambert had been a friend of hers for years and she would love to see her again.

'So that's settled. I'll go up and see Lady Guthrie now and then write the note saying how many we'll be. If the man starts at once there'll be plenty of time for an answer.'

I got up from the table with the confident feeling of one who has arranged everything very nicely for everyone. The young people, Cecil and Lydia, were going to have a lovely time in the boat. Charlie, with most of his guests out of the way, would be able to get on with some work, for Willie, who always travelled with masses of papers which were constantly having to be 'looked through', never presented a problem concerning entertainment. I had reached the door of the dining-room when I realized that Nealie, so unlike her not to show enthusiasm for almost any suggested form of amusement, had taken no part in our discussion of plans. I was brought up short, not actually but in my mind. So that had been Charlie's 'tease' and the cause of Willie's stiff leg! I turned to look at him, wondering how he would appear to someone who, unlike myself, had not known him since he was practically a schoolboy. His hair was fair to reddish and he had what I can best describe as a very Scottish face—bony, without going so far as to be raw-boned, and blue eyes. The whole effect, for he was tall and had a good figure, was if not exactly handsome at least personable.

As I went upstairs I was smiling. The young-old meticulous Willie who, as far as anyone knew, had never been in love in his life was in love with Nealie. But the thing was ridiculous, he was an unknown provincial lawyer—possessed however of a fierce intelligence—and twenty years younger than she. Nealie would never be so foolish as to encourage him. A sentimental friendship at most. But the fact that they had wanted to spend the day together—and it must be arranged so that they should—added a touch of piquancy, maybe of pure happiness, to a morning on which everything was bright already.

I knocked on Lady Guthrie's door and was relieved to see, which I did as soon as I entered the room, that this was to be one of her good days. She was sitting up in bed with a writing-pad on her knee and was busily scribbling away.

'Good morning, dearest.' The charm of her smile made me sorry that I didn't always like her.

I told her that we thought of going over to the Lamberts, 'you and me and Mrs Marsden anyhow, I'm not sure about Nealie.'

Lady Guthrie expressed herself as being delighted with the idea and insisted that my note to Antoinette should be written up here. 'I'll ring for Louise to take it down to the pantry with a message as soon as you've finished.' She reached over and pulled the bell-rope. 'If you run away now, I shan't see you alone again all day. And I've nearly finished my letter to my dear one.' She indicated the pages spread around her on the bed. 'I'll be done by the time your note is ready.'

After Louise had come into the room and left it again Lady Guthrie turned to me with a great appearance of cheerfulness.

'What a difference a little sunshine makes to one's view of the world—that and a modicum of health of course. But when one is well one should not think of being ill.'

She drew herself up so that she was sitting in an even more upright position than she had been before, 'Dearest Anne, what a charming hostess you are. It makes me feel quite ashamed that my wretched health prevents me from enjoying every moment of my visits to you.'

I took her hand impulsively, noticing as I did so how frail but at the same time well-nourished it seemed to be. I supposed that this unusual juxtaposition of qualities was to be accounted for by the smallness of her bones.

'I am a little bit worried and there is something I would like to ask you.'

Thinking that I knew what was coming I looked at her cautiously.

'Do you yourself believe that there is anything, well not exactly wicked but not quite right, about spiritualism?'

Taken by surprise I said, not very helpfully, that I really didn't know.

'It has occurred to me . . . There was in fact something in my dear one's letter yesterday which has made me see the whole thing in a somewhat different light.'

I forbore to ask whether Sir David had found out about Mr Jackson by chance or if she herself had written to tell him about her visits to Paddington.

'He feels very strongly that what he calls "table-rapping" is inconsistent with revealed religion.'

'Then perhaps you had better not have anything more to do with it until you have had an opportunity of discussing it with him in person.'

'I suppose you are right and I suppose that I was guilty of a sin in trying to communicate with dearest Marion, but if she could just have answered one question for me.'

'I'm sure it would be better to leave it alone.'

I got up to leave and she asked me if I would tell Cecil to come and speak to her for a moment.

'Oh, but I think he'll have left by now.' I looked at my watch. 'Charlie arranged for him to fish this morning instead of going stalking.'

How strange that he didn't come and say good-bye.' A slight shadow passed across Lady Guthrie's face but disappeared almost immediately. 'I suppose he heard our voices and didn't want to disturb us. He's always so thoughtful of others. Sometimes I think even too much so.'

I hesitated, could this be the moment, perhaps the only one that would ever occur, when I might beg her to let him go; let him, unhampered by feelings of guilt, marry Lydia or any other girl he wanted. I contemplated throwing myself on my knees in a frenzy of supplication but of course I didn't do it.

'Ever since he was quite a tiny child,' Lady Guthrie was saying, 'he has always been so considerate of other people. In Lisbon he was the little idol of the whole *Corps Diplomatique*: ambassadors and attachés, and their wives and their children, recognized in him one of the sweetest of natures.'

Smiling fondly she went on to tell me how it hadn't even been necessary to teach manners to such a child whose very nature was uniformly courteous and considerate. It seemed indeed that he was incapable of an ungenerous action or falling short of the perfection of politeness. And of course all the servants, starting with his German nurse, always adored him. 'You can see it yourself today with Thompson, such a faithful fellow and absolutely devoted to all of us, but especially, I think to Cecil.'

The devoted Thompson was a retired naval rating whom Sir David had originally engaged as a yacht hand. He now combined that duty with being Cecil's valet and besides was always on hand as a courier whenever any of the family moved from one place to another.

I always feel so much happier when Cecil and I are parted for knowing that Thompson is with him and would let me know immediately if anything dreadful were to happen.'

I said that I could understand that that would be a great comfort, and then as Louise came into the room, left her to the task of getting her mistress bathed and dressed in time, if they were willing to receive us, to go to the Lamberts.

As the door of the bedroom shut behind me I was still thinking about the strange impulse which a few minutes earlier had prompted me to make a direct appeal to Lady Guthrie. I would have begged her to release Cecil but from what? I found that I didn't know. She is *too* fond of him—but that is ridiculous!

I had reached the foot of the stairs and could hear voices coming from the drawing-room—and at times she seems to possess him. 'Possessed by devils!' What had put the idea, which was surely a wicked one, into my head and ten o'clock in the morning was no time for fancies—wicked or otherwise.

Abruptly, I squared my shoulders and pulled my elbows into my sides in the way I used to as a child when enjoined by the nurserymaid to 'come along now do'.

Nealie and Mrs Marsden were sitting together at the far end of the room. As I went over to them I thought what a charming picture they presented. The sunlight streamed through the windows, picking out the highlights of their carefully arranged coiffures—Nealie's hair was already almost completely grey—and reflecting golden tones tinged with palest green on their light summer dresses. They were held for ever—or for as long as I shall be alive to remember it—in the security of a bright moment of time.

'We have been making such plans for the future.' Nealie's eyes were sparkling and she looked so happy that for a moment I thought it must be her own future that she had been planning.

'Mrs Marsden is certain that they are already engaged or so nearly so that it makes no difference.'

I looked at Mrs Marsden and saw that the prospect of her daughter's imminent engagement was the cause of less unalloyed pleasure to her than it was to Nealie.

'Please do be careful for nothing has been actually settled. I know of course that Cecil is very fond of Lydia and it does seem that she cares for him. But they are both so young and if anything were to come of it I'm afraid there would be so many difficulties.'

Feeling that it was very likely my duty to protect poor troubled Mrs Marsden from Nealie's exuberance I said that I thought it would be better not to talk too much about it, just yet.

In order to change the conversation I told Nealie that Lady Guthrie seemed to be about to embark on 'one of her good days' and might even be described as 'rarin' to go'.

'So I was wondering, four does seem to make us rather many, if perhaps you wouldn't mind staying at home and cheering Charlie up at luncheon?'

I put in the last bit in order to make it difficult if not impossible for Mrs Marsden to offer herself as the one who remained behind. Fortunately she was a tactful woman and the thing was settled without further discussion.

The answer to my note having been satisfactory the carriage was ordered for half-past twelve. Lady Guthrie, coming downstairs a few minutes after the appointed time, found me and Mrs Marsden waiting for her in the hall. Nealie had disappeared but, surprisingly, Lady Guthrie did not comment upon the absence.

As the carriage rounded the first bend of the drive, from which there is a view of a long stretch of the river, Lady Guthrie turned to peer in that direction.

'Is that where Cecil should be?' In her eagerness to catch a glimpse of her beloved boy she forgot to ask my permission and called directly to the coachman to go more slowly.

I explained to her that Cecil was fishing the loch.

'Oh' she sounded almost pathetically disappointed, '—then if I had looked I might have seen him from the house.'

I told her that it was just as likely, if not more so, that the boat would be at the farther end which was concealed from the house by a rise in the ground.

'Then we may see him after we have passed the lodge.' Smiling in happy anticipation she turned to Mrs Marsden. 'The high road runs along the side of the loch for about half a mile, such a pretty sight. You may have noticed it on your drive from the station.'

Mrs Marsden agreed that she had. The coachman whipped up the horses again and Lady Guthrie begged that he should be told to reduce the pace as soon as the loch should again be in sight.

We reached the lodge. It was kept in those days by old Mrs Douglas who, although well into her nineties, steadfastly refused to retire on a pension. As the carriage began to slow down I saw that Mrs Douglas—her hearing had remained remarkably acute—was already hobbling about her business of opening the gates. We stopped to exchange a few words with her then we took the sharp left-hand turn into the road and Lady Guthrie, leaning well forward, scanned the loch for a sight of the boat containing her beloved. To her disappointment there was no sign of it. After we had gone about another quarter of a mile and just at the place where there is a slight curve in the road we saw a carriage drawn up on the verge and a group of three or four people standing at the water's edge. As we approached we saw that the party consisted of two young men and a girl and that another girl was standing with her feet actually in the water.

While still unable to make out what they were saying we could hear them shouting to each other and pointing to an object which floated some way out from the shore. Lady Guthrie screamed and my own heart missed a beat when we realized simultaneously that it was an upturned boat. Fortunately the moment of horror passed as quickly as it had come. We were now near enough to hear that the shouts were mingled with laughter, to see, what a low reef had previously concealed from us, that the real cause of the excitement was not the boat but a swimmer—so close to the bank as to be easily within his depth.

As we drew abreast of the young people, too intent on what they were doing to have noticed our approach, their voices broke into ragged and ironical cheers to which Cecil, we could see quite clearly now that it was he, waded ashore.

'What happened! What happened!' The carriage drew up and Lady Guthrie jumped to her feet.

The laughter came to an abrupt end as the young people swung round to face us. Lydia, apparently paralysed at seeing Lady Guthrie, remained up to her ankles in the loch. Explanations, intermingled with introductions, for I now recognized the young men as the sons of some neighbours, followed in some confusion.

One of the Anderson boys and the girl had, like Cecil and Lydia, been out on the loch—I saw now that there was another boat drawn up on the beach. The other Anderson boy had been driving in the dog-cart. They had all met entirely by chance; could we imagine anything so lucky! And there had been a sort of accident—well not an accident really—because they had thought of bathing later on anyhow.

Cecil, dripping wet, standing by the side of the carriage and looking up into his mother's face while he tried to reassure her, looked so young and so happy that my heart went out to him. As indeed it did also to Lydia who had at last summoned up enough courage to come out of the water. She stood looking so abashed at the sounds of Lady Guthrie's vociferous expressions of alarm and displeasure that I at least was left in little doubt as to who had been the instigator of the 'accident'.

I decided it was time, if the thing could be managed without bringing on a positive display of hysterics for us to move on.

'But, dear Lady Guthrie, he can't possibly catch a chill. The water in the loch is really delightfully warm. Very much like the sea at Cannes. Of course if it will make you any happier I'm sure he will promise to go straight up to the house and have a hot bath.'

I thought I saw signs that she might be subsiding and the carriage, the horses having once more become conveniently restive, began to move.

Lady Guthrie, jolted from her standing position, fell back on the seat. She was still visibly shaken. Understandably so when one realized that, on catching sight of the empty boat she had immediately connected it with the idea of Cecil being drowned.

All the same I wasn't going to upset everyone's entire day by ordering the carriage back to the house and giving up the expedition. I smiled across at Mrs Marsden whose only contribution to the foregoing scene had been to tell Lydia to put her hat on.

She and I spent the rest of the drive in expressions of vague sympathy with Lady Guthrie mixed with positive assertions that swimming in the loch, even if the water *wasn't* quite as warm as I said, couldn't possibly kill anybody—or even give them a cold.

Our luncheon at the Lamberts', despite the highly nervous state in which Lady Guthrie declared herself to be when we arrived, went off fairly well. As did the remainder of her visit to Kildonan. She did not after all curtail her stay with us but most disappointingly neither propinquity nor the freedom provided by a larger party—a new batch of guests arrived several days before she was due to leave—resulted in an open engagement between Cecil and Lydia.

Sadly, I decided that Nealie had been right when she said that 'Edythe would be too much for them'.

So now, as I said to Charlie, they would just have to wait until the winter when Lady Guthrie would be safely installed in Cannes.

Charlie answered that if Cecil had an ounce of courage and knew what was good for him he'd grab the girl and elope because he'd never get married otherwise.

I tried to describe my dark thoughts of a few mornings before: 'I don't think it's just a question of Lady Guthrie putting difficulties in the way. It's making him think that he doesn't *want* the girl. She wants him to believe that he's bound so closely to herself that there can never be room for anyone else.' I broke off, frustrated by my failure to explain something I didn't understand myself.

'If she's managed to make him think that there's nothing to be done.'

We let the matter rest there. Cecil and Lady Guthrie left the following morning. Mrs. Marsden and Lydia—the northbound train left somewhat later than the London one—departed an hour later.

As I turned away from saying good-bye to the Marsdens I was thinking how lovely it would have been if the leave-taking had taken place in the midst of exciting plans for the future.

Nealie, who had been present at the Marsdens' departure, asked me why I was looking so sad.

'Because it might have been so different.'

'Might it?' She shrugged her shoulders. 'You know Edythe's really much more tiresome than I used to think. Either that or tiresomeness has grown on her. It does on some people—that's why one ought to be so careful.'

'Not to get entangled with potential bores or not to become one oneself?'

Nealie said that either possibility would be unpleasant. 'Anyhow we all did our best for poor little Cecil so even if nothing has come of it there's no point in spending my last day in grumbling about it. Besides, how do we know that nothing did? I have a distinct feeling that they are *more* engaged to be married now than they were when they arrived.'

'Do you really think so or are you trying to cheer me up?'

Nealie declared that she really thought so and then, jumping up, said that she had no idea it was so late. She had told Willie that she would be down at the river more than half an hour ago. Displaying her usual impatience for the next thing to be done she ran out of the room.

## Chapter Four

Towards the end of September we shut up Kildonan and returned to London. Charlie had a certain amount of business to attend to in the constituency which he wanted to get settled before the start of the new parliamentary sitting. He therefore spent a good deal of time travelling up and down to Hastings. Occasionally we passed a few nights there and, fortunately even more occasionally, for I have never in my life enjoyed making a speech, there would be a bazaar for me to open or a meeting at which 'the member's wife' was expected to say a few words.

The season was marked for us domestically by Alistair's departure to school. It was an event which left Sybil in such a state of lonely despair that I had immediately to find some morning classes for her to attend.

In October we went down to the Marsdens for their first shoot. It was a pleasant party, 500 pheasants on the first day—as I have just looked up in Charlie's game book—but the only thing I remember particularly about it is that Cecil's name was mentioned quite naturally when it happened to come into the conversation. I would have preferred, if of course he wasn't being spoken of as Lydia's fiancé, a deathly hush. It would have been more significant of 'something in the wind'.

In the privacy of his dressing-room I told Charlie that I was afraid the whole thing even the idea of a 'secret' engagement must now be off.

'If it were I suppose someone would have told us.'

'They mightn't have. And I don't think Lydia looks at all as if she is eating her heart out.'

Charlie said that that was a difficult thing to tell about someone just by looking at them.

I objected that as a rule it wasn't. A girl in love with a young man whom her parents wouldn't let her marry usually looked much crosser and certainly didn't talk about him with the cheerful indifference displayed by Lydia.

Charlie said that I was probably thinking of a different kind of girl and that if I didn't go away to my bath and leave him to have his we should both be late for dinner.

The weeks passed and it began to look very much as if Cecil was going to be kept abroad. The letters Lady Guthrie sent from Cannes were filled with news of her own health—not good—and Sir David's if possible, only she always managed to convey that it wasn't, even worse.

Dearest Cecil on the other hand was reported to be having a wonderful time and being admired in all he did by everyone. He was very busy now rehearsing an amateur company in a play, written by himself, which would be produced just before Christmas. In the New Year he and his father, if the latter was well enough to do so, planned a tour of the Mediterranean in the yacht.

As I sat in the drawing-room one winter's afternoon reading the letter which contained this last piece of intelligence I decided that the engagement had definitely fizzled out. I tried to believe that it was perhaps all for the best and managed to find several quite sensible reasons for doing so.

I walked to one of the windows and stood looking out at the Berkeley Square garden. Even in winter it was beautiful and much less depressing owing to a total absence of privet hedges than most square gardens.

Idly I continued to stand by the window looking out on the empty square—no nurses or slowly promenading schoolroom parties on this cold winter's afternoon. The short daylight was beginning to fade and already lamps glinted on several of the passing carriages.

I wondered if my own children, being brought up according to the conventional pattern evolved during the present century, would end by being any happier for it. Their lives had been laid down for them long before they were born. There would be Eton followed by Sandhurst or a university for Alistair; a year in Dresden and 'coming out' for Sybil. It seemed that Charlie and I as their parents had no more choice in the matter than the children themselves. Cecil, alone of his class and generation, had escaped—or at least avoided the convention. He had never been to a private school; the windows of the rooms where he studied with his tutors had not looked out on the roofs of a London mews or Scottish hills, but on the roofs of many cities of Europe and the Near East, the bay of Naples and the Atlas Mountains.

'During all that time he was spoiled and indulged.' I could hear the voices of the relations, including ourselves, mingled in a chorus of disapprobation. It had never occurred to me until this moment that any valid opinion on the subject of education could be opposed to our own.

It is nice to know that one is absolutely right and to believe with Charles the First that things have been arranged by the Almighty in such a manner as to make it impossible for one ever to be wrong. 'Happy the man who goes to his grave without ever having suspected that there may be two sides to any question.'

Had we perhaps been narrow-minded in not allowing that there is something to be said for bringing a boy up abroad; for foreign tutors as against English schools? I would grant that we had. Even so Lady Guthrie *must* have been wrong in not insisting that Cecil should go either to Oxford or a European university. She must have been wrong when she wrote with the greatest complacency that although it had been first intended that he should enter Diplomacy his father so feared, at his own great age, the probable and frequent long separation that the career might bring to pass between himself and his beloved child that it had therefore been renounced: 'Cecil thereafter looked forward to literature as his chief occupation. Meanwhile he was his parents' right hand in all their affairs.'

How could she tolerate such a sacrifice—of a career for which her son seemed to be eminently suited—being made on her behalf? I would never believe that it was Sir David with his long and distinguished career behind him who had stood in the boy's way.

How could she tolerate it unless . . . unless it wasn't true. Could there be some other reason, other than that put forward by the Guthries, which prevented Cecil from entering Diplomacy? I had no sooner formulated the thought than I put it away from me. What dark secret could there possibly be in the boy's life that would not be at least suspected by us? It was Lady Guthrie's almost insane desire to possess her son and keep him for ever chained to her side that was so horrible.

Horrible, but perhaps also understandable? The case as I reminded myself was by no means an isolated one. One had seen the same thing many times before only usually the victim was a poor sad daughter.

'. . . plans a tour of the Mediterranean in *Thalassa*. . . Still standing by the window I began to read over part of Lady Guthrie's letter: '. . . a wonderful convalescence for my beloved husband if only . . . Cecil naturally very concerned about his father . . . Monsieur Coquelin much impressed with Cecil's appearance in the French comedy and declares himself delighted to acclaim him as a confrère . . .' I read on hoping perhaps to find something I had missed. No, there was nothing. Her dearest boy was firmly planted in Cannes. If he left it, it would be only to travel further away from England and the girl with whom a few months ago we had thought him to be so deeply in love.

Folding the letter I watched a cab turn into the square. It was drawn by a bright chestnut which may have been the reason it caught my attention. I continued to watch until the cabman pulled his horse up in front of our door, then, as the footman came in to light the gas and shut up the room, I went over to the writing-table. A cab stopping at the house—with so many people calling to see Charlie on business, besides those who came to leave cards on me was not an event of any particular interest.

Thinking that I would answer Lady Guthrie's letter in here I sat down at the writing-table.

'Dear Lady Guthrie, Your delightful letter, Charlie and I both so very sorry. . . .'

From the hall I could hear the sound of the inner door being opened and then footsteps on the stairs. Callers! I hadn't known it was so late. I got up quickly and went to sit near the fire. It wouldn't do for whoever was arriving to think that they had disturbed me.

The door was opened and Cecil, hardly giving the man time to announce him, came into the room. I looked at him in astonishment and then sprang to my feet.

'My dearest Cecil, what a delightful surprise.'

He bent to kiss me and then, our hands still joined, we stood looking at each other for a long moment. It was as if we neither of us knew what to say next. I moved away, indicating a chair, motioning him to sit down and doing so myself.

'I had no idea that you were in London. I received a letter from your mother only half an hour ago and it didn't say.'

'I came away very suddenly.' He hesitated—I had never seen him so nervous—and then went on, 'I hope that you don't mind my bursting in without any warning.'

'Of course not, don't be silly. But I was so surprised at seeing you that I forgot to tell Robert that I'm not at home. If you would just . . .'

Cecil was ringing the bell before I had finished speaking.

'We'll go into the boudoir. I'll have tea brought in there and we won't be disturbed.'

While all the elaborate arrangements that are necessary to ensure a modicum of privacy in a London house were being made Cecil and I contrived to keep up some sort of conversation. The burden of it, and this in Cecil's company was most unusual, was borne by me. When we were at last alone he repeated his remark about bursting in without warning me in advance.

I decided that if we were to go on saying things we had already said we should never get anywhere and bluntly asked him if anything was the matter.

He turned and looked at me wildly; his mouth moved although no sounds came from it, then to my utter amazement he slumped forward burying his face in his hands.

I looked at him in consternation, longing and yet not daring to put my arms round him in comfort. I waited until his shoulders were still and his face, of which a glimpse was visible through his interlaced fingers, no longer contorted.

'Try and tell me what's the matter.'

'Everything.' He looked up and away from me.

'Cecil, forgive me but has it anything to do with Lydia?'

'Of course.' His lip trembled but he made another and this time a successful effort to bring his voice under control. 'You know we were engaged, thanks to my mother everyone knew that, well, two days ago I had a letter from her breaking it off.'

'I didn't know that the engagement was a settled thing.'

'You mean you didn't guess? But it was all settled at Kildonan on the evening before we left. I proposed formally and for the last time—on the croquet lawn as it happened—and was equally formally, and also for the last time, accepted. The thing naturally was made subject to my being able to obtain her father's permission which I received a week later in the post.'

'Oh Cecil, why didn't you tell us and Lydia, when we were down in Sussex, was so sly that I ended by concluding that the whole thing must be off.'

'You must admit then that she is wonderful at keeping a secret.'

'When, if she hadn't just broken it off, were you to have been married?'

'That was the only thing about it that wasn't completely happy.

I couldn't see how in my present circumstances and when I am not settled in a profession a definite date could be set. Colonel Marsden as you know is a very rich man, but I could never tolerate, even if her father would allow of it, being kept by my wife. Now the thing is broken off and I don't even know the reason for it.'

'So that's why you came to England. You must have started the moment you received her letter.'

'Except that I took the precaution of waiting until the Paris train was ready to leave. Mother had the impression I was going no farther and so, by the way, had the faithful Thompson. He was absolutely astounded when I told him to order the cab to the Gare du Nord instead of the hotel. I shall have to write to my mother this evening explaining that on reaching Paris I was seized with an irresistible urge to travel on to England. By the time she gets the letter I will be on my way home.'

He was smiling and I hoped that he would now be able to go on with what he wanted to say without feeling the need for further questioning. This, after a little more encouragement, he managed to do. He began, but not until he had begged me to assure him that he was not being disloyal in so doing, by reading a portion of Lydia's letter aloud. It struck me as being a platitudinous little note and I noticed that the whole of it was contained on one sheet of paper. He broke off to ask me whether I thought it meant that she was in love with someone else.

'She was, you know, just before I met her again but that's all over and I believe the man is with his regiment in India.'

I told him that from what I knew of Lydia—not after all a very great deal—I thought it unlikely. 'If being in love with someone else was her reason for breaking her engagement to you I believe she would have said so quite honestly.'

'That's what I thought myself. But it's all so odd. She writes that she loves me and yet at the same time she doesn't think we ought to marry. It seems too that her parents are now against it.'

I asked him—it was a question I could no longer resist—what Lady Guthrie had thought of it all.

'I haven't told her.'

His voice was curiously defiant and I remained silent while he told me his reasons for not doing so. They came down really to one. He couldn't bear to upset her and he hated to think what might be the effect on her if she knew how unhappy he now was.

'She has been particularly low all this autumn and winter. She feels things so very deeply, really much more so than other people, but that of course you know.'

I nodded, murmuring agreement. This was not the time to tell him that I didn't believe that Lady Guthrie's feelings were any deeper than anybody else's.

'Besides,' Cecil said eagerly, 'Mother may never have to know anything about it. If only I can get Lydia to see that she's making a mistake. If she really loves me she must be; and you are fairly sure that there isn't another man?'

'I've told you already that I don't believe there is. But Cecil . . . I shouldn't make *too* much of her saying she loves you. Remember it was a difficult letter to write and that she would want to hurt you as little as possible.'

He got up impatiently. 'But why say it if it isn't true?'

'I'm only asking you not to count on it too much.'

He began pacing up and down the room. 'I thought at first I would go straight from Victoria to Carlton House Terrace— you see she writes from there so they may still be in London. And then I thought I'd like to come here first and ask you what you thought. You saw her such a short time ago you might have known something.'

'But she didn't talk to me at all, not even to tell me you were engaged.'

'You must have some opinion though.'

I hesitated for it had occurred to me that it was her parents who had induced Lydia to break off the engagement. If that were so one could easily imagine the scene which had preceded the writing of the letter. The Marsdens gently urging their objections to long engagements. Lydia, stubborn at first, defending Cecil. Of *course* he loved her. It wasn't *his* fault that they couldn't be married at once, his mother's illness made it impossible, et cetera and et cetera. Yes, of *course* she was sure of her own feelings and of his. Gradually though she would have begun to doubt. Why after all didn't he come to England to see her? She couldn't see that there was anything so particular to keep him at Cannes. Perhaps he had grown tired of her or had met somebody else, and having reached that point in her thinking she had decided to write the letter. If he didn't love her he was honourably released, if he did . . . ?

If I was right there was nothing very much to worry about. Given love there was a good chance that it would live up to its reputation and find a way. Cecil had only to fix a definite date for the wedding and Lydia would immediately fall into his arms. Together they would overcome the opposition, if any really existed, of her parents. 'The time when Lydia broke off our engagement' would pass into the domestic history of the young Guthries. It would be a story which Cecil would occasionally tell against his wife who would always deny that there was any truth in it. She could never have been so foolish—and anyhow she hadn't meant a word of it.

Everything having come out so well in my imagination I was impatient for Cecil to start for Carlton House Terrace.

'If you see her at least you'll know.' I heard my own voice, over-bright, less sympathetic than it had been.

Cecil ceased pacing about the room and came to stand by the sofa. 'At least I'll know.'

'That's what you want isn't it?'

'I suppose so.' He sat down heavily in one of the small chairs. 'Do you think it's a try on?'

Uncertain of what he meant I looked at him in astonishment. He presented an aspect so different from the one of a short while ago that one felt it was a stranger who had sat in that chair and covered his face in order to conceal the tears.

Seeing that he had shocked me he went on quickly. He had not been referring to Lydia, she was a darling, but to her parents.

'I think it's one of those "either or" things. You know, either marry my daughter at once or get out of the way and leave her free to find someone else.'

I told him that the same idea had occurred to me.

'I think they made her write it, or anyhow it's possible that they did.' He took the letter out of his breast pocket and began to read it through again this time to himself. It didn't sound a bit like her, that's why he had been so puzzled by it.

'What a fool I am not to have hit on the idea before. Of course it was her parents who had persuaded her to write it. She is very young you know and they probably went on and on at her until she did it.' His face softened as he sought to excuse her and his eyes were shining. 'I'll go to her now and put everything right and you'll forget you ever saw me looking so sad.' He jumped up, came over to me and took my hand. 'Dear Anne how kind you've been to me.'

'But, Cecil,' I was trying to warn him, 'even if we're right and until you've seen her we don't know that we are, it doesn't really change anything.'

'How so?' He was impatient, longing to be gone.

I held on to his hand making it impossible for him, without rudeness, not to hear me out. As shortly as I could I explained what was in my mind: We couldn't get away from the fact that Lydia had broken off the engagement. She might feel that the whole thing was hopeless and that she would rather end it once and for all than allow it to drag on for years. 'If you ask her to marry you now, well say in April, I think, if she does love you, she will accept. If you keep on asking her to wait I think she will refuse. And I think she will be quite right.'

'Then I shall ask her to marry me in April, and if Mrs Marsden doesn't immediately beg us to wait until June you can call me a Dutchman.'

As I rang the bell I could only hope that his confidence would be justified.

'You'll come back and dine with us?'

'If I am not detained *en famille* with the Marsdens, I shall be delighted.'

Cecil did not dine with us that evening. He did however reappear in Berkeley Square at about a quarter to eight. He looked so happy as he came into the library that we knew at once that all was well.

After wishing me good evening he turned to Charlie. 'Anne's told you of course. But whatever she said is no longer true. Hopelessly out of date.'

Charlie, getting out of his chair, said that he was delighted to hear it.

'And you can't,' Cecil said to me, 'call me a Dutchman, because we're going to be married in June—by special arrangement with Mrs Marsden.'

'And what about Marsden's objections?' Charlie asked, 'you managed to overcome them anyhow.'

'Vanished,' Cecil assured us, 'into thin air. As soon as he's exchanged letters with my father—about money I'm afraid—I'm to be formally accepted by him as a future son-in-law.'

Charlie congratulated him saying that he'd been terribly afraid at one time that he wasn't going to come up to scratch.

'That *I* wasn't going to—oh you mean all that business about not fixing a date. How could I when Father was so ill?'

'He's an old man,' Charlie said. 'He may get ill again.'

A shadow passed over Cecil's face. 'In that case . . . but why anticipate things? And I know Mother will do everything she can . . . Poor darling, I'm afraid she's bound to be terribly lonely. But of course we will be able to spend a great deal of time with her.'

Charlie asked if they had got as far as deciding where they were going to live.

'I hope it will be wherever Lydia wants; that's the correct answer, isn't it, but I must say I'll be disappointed if she doesn't like The Manor. I shall suggest taking her and her mother down there tomorrow. No, perhaps not, it can look very sad in the winter.'

I asked him about his immediate plans and was surprised to learn that he intended to return to Cannes in two days' time.

I didn't think that from Lydia's point of view it sounded very satisfactory but forbore to say anything. We talked for a few minutes longer and then Cecil said that if he wasn't to be late at the Marsdens he would have to go.

He was on the point of leaving when Nealie and Willie, for we also were dining *en famille*, were ushered into the room. Nealie expressed her astonishment at Cecil's being in England. Charlie explained his brother's presence by saying that he had been unable to resist a dinner invitation from his fiancée's family.

'Were any of the men you were engaged to ever as devoted as that?'

Nealie said that at this distance of time she didn't see how anybody could expect her to remember but that it all sounded very lovely for Lydia and she was very glad about it.

'And your being here'—she turned to Cecil—'means that Uncle David and Edythe must be a great deal better?'

Cecil, looking rather uncomfortable, said yes, he thought they were, just a little, but that he still wouldn't feel happy about leaving them for more than a day or two.

'Or your theatricals,' Nealie said. 'Your mother writes that you are doing great things with those. Perhaps we ought all to make up a party and go to Cannes for Christmas. Such fun to see you taking the town by storm and being congratulated by Monsieur Coquelin and the mayor.'

Cecil said that she mustn't believe too earnestly in everything his mother wrote. She sometimes let her pen run away with her. He then said that he really must go; not only was he keeping us from our dinner but probably jeopardizing his entire future as well. It would be too sad, and he was sure Nealie would never forgive herself if her fascinating conversation was the cause of his being horsewhipped by Colonel Marsden—'I'm sure he's a very punctual man; he looks as if he is anyway.'

On Cecil's departure we went in to dinner. His affairs, or as much of them as was known to us all, providing an interesting topic of discussion to be enjoyed with the soup. Charlie and I judged it best not to mention the late temporary interruption of the engagement.

Just before the subject was dropped I congratulated Nealie upon having been right all the time. 'He did propose what he calls formally and for the last time, whatever that may mean, while they were in Scotland.'

Nealie said that that didn't surprise her at all. She had had an instinct about it and when she had those feelings they almost never turned out to be wrong.

She sounded so smug that I couldn't resist telling her that the grand proposal had taken place not as she had foretold in the rose garden but on the croquet lawn.

'Well that's very nice too and it leaves the rose garden for somebody else.'

## Chapter Five

In the end Cecil managed to persuade himself that he could extend his stay in England to five days, but declared that that must be the absolute maximum. His mother's health—and, one wondered, perhaps also the imminence of the theatricals—

made it quite impossible for him to be away from home for a longer period.

The day before he left he carried out his intention, despite the sad aspect that it might present on a winter's day, of taking Lydia and Mrs Marsden to see The Manor. Charlie and I were included in the party which was to meet at Paddington station in time to catch the eleven o'clock train for Windsor. We travelled down in a reserved carriage and the first part of the short journey was taken up in describing The Manor to the Marsdens. This led on to the happy discussion of whether it would or would not be an excellent thing for Cecil and Lydia to make it their principal home.

Mrs Marsden was all in favour of it. Lovely country air—so good for Cecil—and yet so conveniently near to London. So conveniently far too, one sensed it was in her mind although she didn't quite say it, from Cannes. Of course they could always take a house in London for the season and at other times there would be more than enough room for them in Carlton House Terrace.

Cecil, although obviously looking forward to showing off his house and very anxious that they should like it, nevertheless begged Mrs Marsden not to go so fast. After all, Lydia hadn't seen it yet; when she did she might think that nothing in the world would induce her to live in it.

Mrs Marsden and Lydia, speaking together and interrupting each other a good deal, assured him that his being so fond of The Manor made it certain that his future wife would like it too.

'I don't see that at all, we have different tastes in quite a lot of things.' The smile he bestowed on Lydia as he spoke robbed the remark of its harshness.

I told Mrs Marsden what great pleasure the Guthries had taken in building The Manor and how it had always been intended that it should be made over to Cecil as soon as he was twenty-one. I said that I thought the idea that it was to be her son's house was what had most pleased Lady Guthrie when it was being planned.

'She practically designed it herself, you know, and I believe it is very like the British Legation in Madrid. Spain was my father-in-law's last post before he retired and they were both extremely happy there.'

The Manor, Old Windsor, (a curiously incongruous name and address for a house entirely Spanish in character) was looking very lovely when we drove up to it that morning. The sun was shining on its pale walls and the 'shrubberies'—really, a beautifully laid-out plantation. The house, although rather near to a road, is perfectly secluded from it. The small park into which the plantation gradually recedes gives the whole a feeling of great spaciousness.

I notice that I am writing as if it all still existed, but in fact I believe that after it was sold the land was cut up and that a number of houses were built on it. It seems very sad when once it was so perfect, and whenever I have subsequently been in the neighbourhood I have made a point of never going to see it and never driving in that direction.

The carriage drew up in front of the long low facade with its few windows which is all that one sees of the house as one arrives. Cecil, who to make more room for the rest of us had been sitting on the box, jumped down. The front door was thrown open with a welcoming, not very butler-like, flourish by Thompson whom Cecil, in order to make quite certain that everything would be ready for our arrival, had sent down in advance.

Since buying the Villa Victoria the Guthries, except during Cecil's last year at Eton, had never spent more than a month or two in every year at The Manor. Even so the house had never been shut up in any more final sense than that which is implied by holland covers on the chairs, dust sheets over the beds and fire irons wrapped in newspapers.

No such evidence of suspended life was to be seen today. We stepped into the long hall to find blazing fires at both ends of it and masses of hot-house flowers. In the drawing-room there were more flowers than one would have thought it possible for any florist to get into his shop at one time. Cecil and Thompson must have raided every one in London and very possibly Windsor as well.

Mrs Marsden and Lydia declared themselves to be enchanted; Cecil, delighted by their enthusiasm, wanted to show them everything and tell them everything at once. Did they realize that the principal rooms of the house were built round a courtyard? They must come and look at the cloisters. What a capital place he had thought they would make, when his mother first showed him the plans for the house, for roller skate races.

'Oh what fun.' Lydia clapped her hands. 'I can imagine what fun it would have been. Did you ever do it?'

'By the time the house was finished I had more respect for Majolica tiles.'

Mrs Marsden, pacing slowly round the cloisters between Charlie and me, started to talk about the hot houses at East Dean. The greater number of them were given over to Colonel Marsden's now famous collection of orchids. She wondered—the young people had now come up to us—if Cecil wouldn't like to start such a collection at The Manor.

'It can be quite fascinating, you know, and you could begin with one smallish house or at the most two and go on from there.'

Cecil, delighted as usual to consider anything fresh, appeared to catch her enthusiasm.

She said what a pity it was that he couldn't come down to Sussex with them when they went there on Monday. 'I know that you saw the houses when you were there before but Arthur would be able to tell you so much more if he thought that you were going in for it yourself.'

'Alas it is absolutely impossible for me to put off my return to France by so much as another day.'

I noticed that he seemed really to regret it. The prospect of visiting Colonel Marsden and his orchids must therefore, at the moment, have appeared to him to be more attractive than that of returning to Cannes.

His mother or the theatricals? I wondered which it was that finally decided him to refuse Mrs Marsden's invitation. Of one thing one could be sure, Lady Guthrie would never, however ill she was or pretended to be, neglect to provide amusements and employments which would have the effect of drawing him to her side and of making the time he spent with her agreeable.

I turned away feeling a slight shiver pass over me. I had been reminded of that story of Maupassant's, I think it is his, in which a French Countess engages a pretty chambermaid for the express purpose, as she is made to say: *'qu'elle veut retenir son fils à la maison.'* She even goes so far, if I remember correctly, as to provide the maid with *les dessous ornés de dentelles.*

The story of course is a shocking one and I would not want anyone to believe that, as I stood in the cloisters at The Manor on that beautiful sunny morning, I had any idea of connecting Lady Guthrie with any such dreadful thing. I mean only to convey that it had struck me that there do exist circumstances in which a woman may be imagined as doing anything in order to keep her son with her.

The housekeeper now appeared to ask if she might conduct the ladies upstairs and show them the rest of the house.

We reached the top of the stairs and Mrs Pomfret opened the door of Lady Guthrie's bedroom which, with Sir David's dressing-room and a bathroom, occupied on this floor the whole of the south side of the house.

Lydia ran to the window. 'The same beautiful view!' She turned towards us as we stood near the bed and I knew, for how easily the young can give themselves away, that she already saw the room as her own. The unconscious grace of the pose and her heightened colour, which imparted an air of translucence to her whole face, made me doubt whether any artist could find a more perfect model for a picture of youthful happiness.

Mrs Marsden and Lydia, having finished their preparations for luncheon, Mrs Pomfret, obviously longing to show off the house, suggested that she should take them through some of the other bedrooms.

'You'll want to see Mr Cecil's rooms I know, Miss, and, if Madam doesn't mind the stairs, the attic where he used to play as a boy.' The arch smile with which the remark was accompanied made it plain that Mrs Pomfret as well as Thompson was in the secret of the engagement.

'You're sure now, my lady,' Mrs Pomfret asked 'that you'll be able to manage your hair by yourself?'

'Quite sure, thank you, and if it all tumbles down I suppose I can ring the bell and that someone will come.'

'Yes, indeed, and if you will please to ring the upstairs' one I shall hear it myself.'

We smiled at each other and she bustled happily away.

Left in sole possession of Lady Guthrie's bedroom I glanced round it curiously, realizing that I had never before fully taken in the extreme 'fussiness' of its furnishing. Such a lot of hangings, such a plethora of little tables—on each one of which stood innumerable ornaments—such a myriad of chairs and wherever you looked an overpowering wealth of frills!

I walked over to the dressing-table and sat down before it in order to take off my bonnet for Cecil had asked me to make myself look as if I had been staying in the house for weeks. The dressing-table, like every other flat surface in the room, was covered with a mass of objects. With my bonnet removed I was glad to find that the box intended for hair pins did in fact contain hair pins. I settled to the task of taking down and repinning my coiffure. It was not in fact a very difficult one, for in those days my hair was so thick that I had not yet had to resort to those nasty things we used to call 'rats' and the little false fringe that I did wear was quite easy to pin into place.

The whole operation was nearly completed when I noticed that, from the angle at which I was looking at it, I could see a portrait of Lady Guthrie reflected in the dressing mirror. The picture was quite well known to me and usually hung in Sir David's sitting-room in Cannes. I concluded that this one was a copy. Amused by the unexpectedness of this encounter with a picture of a picture I continued, while putting the finishing touches to my appearance, to study the face reflected, above and a little to the right of mine. The painted features were just as I remembered them. How well the artist had caught the brooding expression of the eyes—well, perhaps not exactly brooding. I searched for a word which would more nearly describe the look that was at the same time sleepy and intense. Caught up in a welter of words none of which meant what I wanted them to mean my interest returned to the reflection. Strange eyes, and they seemed to be staring at the place where Lydia had been standing when she was admiring the view. The mirrored glance appeared to be focused on the window which had framed the girl when I thought what a perfect subject she would make for a drawing. I now imagined that the eyes held no kindness and that their expression, veiled under the partially lowered lids, was a malevolent one.

'Stuff and nonsense!' I was just about to turn round and look at the picture itself when the door opened and Mrs Pomfret came into the room. Seeing her look of shocked surprise I realized that I must have spoken aloud. Embarrassed, I jumped up from the table.

'You rang, my lady?'

'No, no I didn't. But I must have been an age. Have the others gone down?'

'They are on their way and I believe that luncheon is ready.'

As she drew aside to let me pass I thought that she was still looking at me with some curiosity. Small wonder if she were: a guest discovered talking aloud to herself in her hostess's bedroom cannot fail to be an oddity.

I ran down the stairs, catching up with Mrs Marsden and Lydia as they reached the hall. Charlie and Cecil joined us and we went into an excellent luncheon. The dining-room at The Manor is furnished in the manner of a monastic refectory and is the only gloomy room in the house. Today we were all in so good a humour that it had no power to subdue anyone's spirits.

After luncheon Cecil told Lydia that the best thing of all had yet to be shown. 'You haven't seen my theatre and that is *really* my own for I designed it entirely myself with a great deal of help from Mother while I was still at Eton.'

'The theatre! I had forgotten all about it and yet we have talked of it so often.'

Lydia sounded positively conscience-stricken and Cecil, laughing, told her that well she might. But to cheer up because when she came to live here she would never have it long out of her thoughts, 'What with learning the parts of Lady Macbeth and helping to sew costumes for the pantomime you may come to wish that the place had never been thought of.'

We started to walk towards the theatre which is built into the second smaller courtyard which also contains the kitchen and the servants' quarters.

'You see,' Cecil said, 'it is connected with the cloisters but the auditorium can also be reached through a door that opens on to the back drive.'

Cecil's theatre at The Manor is, I have always thought, one of the prettiest things in the place. It is, like some of those I have seen in the royal châteaux in France, a real theatre in miniature. His delight in it as he showed it off to the Marsdens, explaining the system of lighting and the manner in which the scenery was changed, was very evident. Watching him as he ran from place to place, pointing out the various parts of it, anxious that nothing should be missed, I was touched by the almost childlike quality of his pleasure. There was something so warming in it that I never forgot it; only later, when Lady Guthrie wrote that it was the promptings of his charitable instincts that had decided her son to build the little theatre, the memory was spoiled for me. Warmth gave way to chill. Of course Cecil hadn't built his theatre, as she claimed he had, for the amusement of the poor, the village people and the inmates of the workhouse and it would have been intolerable if he had.

By the time the theatre had been fully inspected the daylight was beginning to fade. Cecil begged nevertheless that we should make a short tour of the grounds.

'Just five minutes to the end of the plantation so that Mrs Marsden may see where it joins the park. It cannot be seen from the drive or I would suggest that we go in the carriage.'

'Please.' Cecil appealed to me, saying that he had already sent a message to Mrs Pomfret to have all our mantles and things brought down to the 'Priors's Lodging'—this was the nickname for a bedroom and dressing-room on the ground floor. 'It can't take you more than a moment to put them on and be ready.'

There was no gainsaying him. Mrs Marsden was duly shown the park. We then departed for the station. The expedition, for which Cecil had thought of everything, had been a complete success.

## Chapter Six

ON THE FOLLOWING morning, which was Sunday, Cecil, on his way to Victoria, called to bid us good-bye. I was sorry to see that he looked worried and that all the joy of the previous day had departed.

Charlie—we were breakfasting when Cecil arrived—got up from his chair, saying how disappointed he was to see that Cecil had not after all decided to remain a little longer in London. 'At least I suppose you have not'—he looked towards the window—'for I think I can see what looks like a box on the roof of the cab and a shadow that may very well be Thompson lurking inside it.'

'I can only stay a few minutes.' Cecil took the chair the footman had drawn up for him. 'There has been a telegram from Cannes saying that my mother is very much worse. In the circumstances I will not be able to spend a night in Paris but will travel straight on.' Charlie and I said how sorry we were about Lady Guthrie and hoped that there was no immediate cause for alarm.

'Until I arrive there I won't know.' He looked utterly wretched. 'I only came because I wanted to catch a last sight of you both before leaving and to thank you for yesterday, because if you hadn't been there to make it so pleasant, nobody else would have found it enjoyable.' He got up to go. 'I wonder when or if ever we will all meet there again. That is the trouble about being happy—one misses it when it is over.'

As Cecil stooped to kiss me I begged him not to be so despondent. Charlie, patting him on the shoulder, said that when he got to Cannes he would probably find that the news was not nearly so bad as he now feared—'She's liable to these relapses—you ought to be accustomed to them by this time.'

'Unless she was really ill she would never have allowed them to send the telegram.' He hesitated and then, almost as if he was being forced to speak, went on: 'You know I was thinking last night that it might have been better if Lydia and I had been married in the summer. You don't have to tell me that it was impossible.' In order to avoid the objections that he obviously expected us to raise he was speaking very quickly, running his words into each other. 'Of course it was impossible when, if you don't count the years when we were children, we had only known each other for a month or two. And then, my father being so ill. I could never have left Mother to contend with it all alone. It would have been horribly selfish.'

Speaking as quickly as Cecil and probably sounding as angry as I felt, I told him it was nonsense to talk about selfishness. He had a perfect right to his own life and if any sacrifice was going to be involved it belonged to his parents. If he denied it them he was taking away that which nature, the Almighty himself, had given. 'You encourage your mother in what is wrong and that is a very dreadful thing. She is storing up great unhappiness for herself and it is you who are to blame.'

Out of the corner of my eye I could see that Charlie at the other end of the table had taken refuge behind a Sunday newspaper.

'You talk,' Cecil said, 'as if she had done something wicked and yet you know that isn't true. Mother has sacrificed her whole life to me and my father. She has never done one selfish thing, entertained one selfish thought.'

He sounded as if he was too bewildered to be angry, as if he believed with absolute certainty in what he was saying. And yet he couldn't possibly be so stupid!

Our eyes met and it was I who first looked away.

Cecil, still standing by my chair, had started to say something more about having to go, when the door of the dining-room was unceremoniously thrown open and Sybil rushed into the room. In her holland pinafore worn over the plum-coloured merino frock and with her fair hair hanging down her back she really looked very pretty. The fact that her fringe—her hair was inclined to curl—had as usual refused to stay correctly flat enhanced rather than detracted from her appearance.

'Uncle Cecil, Uncle Cecil, I nearly missed you again!' She threw herself into his arms. 'I never know when you are in the house and you never come up and see me.'

'Sybil, Uncle Cecil is just going. Say good-bye to him quickly or you will make him late for his train.'

'Going! But only into the country I hope. You will be back very soon?' She stood holding on to his hand, looking up into his face.

'No, Sybil, I am going back to France, my mother is not well.'

'Oh.' Her lower lip shot out, but at a look from me she recollected her manners enough to say that she hoped Aunt Edythe would very soon be better.

'I hope so indeed and I will give her your best love and,' lowering his voice he spoke to me over Sybil's head, 'I shall not repeat to her any of those disagreeable things you were saying.'

Finding that she was not going to be able to detain her uncle any longer Sybil came over to make her formal 'good mornings' to me.

Charlie went into the front hall to see Cecil off.

Thinking they might have something to say to each other in private I kept my arm round Sybil to prevent her from following them. She wriggled a little but finally stood still.

'It's too bad, isn't it, that Uncle Cecil always has to go? How tiresome it must be to have a mother who is always ill.'

'Very sad indeed. Now if you sit down quietly in that chair'—I indicated the one Cecil had vacated—'you may stay and talk to us while we finish our breakfast.'

'Poor fellow'—Charlie came back into the room—'He seems very upset.'

'Do you think it likely that she is really ill?' As I spoke I looked towards Sybil, hoping that Charlie was not going to say too much in front of her.

He shrugged his shoulders. 'It's possible, but if she is it won't be according to precedent.'

Morning Service at St George's ran its usual quite interesting course. After it was over Nealie returned with us to Berkeley Square where she and I, while waiting for luncheon to be ready, settled ourselves in the boudoir.

'Tell me all about the jaunt to Windsor and what, if anything, has been settled about the wedding.'

'Oh Nealie! And on the way back from church you were saying how ridiculous it was of Charlie to accuse you of liking to gossip. You sounded so earnest about it that I began to believe that you might have reformed. Anyhow, the latest news is that Lydia was delighted with The Manor and that she and Cecil are to be married in June. But the last part you knew. I think it was mentioned the other night.'

'Has Edythe agreed to it?'

I said that I didn't think there had been time for an exchange of letters before Cecil left England and that in any case Lady Guthrie was now again very ill.

'Naturally! But as it won't be June for another six months I don't know why she gave herself the trouble.'

'Now you are being unkind. I know that we always say that she puts it on, but I was wondering in church this morning if she mightn't really be much more delicate than we believe.'

'Personally, I don't think so for a moment and neither, whatever you may be saying now, do you.'

'There was a telegram for Cecil before he left and he said that she would never have allowed it to be sent unless she had been too ill to prevent it.'

'He would say anything that would make her sound less selfish than she really is. I think she's a very disagreeable woman and I may say that I've known her for a good many more years than you have.'

'You're always so violent.'

The words had slipped out before I realized how offensive they might sound. I looked at Nealie and saw that she was offended so with the idea of changing the conversation as quickly as possible I began asking her about her plans; whether she would be going back to Leicestershire next week or would wait until after Christmas?

Nealie said that she thought I knew that she had only left Leicestershire because of the frost. Surely I didn't think that she would take an expensive hunting box, send a pair of carriage horses as well as four hunters up there and then choose to come to London?

In fact, that is-exactly the sort of thing that Nealie is quite likely to do. She spends money without thinking about it and if anyone suggests that she is being extravagant is at a loss to understand what they mean. I think indeed that throughout her life she has never known more than two things about money; it can be made and it can be disembursed. In no circumstances whatsoever would it occur to her that it might be saved—and what fun she has had and what pleasure she has given in its spending!

'If the weather doesn't change soon I shall begin to wish that I hadn't bothered with the English hunting at all but had either stayed in London or gone over to Glenveagh.'

Glenveagh was the house in Ireland to which Nealie and Mr Adair had moved after his family house had been burned down—set fire to, some said, by one or another of the people who hated him. Originally a small and, during the last hundred years, dilapidated castle, Glenveagh had, from the moment she got her hands on it, been extensively altered and added to by Nealie. As with all her other houses it was in a continual state of being enlarged. One of its chief charms, anyhow for Nealie, was the ghost of a 'man in grey' who was reported to walk on the terrace, and whom she claimed to have seen on several occasions.

Nealie had had, or anyhow believed so, for who can tell about these things, several psychic experiences during her life. Some of them had frightened her a good deal. Others, like the time she saw the red glow in the sky on the night that Mr Adair's house was burning—and she fifty miles away with two mountains between her and it—she liked, as she proceeded to do now, to recall.

'I was in Dublin at the time and when the telegram was delivered in the morning I knew at once what it would say. They try and explain that sort of thing now by calling it telepathic communication, but I don't see that it makes it any easier to understand.'

I said that I had never had that kind of experience or at least I didn't think so. As I spoke, something stirred uncomfortably at the back of my mind. The memory of something that had never happened or had happened outside consciousness? The feeling, unaccountable and unpleasant, remained with me for several minutes. I tried to tell Nealie about it but it was too difficult to put into words. Misunderstanding what I had said, she was soon launched on an exposition of psychic phenomena and her own interpretation of what was meant by a sixth sense.

'There is no doubt but that one does sometimes see quite plainly what is the best thing to do and only finds reasonable reasons for it afterwards.'

'So that'—Charlie had come into the room in time to hear the last two or three sentences—'is how you manage your intrigues and why you believe you are able to arrange people's lives for them so much better than they can themselves. I suppose it was a sixth sense which told you that Willie should come to London?'

'That,' Nealie said indignantly, 'was his own idea entirely. I only wrote to Sir Terrence about his joining the firm after Willie had made up his mind about leaving Scotland. And a very good thing that I did for now he has been given the promise of becoming a partner.'

'So far then your meddling has done Willie nothing but good? I can't say that it's done the same for me because until you lured him away to London he was doing very well for me in Scotland.'

Charlie said that it was too bad that Willie couldn't be in two places at once so that Kildonan might continue to benefit from all the sound advice which was now, as far as he could see, being given out exclusively to Nealie.

Nealie, who still didn't seem to notice that she was being teased, said that that was nonsense because Willie, placed where he was at present, was going to be much more useful to all of us than he could ever have been had he remained in Scotland. 'So instead of grumbling you should be very grateful to me.'

'At least I appreciate that the change, from Willie's point of view, is a very good thing.'

'And from ours too,' Nealie insisted. 'Just imagine if anything really awful like a Tichborne claimant happens to us we'll have Willie as well as Sir Terrence on our side.'

'That settles it of course,' Charlie said, 'and makes me almost sorry that I haven't got a long lost brother who might come back and claim Kildonan.'

With an abrupt change of subject Nealie asked Charlie if he really believed in his heart that Lady Guthrie would ever let Cecil marry anyone. 'Anne says that she will and thinks I am being unkind in doubting her.'

Charlie shrugged his shoulders. 'Who can tell. But if I ever had to give an opinion I'd say that Cecil's best chance of getting the thing settled without endless delay would be to elope with the girl immediately.'

'He'd never dare, and I think his only chance is for Edythe to die. It's like somebody serving a life sentence, except in this case it's for the duration of somebody else's life.'

I begged Nealie, I suppose the influence of Sunday morning was still upon me, not to say such dreadful things.

She protested that she hadn't wished for Edythe's death only said, what was obvious to anybody, that until it came about Cecil would always be her slave.

I said, and could hear my own voice tiresomely priggish, that if she insisted upon looking at the thing from that point of view we could all be glad that time was at least on Cecil's side.

'Oh time!' Nealie dismissed it contemptuously. 'The moment young people are in question everyone talks as you do. It's the greatest nonsense; time is always on the side of the middle-aged and against the young because for them it's so long. And I'm certain, whatever is supposed to be arranged now, that Cecil won't be married next June and that Edythe, unless something happens to prevent it, will end by getting her own way over this as well as everything else. If necessary she'll go on being critically ill for another forty years, but as she's too selfish ever actually to die, Cecil will still be tied to her when he's sixty.'

Nealie, who had got up while she was speaking, stood in the middle of the room, her eyes flashing, and looking magnificent.

## Chapter Seven

When Nealie, in December 1887, said that Cecil would not be married in the following June I had not taken her seriously and Charlie had dismissed her diatribe against Lady Guthrie by telling her that he had never had any idea that she was so interested in his stepmother's health. Events, however, proved her to be right, for during the next two years everything seemed to combine to delay Cecil's marriage to Lydia. The date originally set for it had to be given up owing to his catching smallpox in the spring of that year.

'The infection,' as Lady Guthrie wrote in her introduction to *Letters and Diaries*, 'had been contracted in the East End of London where he had been busy amusing the poor children and cheering the sick. Feeling very ill but not knowing what was the matter with him he travelled out to join his parents in Venice. He arrived there with a high temperature and very nearly died.' His convalescence was extremely slow. Made slower still, quite likely, by Lady Guthrie for she insisted, almost as soon as he was able to leave his bed, on taking him on a long journey. During its course they visited Syria and several places in the Middle East the climates of which one would not have thought of as being particularly beneficial to the invalid. It was more than a year before he was fully recovered and the wedding, according to his mother, could again be thought of. After a lot of what Nealie called unnecessary fuss it was then agreed between the parents that the wedding should take place in the autumn of 1889 and preparations for it were set *en train*. At which precise moment Lady Guthrie's health failed her and she in her turn was said to be dying.

'But you'll see,' Nealie promised, when told about this latest contretemps, 'she won't do anything of the kind and what's more she'll take her time about not doing it.'

Again, Nealie was right. Lady Guthrie did not die and it wasn't until the following spring that she admitted to being well enough to come to England in order to be present at the marriage.

In the meantime Cecil paid a short visit to the Marsdens at a house they had recently bought in Northern France and from there wrote to Lady Guthrie:

> 'Tuesday Night, Midnight. Darling Mother, How good you are to let me stay on here some days longer! You are the most perfect mother of modern times! I do hope you are better? My father is so happy to be with you again!
>
> 'This is a real treat to be staying under the same roof as her again, she is so sweet, and I feel she cares and has shown it to me. I cannot tell you how overjoyed I am to find myself right in so many surmises about her: her sensitiveness and power of affection is a delight. I hate tough-skinned women. I do think she will be a delicious little wife, and she has such charm besides. She is so sensible and practical, and will prevent my launching forth into extravagance.
>
> 'I am sorry to say I don't think she cares for music—a great pity, it is so nearly allied to poetry, and its appreciation is so intimately connected with enjoyment of many other subtler influences of life. She is low and depressed and not well. I think it is very difficult for me, who have always been surrounded by such loving care and sympathy by you and my father, to realize how fearfully lowering it must be to have coldness and restraint instead of that motherly love which is the most entirely unselfish and divine of earthly affections.
>
>                 'Your own boy, Cecil.'

The reason, both for Lydia's general lowness and Cecil's complaint as to the lack of sympathy shown towards her by her parents, became obvious when, shortly after Cecil returned home, Colonel Marsden withdrew his permission, which I do not think had ever been given except reluctantly, for his daughter to marry. It was understandable enough that he should not be in favour of the marriage. Cecil, even discounting his mother's anxiety on the score, was not strong. The continual postponements, always coming from the Guthrie side, were not flattering to the Marsdens. Then, there was the disagreeable question of money. Colonel Marsden was a very rich man and Lydia was his only child, while Sir David Guthrie although reasonably well off had no great fortune. The pension which made up quite a large part of his income would die with him and as Lady Guthrie, one of a family of seven children, was practically penniless most of what her husband had to leave would have to be tied up on her for her life. None of which had much to recommend it to the father of an heiress.

But why, as we asked ourselves when we first heard what had happened, had Colonel Marsden decided to put his foot down now rather than earlier? We eventually discovered that although the Guthries had at first promised to make Cecil a handsome allowance they had lately begun to waver. They would do their best to provide him with the sum that had been promised but they didn't know whether it would be possible to put it formally into a marriage settlement. They, or rather Lady Guthrie, for it was unthinkable that any negotiations on the subject were conducted except through her, had so many expenses. These expenses were heavier now, what with one thing and another, than they had been when the settlement was first discussed. It was easy to imagine the kind of letter that had arrived from Cannes, and it takes no effort of the imagination to understand why Colonel Marsden ended by losing his temper.

If he couldn't actually prevent Lydia from marrying he could and would, as he stated in a furious letter to Lady Guthrie, refuse to give her anything at all if she insisted on going against his wishes. Lady Guthrie replied that in that case Sir David must refuse to settle anything on Cecil. The result for the time being, for it was unimaginable that either side would give way immediately, was deadlock.

If the thing had happened to some other young man he might possibly, as Charlie had long ago suggested as a solution for Cecil, have ran off with the girl and married her out of hand. Cecil, however, and I'm sure it was another reason for Colonel Marsden's objections to him, had not been trained for any profession and was quite incapable, rendered so by his mother, of earning any sort of living.

I did not see a great deal of Cecil during this period. He did however come to us in Scotland for a few days in the summer of 1890. The engagement had then been 'off' for several months and he was, not unnaturally, although he did his best to hide it, very low and unhappy. We did our best, although how foolish to try and heal unhappiness with picnics and days on the moor, to cheer him up. I like to think all the same that we perhaps succeeded a little.

For me it was another summer which marked a domestic milestone, for Alistair, having left his private school at the end of the preceding term, was due to go to Eton in September. This event necessitated, for he had taken a low place in the school, a holiday tutor. The young man selected for the job, Alan Helbert, succeeded in bringing our son on in what the headmaster of his private school called, his weaker subjects—which as far as any of us could make out was all of them. Charlie and I, as well as Alistair, found Mr Helbert extremely pleasant and he returned to us on several subsequent occasions, whenever, in fact, low marks on Alistair's part rendered his presence necessary. Only Nealie persisted in saying that there was something about him that she didn't like.

Colonel Marsden had proved himself to be a stern father. Having done so, and having written what he intended to be a final letter on a disagreeable subject, he must have gone thankfully back to his orchid houses. As a place where marriages took place only at his direct instigation they must at that time have been particularly agreeable to him.

A stern father, but not one capable of remaining adamant for ever! He was fond of his daughter and she was very unhappy. She vowed that if she couldn't marry Cecil she wouldn't marry at all. Her mother declared Lydia was going into a decline—or if not quite that, had at least lost a great deal of weight. Gradually, it took him nearly a year to do so, Colonel Marsden began to give way. A letter arrived for him from Cecil and was answered. Shortly afterwards the engagement was renewed, a settlement of a kind was drawn up and a date set for the wedding. But this time, and that at least he would adhere to, there were to be no delays. Cecil and Lydia could marry in October 1891 or they could not, as far as Colonel Marsden was concerned, be married at all. He intended, as he clearly stated to the affronted Lady Guthrie, that nothing, short of the death of the bridegroom, was going to lead to any more of these ridiculous postponements.

This 'now or never' attitude adopted by the bride's father made the bridegroom happier than he had ever been in his life. As soon as the thing was settled he rushed off to stay with the Marsdens in France and from there wrote to his mother:

Dearest Mother,

So grieved for this continual pain you tell me of in your dear letters . . . I had the weirdest journey, missed my train hither and had to roost at Versailles. I proceeded hither on the top of a bus Sunday morning, all of a heap, amongst packages and packing-cases in a very useful Scotch mist. Yesterday we made things cheerful in various ways . . . After a theatrical dressing we started off in a four-in-hand of ponies for a fair at where we rode the horses of wood, I doing one or two acrobatic acts, and kissing my hands affectionately to the mob, which came to an abrupt conclusion owing to my hostess—she objected to my extravagance! We returned as gaily as we went.

Last night I was tired, as you may imagine, but I am so, so happy, all so kind and affectionate to me. I know I ought to have written to you yesterday, but I really had hardly time allowed me to blow my nose . . . My flower's charm is wonderful. I am sure she will be a wife to love with all one's heart. She is not extravagant—is not that wonderful! You will be happy in our happiness, and it is so great.

> Darling Mother,
>
> Your own boy, Cecil.

Intensive preparations for the wedding started a full month before it was due to take place. It was to be in the grand manner, although of course big weddings were then much smaller affairs than they became later. In those days, although the custom was already beginning to change, people invited only their relations and more intimate friends to see them married and didn't bother with persons whom they had only met once in their lives.

Cecil, always anxious for perfection and always concerned for a good theatrical effect, took an enthusiastic part in planning all the details of the arrangements. He came over from France at the end of September, settled himself at his club, and spent the ensuing weeks rushing between London and Windsor. It was so important that the bridesmaids' dresses should be of exactly the right tone to blend with the flowers with which he was going to decorate St George's. It was equally important that the minor alterations that were being made to The Manor should be done in exactly the way he wanted them. Nothing must be omitted that would make the wedding ceremony, the honeymoon journey to India and Ceylon, and the return to The Manor less than perfect in every particular.

If there was any flaw in all this perfection it was the minor one of Lady Guthrie being said to be equally busy putting the finishing touches to the wing she had lately added to the Villa Victoria. We all wondered how much time she would in future manage to make the young couple pass under that roof. But what after all did that really matter when everything else had at last come out so well?

Charlie and I had spent the greater part of the month between Berkeley Square and the various shooting parties to which we had been invited. Parliament was in session and as Charlie was then Under Parliamentary Secretary for the Colonies it was very often difficult for him to get away from London and often we had to leave our friends' houses the moment shooting was over on the last day.

It was on our return from one of these scrambled visits that we were met with the news that Mr Cecil's man had called round twice during the afternoon to ask that Mr Guthrie should go to his brother at the Bachelors' Club as soon as possible.

'You mean tonight?' Charlie, hungry for his dinner and with a long evening of work in front of him, sounded annoyed.

The butler said that he imagined so and that Thompson had appeared to think that the matter was urgent.

'Perhaps he is ill and Thompson didn't say so.' I made the suggestion because I couldn't think of any other reason why Cecil, whose formal manners were usually so punctilious, had omitted the courtesy of a written message.

'No, my lady, I particularly asked Thompson if Mr Cecil was confined to his bed or anything of that kind and he said, no.'

'In that case,' I turned to Charlie, 'why don't you send round a message to the club asking Cecil to come here? And if you liked we could ask him to stay to dinner. Nealie and I half arranged that she should come in afterwards on her way home from the Somersets—their dinners are always what she calls so abominably early—but otherwise we shall be alone.'

Charlie, who had not yet taken off his overcoat, hesitated, finally made up his mind and turned back towards the door before which the carriage still stood. 'I might as well go. If Cecil comes here we almost have to ask him to dinner and the thing will drag itself out and I shall lose half the evening.'

I went on upstairs to sit for a little while in the boudoir. I was chilled from the journey and hoped that my maid, whose cab had just arrived, was not going to take too long over the unpacking. Pulling a chair as close to the fire as possible I thought how sad it was to come home now that Sybil, who in April had departed with Miss Wilson for Dresden, was no longer here to welcome our return. Fondly, I remembered how wildly excited she had been when she left. The idea that she was to be separated from Charlie and me for nearly six months not appearing—as was only natural—to affect her spirits in the least. Her only worry, voiced as her train started to draw out of Victoria, being that something might happen to prevent her returning in time to be Lydia's bridesmaid.

'Mama you promised. You won't write and say when the time arrives that it isn't worth while my coming home for only a few weeks?'

'I never do break promises. I consider them to be sacred.'

The train had been moving quite fast and I think it probable that Sybil didn't hear me. A gentleman standing close to me on the platform must, however, have done so. As I turned to walk back to the barrier I saw him looking at me with that cautious expression of doubt, mixed with amusement and apprehension, that is usually reserved for revivalists.

Thinking of Sybil as a bridesmaid brought me back to the subject of Cecil. I wondered, but with no great sense of urgency or any premonition of anything really dreadful, what had gone wrong. Probably, so I decided, nothing at all. Thompson and our butler between them must have managed to imbue the message from the club with a misleadingly dramatic quality. Charlie, thinking ahead to his hot bath, was most likely already on his way home. Having found out that it had been unnecessary for him to leave it in the first place, he would be cursing his brother's importunity and brooding over the small amount of brain possessed by all servants; his own and Cecil's in particular.

'Your bath, my lady.' The maid stood at the door of the boudoir.

I looked at the time. She had not after all been very quick. Charlie had been gone for more than half an hour. At that moment I heard him in the front hall. I got up and crossed the room. Someone was running up the stairs, then Charlie, brushing aside the maid, was in the room. He shut the door behind him.

'She's broken it off.'

'Who, Lady Guthrie?'

'No, Lydia.'

'It isn't possible!' I was horrified, not knowing if I could believe what I heard.

Charlie sank down on a chair. He was breathing very fast and I wondered if, having dismissed the carriage, he had run the whole way from Hamilton Place.

'It isn't possible; there must be some mistake.'

'No, Colonel Marsden has been to see him and he brought a letter from Lydia. Cecil, well you can imagine, is practically demented.'

I sat down, still not believing what I now knew to be true. 'Poor little Cecil, what are we going to do?'

'He'll have to come here.'

Charlie looked thoroughly exhausted and I asked him if he had told the footman to bring up the whisky decanter. He shook his head and I rang the bell. Then he began to tell me a little of what had happened and what arrangements he had so far been able to make.

On going round to the club he had been taken up to Cecil's bedroom where he had found his brother in a state of what he described as near collapse.

'That idiot Thompson hadn't had the sense to send for a doctor. Or as a matter of fact I believe he did suggest it but gave up the idea immediately when Cecil objected to it. Anyhow as soon as I saw how things were I sent for Symonds. Fortunately he was at home, and I waited until he came.'

'And what did he say?'

'He called it nervous shock and suggested bed and a sedative.'

I told him to hold off until we could get Cecil over here. Symonds is waiting with him and will bring him round in his own brougham as soon as we send to say that the bedroom and everything is ready.

I am afraid it will be a nuisance but there wasn't anything else I could do.'

'Of course he must come here.'

The footman came in in answer to the bell. I told him to bring the decanter and said that a spare room, the one at the back which was the quieter, was to be prepared for Mr Cecil immediately.

'He is not well so he will be going to bed as soon as he gets here. If he has any dinner it will be on a tray and ours must be put back for at least half an hour.'

The man withdrew and I turned to Charlie. 'Why did she do it?'

Charlie shrugged his shoulders. 'I don't know. Cecil was all but incoherent and the girl's letter, which he showed me, was as vague as it was possible to make it. Vague only as to reasons. I'm afraid the fact that she was not going to marry him was almost brutally clear. I shall have to try and see Marsden later on this evening and find out what happened.'

I got up, saying that I would go and see that everything was being done as quickly as possible.

'It shouldn't take very long so if you like to send round to the club now I promise it will all be ready when he arrives.'

As I passed Charlie's chair I paused to kiss the top of his head and to lay my hand against his cheek. Sorry as I was for Cecil I wished that it wasn't always Charlie who was expected to do something about it when things went wrong. Here he was with his carefully husbanded evening of work, for the sake of which we had rushed away from the country and the company of amusing friends, completely destroyed. He would make up for it, as I knew only too well, by working through the early hours of the morning; going to bed at last only when complete exhaustion made it impossible for him to work any longer.

The next hour—or it may have been longer or less—was passed in all the activities contiguous upon getting Cecil from the Bachelors' to Berkeley Square and finally settled in a bedroom. Watching him being helped into the hall by Dr Symonds and Thompson I was shocked by his appearance and it proved to be necessary for him to be carried upstairs. A trained nurse, previously summoned by Dr Symonds, arrived only a few minutes after the doctor's brougham.

I have noticed before that during any crisis, especially one with an emotional content, time seems either to stop completely or to pass so quickly—like a watch that is running down—one does not keep up with it.

I know that at some time during the evening we sat down to dinner. Dr Symonds, whose own dinner must have spoiled long before, was with us. He had just come down from seeing Cecil. Anxiously, when the servants were out of the room, we asked him what he now thought of his patient.

At first, as is the way of doctors, he was inclined to be non-committal. Then, having evidently made up his mind to be frank with us, he said that he thought it possible, although he had not been able to get him to admit it, that Cecil had taken more chloral than was good for him.

'Oh, no!' I was unable to repress my cry of horror.

'If he did,' Dr Symonds turned to Charlie, 'it must have been just before you reached him. I blame myself now for not thinking of it sooner. I have to tell you this but it is my honest opinion that the half hour more or less that was involved can have made no difference.'

'How serious?' Charlie's eyes were on the doctor's face.

'His chances of recovery are almost certain. For anyone with a sound constitution there would be no doubt of it.'

Charlie, reminding Dr Symonds of his father's age, asked if he should telegraph to Cannes.

'In the circumstances . . .' the doctor hesitated, 'Lady Guthrie as I remember'—he had attended her on one occasion when she had been in London—'is an hysterical subject.'

'She is subject to mysterious illnesses for which no cause has ever been discovered.'

'Then I think you are justified in not telegraphing tonight.'

'Very well,' Charlie accepted the responsibility, 'and in the meantime we had better get on with our dinner,' and he rang for the next course.

As soon as the meal was over Dr Symonds went upstairs. He was gone a very short while and when he came down to us in the library he brought a satisfactory report. Cecil was sleeping more or less quietly. If no complications set in he ought to be all right.

Charlie asked what complications one could expect.

'It's hard to say.' It was obvious that Dr Symonds had hoped to leave the possibility in an indefinite state. 'His heart isn't as strong as it might be—and of course pneumonia—although at the moment I don't believe there is any great danger of it. Naturally, the shock itself, his engagement being broken, is likely to take its toll.'

The butler came in to announce that Mrs Adair was in the hall. Was he to show her in or, and he cast a meaning glance at Dr Symonds, say that we were engaged?

I directed that Nealie should be taken up to the boudoir and told that I would be with her in a few moments.

Dr Symonds, probably anxious to escape from further questioning, said that he must be off. The nurse had her instructions. If there was any unforeseen change in the patient's condition during the night he was to be sent for. He very strongly advised against anyone other than the nurse going into Cecil's room.

When the doctor had gone I asked Charlie if he was coming upstairs to see Nealie—'We need to be cheered up or calmed down and she's the one person who can do both.'

'I don't want this affair discussed until after I have seen Marsden. I'm going down now to meet him at Brooks's.'

'The note that was brought in while we were at dinner was from him?'

'The answer to one I sent earlier. I don't want to keep him hanging about, so you must make my excuses to Nealie.'

'But what can I tell her—we can't make a mystery of Cecil's being in the house.'

'You must say what you think best. No one must ever know about the chloral; that much at least is obvious, I don't have to tell you.'

When I got upstairs I found that Nealie already knew that Cecil had been brought to Berkeley Square and that a nurse was in the house. The butler had 'let it out' in the course of making up the fire.

As I came into the room she got up to greet me. She was looking wonderful in a brown velvet dress trimmed with masses of ecru lace. The diamond dog-collar which she had lately taken to wearing and the small tiara, affectionately known as 'the third best' glinted as she moved.

'Tell me, Anne, is he really as ill as Purvis made out?'

'As I don't know what Purvis said I can't tell you. At least Dr Symonds doesn't think that there's any immediate danger.'

Of course Nealie wanted to know all about it: when had Cecil been taken ill, and what was the doctor's diagnosis?

I put her off as best I could and when she saw that I didn't want to be questioned she let the subject die away.

'You must be very worried all the same. I think I had better go.'

I told her that Charlie had had to go out on some kind of business and that if she didn't think it too late and wasn't tired I would be glad of her company—'If I did go to bed I shouldn't sleep for I would be listening for the nurse with one ear and for Charlie with the other.'

Tactfully, she forbore from asking me if Charlie's business had anything to do with Cecil, but I think she suspected that there might be a connexion between the two.

An hour passed while we talked on indifferent subjects. Once I crept to the door of Cecil's room but could hear no sounds from within. On a second occasion I tapped very lightly; the nurse came and whispered that he was sleeping peacefully. Coming out on to the landing she begged that I wouldn't worry, that his pulse and temperature were both satisfactory.

She smiled at me reassuringly. 'He isn't going to die my dear. I've seen so many and it gets so that one can tell.'

I thanked her and went back to Nealie. I told her that the news was good and we agreed that we both had more faith in nurses than we had in doctors.

Nealie again suggested that she should leave. 'You look worn out and now that you have such a good report of Cecil you may be able to sleep.'

The door opened and Charlie, somehow I had missed hearing his key or his footsteps on the stairs, came into the room.

'How good of you, Nealie, to be still here,' he kissed her affectionately, 'and looking so magnificent as if there were no troubles in the world.'

'How horrible you make that sound, but I was just going. I have to ask for a cab as I didn't keep the carriage. I have had it out late every night this week and Prior was beginning to be cross. He seemed to think that one more hour would have resulted in both the horses being found dead in the morning.'

She had risen to her feet but Charlie, standing beside her, did not move. Instead he reached for her hands and pushed her gently back into a chair.

'You have been kept so long as it is that you may as well make it a little longer. Anne has told you what has happened?'

'Only that Cecil is ill, but now the nurse appears to think that he is better.'

'One can be glad for that anyhow and if that's all you know I must say that you are both more discreet than I ever gave you credit for.'

He came over and kissed me and then went and stood by the fire while I told him what the nurse had said.

He looked relieved and said what a good thing it was that we hadn't telegraphed. 'Sending to my father,' he turned to Nealie, 'would have been just as bad, for of course Edythe has all the household arrangements made on a pattern which ensures that nothing can be kept secret from her.'

Nealie said that Uncle David must very often miss his despatch boxes—'I wonder if she ever approached the Foreign Office on the question of getting duplicate keys made for herself?'

'If Anne hasn't told you you might as well know it now, for the thing is quite definite, the engagement has been broken off.'

Nealie, as I had done earlier, protested that it was impossible. Convinced that the impossible had come to pass she posed all the questions that had been in my mind, and for which there had been no time, when the news was told to me.

Charlie, sitting down, said that he was sure that it wasn't necessary for him to ask that neither of us would repeat anything of what he was about to say. 'I asked you to remain, Nealie, so that you can help us to decide on what we are going to tell Edythe, and, although this will surprise you until you hear what I have to say, what we are going to tell Cecil.'

'I hate to think of her triumphing over him. She must be told as little as possible and none of the truth. Above all, absolutely nothing that would make her decide to come to England. Nealie's eyes were flashing. The Civil War, 'up the Yankees' spirit, which Charlie so often teased her about was at its highest.

Charlie said that Lady Guthrie coming to England was perhaps the least of our worries—'she is reported to be in a very suffering state and in fact unable to leave her bed for the past fortnight.

'She'll get better the moment she knows he isn't going to be married. But do go on and tell us what's happened.'

'I was about to do so when you interrupted me, but it isn't going to be easy.'

Charlie then told us, I imagine more or less in its entirety, what had passed between him and Colonel Marsden. 'First of all there is, but don't say anything yet because it's not the most important part, another man in the case. For Lydia's sake and for Cecil's as well, for it is likely that she will marry the fellow, I am glad of it.'

'How can you say that!'

Hardly noticing the interruption he went on: 'If she is married to someone else Cecil has lost her irrevocably not only in fact but in the eyes of the world and there can be no more of this on-and-off business.'

'But they were to have been married within a month!' This time it was I who had interrupted.

'There could have been no marriage, there is indeed a very grave reason against it. Nealie must forgive me for putting it plainly but the fact is my brother is incapable of having children. He is incapable now and possibly may never be capable of it.'

'Charlie, did you know this before?'

He hesitated. 'You might say I suspected it and yet didn't want to know it. Had I been sure I would have begged him to break off the engagement, had he refused I might have gone to Colonel Marsden. How can I tell what I *would* have done—and none of that matters now anyhow.'

'It's appalling.' Nealie sat staring in front of her, her position frozen.

I remembered the rumours which had surrounded the death of her first husband. Long ago Charlie had told me about them. We had never known, for these things were spoken of even less then than they are today, whether or not there was any truth in them.

How could Cecil have let the engagement go on?' Nealie still sat without moving any part of her body.

'It was very wrong,' Charlie shifted his position, 'but there are circumstances attached to it which make one disinclined to condemn him utterly. I think it more than possible that Cecil didn't know about the thing himself until after Marsden had given his final permission for them to be married. By that time everything was arranged, for everyone, always excepting Edythe, had been made happy. The woman upon whom all his hopes had rested for nearly five years was—and by that time it must have seemed to him it had only been brought about by a miracle—going to be his wife. He knew that he was cured and that there could be no danger to her. He knew that he could be a husband although not a father and that in time even that potential might be restored to him. The temptation to say nothing was very great.'

'I see.' Nealie drew a deep breath. 'How did Colonel Marsden come to know of it?'

'I've already told you that I myself, had I been sure of it and had Cecil refused to do so, might have gone to him.'

'But it wasn't you and so there is only one person whom it could have been.'

'The letter was written by my father.'

'We all know what that means,' Nealie said, 'but what I can't make out is why the letter wasn't written sooner?'

'The reason given by my father was that the thing was not known to him until very recently. He said, as far as I can remember the wording of his letter, that Cecil not, he gathered, having done so, he felt it to be his duty to lay the facts before Marsden.'

'Edythe's name was of course not mentioned in any way?' Nealie thought for a moment, 'but I'm sure that the letter must have been written at her instigation. It's possible even that she told Uncle David that Cecil, unable to bring himself to the point of telling Colonel Marsden himself, wished his father to do so on his behalf.'

'She may even have written the letter herself.' I have never heard Charlie's voice more bitter. 'The writing seemed to be my father's, but so much stronger than it has been lately that . . .' he broke off.

We were all silent for a few moments and then I asked Charlie what he had meant when he said there was another man.

He answered that Colonel Marsden had been frank with him on the point. The young man was one whom Lydia had met when she first came out. She had been on the point of becoming engaged to him when Cecil had reappeared on the scene. The young man, Charlie told us his name, and I remembered that I had already heard something of the story from Cecil, had been discarded on the instant. He thereupon transferred to the battalion of his regiment then stationed in India. Six months ago he had returned, as much in love with Lydia as when he went away, and Lydia had fallen in love with him.

'Marsden believes, and from what I know of her I agree with him, that Lydia would, if things had gone forward in the way that they seemed to be doing, never have broken faith with Cecil. She would have married him in spite of the fact that she was no longer in love with him—and they would both have stood an excellent chance of being unhappy.'

'I think I can understand it,' Nealie said. 'In Lydia's place I would always have felt that somehow in the end Edythe would succeed in getting the marriage postponed.'

I asked when Colonel Marsden had received Sir David's letter. Charlie said it had been yesterday evening. 'You can imagine what a shock it was to him and Mrs Marsden and how difficult it was for her to break it to Lydia and explain to her what it was all about.'

Nealie said that she didn't think that girls were usually as ignorant as people were wont to believe—'I know that I wasn't.'

Charlie remarked that as Nealie and her sisters had been brought up on a farm in the wilds of America that wasn't to be wondered at, but that with English young ladies the case was very different.

'Upper New York State was never the wilds in *my* day, *nor* in your mother's. Aunt Lizzie as well as ourselves had an excellent education.'

'So I have often heard you say and the local Indians were quite tame and used to come up to the house in the politest manner in order to be done out of their lands by our grandfather.'

Nealie said that it hadn't been like that at all as Charlie, when he wasn't trying to be amusing, knew perfectly well.

'Anyhow,' Charlie ignored her and went on, 'Mrs Marsden had a very distressing time of it with Lydia. The girl, not surprisingly was completely bowled over. I suppose that there were tears and probably hysterics. In the course of a very painful scene it came out, Lydia had never said anything about it before, that she was in love with this other man. She told her mother that believing it was her duty to honour her engagement to Cecil she had put all thought of the other man away from her. I think she thought it was very wrong of him to speak to her when he knew that she was to be married to my brother.'

'Very noble,' Nealie said, 'but then the young always have such high ideals. I suppose that it's natural. Having lived for a shorter time than we have they have had less to put up with.'

I told Charlie that I was surprised that Colonel Marsden had told him so much—'after all, Sir David's letter gave them more than enough reason for ending the engagement.'

'He said that he preferred, and that it was his daughter's wish also, that we should know the truth. He knew that it would go no further and I then asked his permission, which he gave, to tell Nealie. How much of it should be passed on to Cecil was left to us to decide.'

'And what are you going to do?' Nealie and I asked the question together.

'I don't know and of course there can be no question of saying anything while he is so ill.'

'Whatever happens,' Nealie said, 'you won't tell Edythe about the other man?'

'I shall not but Cecil, if he learns of it, may do so.'

'If only she had not put so many obstacles in their way at the beginning!' I was thinking of the day, four years ago now, which we had spent at The Manor. 'He was so happy and so was she—and her mother and you and I because of it.' I turned to Charlie. 'They were going to be married in the following June and then because of the small-pox they couldn't be.'

'She could have gone to him in France and the voyage of recovery would have been their honeymoon.'

I looked at Nealie and saw that she was crying.

## Chapter Eight

THE ILLNESS which Cecil sustained as a result of his great loss was, as Lady Guthrie said in *Letters and Diaries*, a long one. She of course never knew, or I do not think she did, that he was suffering not only from emotional shock but also from the ill-effects of an overdose of chloral.

Charlie, after the first day had assured us that there was no immediate danger, had written to Lady Guthrie. Of what use was it, as he said, to worry his father if he knew nothing about the letter he was supposed to have written? Charlie told Lady Guthrie that the letter's reception had resulted in the breaking off of the engagement. He said that she would not be surprised to learn that it had been a terrible blow to Cecil, who was now staying with us. The doctor had advised complete rest and Thompson was looking after his master splendidly. Charlie did not mention, again of what use was it to worry people unnecessarily, that there was a nurse on duty at night.

On Friday Cecil was judged to be a little better and Charlie decided that he must talk to him. The time he chose was eleven o clock in the morning. He asked me before he went into the bedroom to remain indoors saying that after he had seen Cecil he might want to consult me.

'I suppose I shall find you in the boudoir?'

'Writing dull letters to dull people. It's only the tedious ones that are always waiting for an answer. The interesting ones seem to get themselves written without my noticing it.'

I had been writing for rather less than half an hour when Charlie joined me.

'It didn't take very long?'

He sat down looking tired and very sad. 'I don't know whether I have done good or harm. Tell me, when you have been in to see him, has he said anything to you?'

'Nothing of any significance and when I offer to read to him he seems to welcome it as precluding conversation.'

Charlie leant forward, his elbows on his knees, his chin supported by his hands. 'As soon as I started to speak he more or less broke down and then he went on and on blaming himself for everything. It was impossible to stop him.'

'And yet what he did was very natural. I suppose there are many young men living alone in Paris and in his situation who would have done the same?'

Charlie hesitated before answering. 'You know my brother has been brought up abroad and in many ways thinks as a Frenchman. As he sees it any unmarried man—I didn't inquire what would have been his principle as a married one—has a perfect right to amuse himself as he did. He does think however that his own case is exceptional.'

'Why should he believe himself to be different from anyone else?' I got up from the writing-table and started to walk about the room.

Charlie said that now that he was beginning to get the thing sorted out in his mind he thought that Cecil believed that his fault lay in the fact that he had deliberately tempted fate. 'He thinks that all his life he has been consistently unlucky and that when at last God gave him this wonderful prize a sacrifice was demanded of him in return. He thinks that what is given freely to others must be paid for by him.'

'But all this is purest superstition.'

'I don't know,' Charlie sighed. 'I suppose it is. And I'm not sure even now that I fully understood what he was trying to say. It was all mixed up with his feelings for his mother. Whether or not he feels that he has yet paid the price for the honour of being her son I wouldn't know.'

'He must surely realize that by preventing him from marrying when he was younger and when he and Lydia were both so deeply in love, she has ruined his life.'

Charlie shrugged his shoulders. 'You know he will never hear a word said against her or criticize her himself in any respect.'

'Did you say anything directly to him about Lydia? I suppose that if she is going to announce her engagement to someone else it would be better for Cecil to be warned of it in advance.'

'She can't possibly do that yet, but when I started speaking about her he became so upset that I thought it better to leave him. I shall try and see him again in the late afternoon. Maybe, if I can get away from the House, just after tea.' He got up. 'You'll be in then, I suppose, or is it a charity committee day?'

'No, it's a nice day, no charity committee, no receptions and not a single call that won't wait until tomorrow. The weather is perfectly horrid and I shall spend the afternoon alone with three books from Mudies. They've been in the house for more than a week without my having had time to open them.'

Charlie said that it sounded a delightful programme and that he envied me.

When he had gone I went back to the dull letters. Having been brought up in the illogical belief that novel reading is an unsuitable occupation for the morning hours I have never been able to discard it.

Immediately after luncheon I went up to Cecil's room. I knocked and Thompson, coming to the door, said that he was just settling his master for his afternoon nap. I thought the man looked tired and suggested to him that he should go and get some rest and that I would sit with Cecil while he slept. 'I might as well read my book here as downstairs and if you place the screen between his bed and the window he won't be disturbed.'

Thompson said that that was what he had been doing as Mr Cecil couldn't bear to have the curtains drawn during the day.

Cecil called from the bed to say that it was unnecessary for anyone to be with him. But that he was grateful for my offer, for without it he would not have been able to persuade Thompson to leave him. 'If he doesn't get out of this room soon he will end by being much more ill than his patient.'

I went to get my book and when I crept into the room five minutes later Cecil was already nearly asleep. I settled myself in the low chair by the window and the next hour passed very happily in the sole company of Miss Rhoda Broughton.

At the end of the hour I heard moans coming from the other side of the screen. I went over to Cecil and saw that he had slipped so far down in the bed that his head no longer rested on the pillows. He was sleeping restlessly, turning from side to side and as I stood there the moans changed to cries of distress. His face was very red and I judged that the fever which this morning had been low must have risen by several degrees. I was just wondering whether I should awaken him when his eyes opened. He lay quite still on his back, staring at me, obviously not yet fully conscious. Presently a look of recognition came into his face and in a voice which was much stronger than it had been earlier he begged me not to be so scared.

'You look as if you had seen three ghosts and a street accident all at once and didn't know what to do about any of them.'

The tone of his voice, sounding like a well person and not a sick one, and the smile which accompanied it was somehow more worrying than the cries and moans which had preceded it. Trying to hide my disquiet I stooped over him, attempting to pull him further up in the bed. He didn't seem to be able to do very much to help me and it took me some minutes to get him and the pillows back into their proper relative positions.

'We were wrong to let Thompson escape,' Cecil was still smiling, 'for he can pick me up like a baby. I had no idea all the same that you were so strong.'

'I am a very good nurse and have had a lot of experience.'

'Really, I thought that Charlie was never ill. He had all the luck there, for when he was born my father was only forty-six which was not so bad. By the time I arrived he was getting to be an old man.'

'Cecil!' But I didn't know what I could say to him.

'Now you are looking frightened again but I was only talking about heredity. It can be a very interesting subject. In our family, as I was saying, Charlie had more fortune with it than I. A strapping American mother, even if she did manage to die as a result of his confinement, was a better proposition than a poor sickly Irish girl. A girl who, at the time of her marriage, should by rights still have been in the schoolroom. I am sure she must have mentioned the matter to you. Some people say that the schoolroom was situated in a bog but that of course isn't true.'

I looked at him helplessly, not sure of what to do. Ought I to send for Dr Symonds? And if he came I would be able to tell him that his patient had been talking about heredity! I looked at Cecil closely. The signs of fever which I had noticed earlier had disappeared. Thinking I would take his pulse rate I reached for his wrist but he snatched it away.

'I do not think you can be quite as good a nurse as you say. My temperature is quite normal now but if you insist on teasing me it will go up. But we were talking about my mother.' His voice broke on the last word.

'Can I give you some barley water?' I started towards the table where it was kept. The bed, having been moved in order to make things easier for the nurse, was now on the opposite side of the room from the bell-rope.

I had hardly moved when there was a cry of rage from Cecil. 'Anne, I have already asked you not to tease me. There is nothing to ring for'—so he must have sensed that the bell had been my objective—'do please sit down and let me talk to you quietly.' As he indicated a chair near the bed he was shouting at the top of his voice.

I hesitated, but thought it was better to do as he asked.

'I have been lying here for two days with neither you nor Charlie coming anywhere near me. Now when at last I get a chance to talk to you, you do nothing but fidget about the room like a demented chicken.'

'It's unkind to say that we haven't been to see you.'

'Is it? Yes, I suppose so,' he passed his hand over his forehead, 'but what with the nurse and what with Thompson our conversations have been very disjointed.'

I nodded, glad to notice that he seemed to be calmer.

'It's not Charlie's fault about having all the luck. I am sure he would have shared it with me if he could. And yet I don't know, his mother was very rich. If her fortune had had to be divided in two I don't expect he'd have liked it.'

I begged that if we were to talk it should be about something else.

'Yes, of course, that wasn't what I wanted to say anyhow.' Suddenly, although a few minutes earlier he had hardly been able to move, he sat bolt upright in bed. 'Do *you* believe that Lydia loved me for all those years?'

'Of course, dearest.'

'Then you're as idiotic as Charlie.' He slumped down. 'She loved me for three years, perhaps even four and then she began to tire. She began to notice I was weak and she wanted someone strong. In other words,' he made a gesture in the air, 'by the time the thing was announced and the banns were called she had had enough.'

It all seemed so diametrically different from the conversation Charlie had reported having with Cecil in the morning that I didn't know what to say.

'She had stopped loving me but I still wanted her to be my wife. I wanted our marriage more than anything else in the world and there was nothing I wouldn't have done to bring it about.'

He paused and I thought he must be thinking of the facts he had not laid before Colonel Marsden.

'Listening to Charlie was really very amusing.' The mockery, grating on my ears, had returned. 'He was so careful as to what he said that he ended by saying nothing. In the end he panicked and rushed out of the room, to discuss it with you I suppose, for I heard him go into your sitting-room.'

'Cecil!'

'Your loyalty is admirable but it doesn't make him any less of a bore. Nice for the shorthand writers in the House of Commons, of course. Knowing what Charlie is going to say before he starts speaking must make their work so much easier.'

Jumping up I said that I would not listen to anything further.

'I think you will, because the rest of what I am going to say is about my mother. You have always been very interested in her, haven't you?'

Our eyes met and he continued to stare until I looked away.

'That's better'—his voice which had seemed to contain sinister undertones became quite ordinary—'and I apologize for what I said about Charlie. He has always been very kind to me and really he isn't stupid at all. When I pretend he is it's because I'm jealous of him.'

I sat down uncertainly.

Cecil, looking at me from time to time to see what effect his words were having, continued to talk. He said that he had suspected from the first that it was his mother and not his father who had written to Colonel Marsden. He had said the contrary to Charlie in order to put the supposition to the test. 'When he went out of the room without answering I knew I was right.'

'But, Cecil, Charlie didn't *know*, like you he only suspected.'

'Suspicion or knowledge? What does it matter when we all know without being able to prove it that the thing was done by my mother.'

'I suppose that . . .' But Cecil, ignoring me, was still speaking.

'What none of you know is whether or not what she wrote was the truth.'

Appalled, I protested that nobody on earth would do such a devilish thing.

Cecil, his voice almost bored, asked me if I thought that anyone on earth would be devilish enough even to hint that such a thing had been done if it hadn't.

'And which is the truth?'

'I don't see how you are ever going to find out.' He lay back against the pillows with his hands clasped on his chest.

'If it isn't true, why did you let Colonel Marsden believe that it was?'

He asked me if I had forgotten that Lydia had ceased to love him long before the letter was written. 'In one sense she must have welcomed it as providing her with an unassailable reason for breaking off the engagement. But if you think for a moment you will see that if the letter was a lie she had an almost equally good reason for doing the same thing. Only a devil, as you have just said, or someone who is mad could have written it. Madness in the family is another very respectable reason for refusing to marry. I think it unlikely that Lydia is particularly anxious to have insane children.'

He had been talking faster and faster, his voice rising with each word, now, horribly, he began to laugh.

'But, Cecil, which is it?'

'The joke is that you will never know.' He continued to laugh hysterically.

Terrified I rushed to the bell. I pulled it four or five times, imagining, although the thing was impossible, that I could hear the sound of it pealing through the house.

Suddenly, several people were in the room. I directed that one of them should go for the doctor. I turned and saw Thompson kneeling beside the bed. He was supporting Cecil in his arms, patting him on the shoulder, trying to soothe him as a nurse does a child taken with a fit of crying.

The man turned his head, saying that the doctor had said this might happen. 'There are some pills in the blue box on the table which we were to give him if it did.'

I found the pills and took them with a glass of water over to the bed.

Cecil, still laughing, tried to refuse to take them but Thompson, firm but very gentle, managed to persuade him.

I took the glass back to the table and stood there waiting. The laughter changed to sobs then to sounds that were neither one nor the other and finally ceased altogether. The man eased Cecil back on to the pillows where he lay, fully conscious but perfectly quiet.

During the week which followed that dreadful day Cecil continued to be very ill. His temperature alternated between extremely high and very low. I suppose that I had seen the beginning of that condition when he woke from sleep in an obviously high fever which had appeared to abate within a few minutes.

At the end of the week there was a decided change for the better. The doctors—Dr Symonds had decided upon calling in a second opinion—declared themselves to be satisfied. Provided there was no relapse the thing, so far as physical symptoms were concerned, was over.

While the fever lasted it had not been possible to hold any conversations with Cecil which went outside of the limit of asking him if there was anything he wanted. Even when he was better Dr Symonds said that he was not to be encouraged to talk about anything which was likely to upset him.

We did our best to follow the instruction. The result, in my case at least, being a series of short visits paid to the patient's room during which I made would-be cheerful remarks on the dullest imaginable topics. When I failed to keep it up I would say that I was sure I was tiring him and go away.

Cecil, which was not surprising, never said anything to try and detain me. In fact he never seemed to be more tired by conversation than by the lack of it. He would just lie in bed or, as the days went on, sit wrapped up in a dressing-gown before the fire and be tired all the time. I noticed that although I was careful to keep him provided with books—both the kind I thought he would like and the ones he mentioned himself—he read hardly at all.

This state of complete depression lasted for at least three weeks. I was beginning to despair of it ever lifting when on going into his room one morning I found that the lassitude which I had grown to expect was much less in evidence than it had hitherto been. He was sitting in a low chair recovering from the exhausting process which Thompson called, getting him ready for the day.

I said good morning and in the usual falsely bright voice asked him how he felt.

He said he was better and added that he would be obliged if I would now stop addressing him as if he was a collection of elderly paupers in a hospital ward.

'Oh dear, I'm sorry.' I sat down in the chair on the other side of the fireplace.

'People always do it,' Cecil said. 'I think the reason is that when one is ill one is apt to look much stupider than usual. The only hope of putting any sense into stupid people or foreigners is to shout at them, so one's friends shout.'

I again said that I was sorry and Cecil said that he hadn't meant to scold me in particular but had been considering human relations as they were concerned with sick visiting.

'It makes me nervous,' I said, 'unless of course one is doing something for the patient, like smoothing his pillow and so on, but then of course one stops being a visitor and becomes a nurse.'

'Dear Anne, in either capacity you are delightful and very kind. I know what a nuisance I have been to you and Charlie all these past weeks.'

I tried to stop him but he interrupted, saying that he insisted upon thanking me and that if I refused to listen he would send his temperature up again and we would never be rid of him.

'Can you imagine what it will be like? Three very old people, one of them me who has been a permanent invalid for fifty years now lying in this very room and the other two, you and Charlie, hobbling in and out to see me.' Suddenly his manner changed, 'Anne, there's something I want to ask you about, something that happened just after I started to be ill,' he paused, wrinkling his forehead, 'it's so difficult to remember things.'

In view of what the doctor had said I thought it unwise to encourage any line of thought that might end by reminding him of his outburst of three weeks ago. I tried therefore to change the conversation but he was not to be put off.

'When one has a high fever it's impossible to distinguish conversations that have actually taken place from those that have come to one in dreams.'

I said that I thought that everyone had had that experience at some time or other. I picked up a novel—one of those I had chosen—which was lying on the table at my elbow, and asked him if he had yet started it.

'Now we are back in the workhouse. The poor old people, all so grateful at being made happy by the charitable lady with her bright face and cheery manner.'

'At least they'd be grateful,' I made a face at him, 'and if you describe them any further I shall end by being quite fond of them.'

'I do remember some of that conversation. It did really happen. I began by telling you that you weren't a good nurse and I went on, didn't I, to abuse Charlie. You were very angry and said that you wouldn't listen to me.'

'All this is something you've dreamed.' I willed him to believe what I was saying.

'Are you sure?' He was looking at me closely, trying I supposed to find out the truth. 'I don't suppose that Lydia is so very different from a great many other girls.'

This, to my relief, was not what I had been expecting. Thinking that it might help him to talk about her I nodded, waiting for him to go on.

'She was different though in that she loved me and because it was she and not the hypothetical others—who don't exist anyway—who wasted five years of my life.'

'They can't have been quite wasted.'

'I didn't use them as they should have been used. I let myself drift from month to month, never settling to any serious work. It never seemed worthwhile, you see, to settle down as a single man. Our marriage during all that time never seemed to be more than a few months ahead. I promised myself that after we were married things would be different. In the meantime I thought I might as well enjoy myself and bring pleasure to my mother by spending as much time as possible in her company.'

'I can see how it happened.'

'My father being so old means that every burden has to be shouldered by her. It seemed so cruel you know to take the comfort of my support away from her before other ties made it a necessity.'

As gently as I could I said that I thought he often carried his consideration for his mother to too great a length.

'As if that could ever be possible when she has always been so wonderfully unselfish about everything. She talked so much about our happiness, mine and Lydia's, and never thought about her own. I had another of her wonderful letters this morning. She is quite broken-hearted and even suggests, ill as she is, that she should come to me.'

As he spoke he was looking at me very carefully but I said nothing.

'Perhaps it is impossible for anyone who has not lived as closely with her as I have always done to appreciate her full worth, the extent of her many sacrifices.'

I knew that he wanted me to say something that would be flattering to Lady Guthrie but the words wouldn't come.

'I said just now that there was something I wanted to ask you. Did I or did I not when I was talking that nonsense about Charlie, say anything on the subject of my mother?'

'When you were delirious? Yes, I think, perhaps, but you were very incoherent.'

He sat for a moment without speaking. Suddenly he looked up. His face was turned towards me but his eyes were focused several feet above my head.

'If I did say anything—I am not going to repeat what I believe it may have been—I want to deny that there was any truth in it. You say that I was incoherent and there is no way for me to know whether you are telling the truth.'

'You were incoherent.'

Our eyes met and the word truth hung in the air. It brought us so closely together that for a moment we became one person, yet each of us was alone with a question which would never be answered.

## Chapter Nine

Two days after that haunting and inconclusive conversation Cecil left for France. I went to the station to see him off. He was still looking very unwell and, as I stood on the platform waiting for the train to leave, I hoped that the long journey to Cannes wasn't going to prove too tiring for him.

Standing in the doorway of the carriage he smiled down at me. 'You know I can never thank you enough.'

'We agreed that you weren't going to try.'

He turned away from me to where Thompson hovered in the background. The next moment he was thrusting an enormous bunch of roses which still trailed several sheets of tissue paper into my arms.

'Oh Cecil, I thought it was the people who were going away who were given the flowers!'

He leaned forward to kiss me but there were so many roses that our embrace became entangled in them. The train, Cecil's timing had as usual been perfect, began to move. A porter ran a few steps down the platform, shutting the door of the carriage with a resounding slam. It was a sound of departure which for the next three years would continue to remind me of Cecil.

Soon after his arrival in Cannes I received a letter from Lady Guthrie. She reported his health as being completely shattered by his bitter grief and added that she and his father were urging him to take the *Thalassa* on a long voyage through the Mediterranean: 'It will be very sad for his parents to lose him again so soon, but he and I are agreed that his hurt will heal more quickly if he is allowed for a little while to be alone. You who know his character so well will not be surprised to learn that he had no harder word for his five years' betrothed than the expression of the hope that she might be happy.'

After I had finished the letter I did not immediately put it away but sat for a little while looking at the familiar writing. What, in view of what Cecil had told me and afterwards retracted, was one to make of it?

In December he started off on his voyage of recovery. In *Letters and Diaries*, Lady Guthrie, as usual describing his activities as they affected herself, does not write as most people would have done, that he visited such and such countries. But that 'his letters to his mother were from Spain, Algeria, Sicily, Corfu and Albania'.

The curious description continues: 'In Greece he had shooting and riding, he made collections and took photographs . . . In this comparatively long parting of four months Cecil had one perpetual preoccupation—the post from his mother and to her; town and port were sought by him for the sake of this communication; at any hour of the day or night that a mail might be caught he took the always precious opportunity of a word with her who never left his thoughts, and to whom he referred everything that seemed to him beautiful or desirable in any place he visited.'

How difficult it is even with those we know very well to piece people together from the fragments which they themselves allow us to see. Turning from Lady Guthrie's words to the extracts, selected by her, from Cecil's letters I find that they seem to corroborate much of what she says. Even so I am not satisfied. The truth appears and disappears like a shadow when clouds pass across the face of the sun.

'Dearest Mother . . . your own boy, Cecil . . . *On board the* Thalassa, *Oran, Dec* 10. Mother Darling, The book on Algeria which I will bring you will give you a far better idea of these beauties than any description of mine. I also took one or two snapshots with my Kodak but fear the weather's gloom . . . The weather has turned very stormy so we may possibly be delayed for another day or two. As there is little or nothing of any interest here this is to be regretted, but I do not find time hang heavy on my hands. I hardly know how to get through the letters and photographic developing that must be done. . . . Thalassa, *Algiers, Dec* 15th. Darling Mother, Your letters are very sad reading still, my poor suffering dear, to anyone who knows how brave you are to bear pain and worry. . . . Thalassa, *Syracuse*. My dearest Mother . . . I should be really pleased to show you round Tunis, though Goletta is a wretched place to stay ... I got some attar of roses and marvellous violet essence for you, also amber for our Turkish coffee. If you wish the draperies and a fine embroidery cushion sent, please write to me at Corfu—Your own boy, Cecil.'

In all the letters—as they are printed—I can find only one short sentence in which he refers directly to his lost love: 'My morale is brighter already, the fresh air and new scenes help me to forget and at any rate to forgive today.'

One wonders if that was all or whether other references were deleted because they were too revealing of the writer or too painful to the recipient?

On the subject of women in the abstract he has much to say: 'More and more, it seems to me the lovely task of woman to ease the pain and rush of life, to share its joys and to divide its griefs.' And then, writing in French, he complains that although everything has already been said on the subject of woman, no one has yet succeeded in describing man's inexpressible delight in a beloved woman or the bitter hatred with which he longs to destroy the woman whom he used to love: 'Yet the hatred will always be mixed with regret; regret for time past when she was dear to you, when her kisses were always in your thoughts, capturing your whole being in perfect forgetfulness of yourself—if such a thing is possible—male egoist!'

In other letters he speaks of his hopes of becoming a writer: 'Thalassa, *Corfu, Jan* 6th 1892. Darling Mother, I am very much excited by your Provencal cottage. Are we going to picnic there, or sleep? And shall I be allowed to go up there with you, accompanied by Thompson carrying reams of MS. paper and ink? It sounds just the place to write; and we will talk there, and you will tell me stories of which I will make *nouvelles*, and then you will be pleased to think that, as in all else, you have helped and guided my literary work ... My very tiny griffonnage reminds me that perhaps it is trying to your poor eyes. Oh how I wish they would be well, for reading is the only thing to divert your thoughts. Perchance if I read to you, you may be strong enough to bear it. Then you will lie on the sofa, and I (11 stones, 10 pounds and 5 feet 11) will negligently loll by your side, edging up to the green-grey lamp for better lighting, as in the old days, when I dreamed already of the pretty books I would write. The Browning period followed, and the Rossetti, and the Balzac, and the Bourget—until the present.'

The picture the paragraph evokes is rather pleasant. It is saved from priggishness by the sentence that immediately follows it: 'We had a really good duck-shoot last evening for our last—bringing down fifteen duck, of which we lost some by reason of the darkness . . . Your own boy, Cecil.'

A pleasant and easy correspondence! Reading it one catches at straws in an effort to understand the relationship existing between this mother and son. Do ordinary young men write their thoughts upon love and women to their mothers? Do they give themselves the trouble when the proposed companion is to be their mother of drawing pretty pen pictures of an imagined *déjeuner sur l'herbe*? I know my own sons never did anything of the kind but what does that prove? Only, Lady Guthrie would say, that I had failed as a mother.

'A woman without a son is pitiable but a mother who does not have her son's full confidence is in almost as bad a case. I find it impossible to imagine how bitter it would be.'

I can see her now, sitting upright on a sofa as she delivered the dictum. Her eyes are mournful but there is pride about her as well, for isn't she possessed of a son who will always treat her as a confidante and a human being?

The carriage door slammed shut in October 1891, the train which I watched depart took Cecil out of my life for the better part of three years, for I did not see him again until the summer of 1894. The intervening years had been spent by him in Cannes, in travelling—sometimes with his parents and sometimes alone—and in Paris where he was beginning to have many friends in the literary world.

His own ambitions of becoming a writer were much encouraged when the *Gaulois* decided to publish two of his *nouvelles*. These were the first of his writings to be published. Naturally we were all delighted and began to hope that Cecil, at long last, was settling down to a career.

During the same period of time two events, both of which occasioned a good deal of domestic upheaval, occurred in my own life. I refer to the birth of my younger son in December 1893 and Sybil's 'coming out' early in the following year. I do not consider that my 'timing'—always inferior on no matter what occasion to Cecil's—was good and the coincidental general election, in which Charlie was again returned for Hastings, didn't as may be readily imagined make things any easier.

It was a great relief to me when with a new son, a newly grown-up daughter and Charlie still safely a Member of Parliament we managed at the end of July to get up to Kildonan. There would be nearly two weeks of peace and quiet before the shooting and the entertainment which was part of it would begin. Our first party, planned for the twelfth, was to include Cecil and I was much looking forward to seeing him after so long an interval.

About ten days before everyone was due to arrive I received a letter in the afternoon post from Lady Guthrie.

She was unexpectedly in England. Her mother had been taken suddenly ill and she had deemed it to be her duty, in spite of her own extremely unsatisfactory state of health, to go to her: 'Fortunately when I arrived I found my dearest mother very much better, and I would so like, since I am in England, to take this—perhaps my last—opportunity of seeing dear Kildonan at least once more. If it would be perfectly convenient to you and Charlie, Cecil and I could travel up to you on the night of the sixth and he could bring me back to London a week later. If he comes with me as far as Dover I am sure that I will then be able to manage by myself although a journey across Europe in this heat will, and especially with no proper escort, be extremely trying.'

'Oh dear!' I handed the letter over to Charlie. 'I can't see any possible way of getting out of it so we'll just have to make the best of it. After all, a week isn't so very long.'

'So like her,' Charlie was looking resigned, 'and why does everything that she wants to do always have to interfere with something of Cecil's. He's to be allowed a couple of days' shooting up here and then he's to be dragged down South again just in order to see her on to a boat.'

Lady Guthrie and Cecil arrived, as threatened, on the sixth of August. I had not, as I have said, seen Cecil for nearly three years or Lady Guthrie for seven. In the interval my feelings towards her, mainly, naturally, owing to the circumstances which had surrounded the breaking off of the engagement, had undergone a considerable change. As I waited for the carriage I realized that whereas before I had been accustomed to think of her as a selfish and often foolish woman I now regarded her as a veritable ogress. In my imagination, untouched by any sight of the reality, the soft features had become witch-like; the *embonpoint* had turned to layers of repulsive flesh. My first sight of Lady Guthrie, not very surprisingly, proved me to have been completely wrong. The appearance of the woman who was ushered into the drawing-room differed very little from that of the one who had last left it in 1887.

'My dear child, such an abominable journey,' Lady Guthrie, pausing just inside the threshold, held out her arms to me. 'How very wonderful to see you again. I have thought so often in these last years that I should not live to do so.'

Murmuring words of welcome I was clasped for a long moment against her corsage of palma violets. Released, I turned to Cecil who stood just behind her.

'Isn't my mother looking superb, young and beautiful as ever as you see?'

I agreed—by repeating the same adjectives as he had used. I didn't see why I should be troubled to think of new ones.

Lady Guthrie begged us both not to be so foolish. 'I'm getting to be an old woman and I know it.' Shivering a little she took a chair next the empty grate. 'Very lovely to be here,' she looked round the room, 'and nothing changed in all these years. It makes it a little like coming home. My dear one living here so much as a child is another reason I suppose for it giving me that feeling. So sad that he could not make the journey with us but the doctors absolutely forbade it.'

'How is Sir David?'

'As well as at his age he can hope to be. It was a great joy to him to see Charlie for those few days last month but of course he was disappointed that the time allowed for the visit should have been so short. He thought too that it would have been nice to see you and his granddaughter.'

'My dear Lady Guthrie, in the middle of her first season!'

'For him there may not be so very many more,' she shook her head reproachfully. 'Oh well, if my dear one himself is to be allowed no glimpse of his family I can at least describe them for his benefit. How is the baby? I have brought him a beautiful present which you shall have as soon as I'm unpacked.'

I thanked her and said that Ian was very well.

'And poor little Alistair? I hope he is now getting on better with his work, it would be such a pity if he had to leave Eton.'

I told her that Alistair, no longer so very little, was working hard, doing so well in fact that for the first time for several years a tutor had not been suggested for the summer holidays. 'Charlie and I are so pleased with him and if he goes on in the same way there will be no doubt of his doing well at Sandhurst.'

Lady Guthrie said how sad it was that there had never been any chance of Alistair being able to get into the Foreign Office. 'He seemed so intelligent too when he was quite a little boy and it would have made my dear one so happy to think of being followed in his career by a grandson.'

I did not say that Sir David would probably have been made happier still if Cecil had not been prevented from doing exactly that. Instead, I offered her the baby as a future Guthrie Britannic Minister.

We talked for a little longer and I happened to say something about the new alms houses that Charlie was then having built in the village. We thought the design for them so pretty and they would provide the old people with much greater comfort than they had had in the old ones, which had really ceased to be fit for human habitation.

Lady Guthrie, professing herself to be much interested, said what a good and charitable man Charlie was. 'Very nearly as good as you, my darling,' she smiled at Cecil, 'although I know how you hate to have it mentioned.'

'I told you that she was the same as ever—' Cecil got up, '—incorrigible when it comes to praising her "dearest boy".'

He went over and took his mother's hand and I saw a look of understanding pass between them. It made me, although I would have found it hard to say exactly why, feel slightly uncomfortable. It was as if, for that is the nearest I can come to it, I had come into a room in which two people believed themselves to be alone.

I got up and more abruptly than the occasion warranted apologized to Lady Guthrie for having kept her so long in gossiping; most selfish of me when, as the result of the abominable journey, she must certainly be very tired.

'You will be wanting to have a bath and rest before luncheon, unless of course you would like to spend the rest of the day in bed?'

'Well, perhaps,' and Lady Guthrie, making a great effort of the thing, allowed Cecil to help her to her feet.

On the way upstairs, making trivial conversation to Lady Guthrie, I was thinking how strange it was that Cecil's attitude towards her had not changed in any outward particular since he was a child.

'The same room as before.' I held open the door. 'I do hope that you've got everything you want.'

Uttered in the presence of Louise, who would certainly have torn down the house rather than let her mistress lack for anything, the conventional phrase sounded even more foolish than usual.

'And nothing is changed,' Lady Guthrie looked contentedly round the room.

Absence of change—why was it so important to her? I remembered the well-nigh incredible things Cecil had said during his fit of delirium. 'And the joke is that you will never know whether what she wrote about me was true or false.' Later, he had stumblingly tried to find out whether or not the words had in fact been spoken. If they had he wished to deny them. Or did he know all the time that, for once losing control of himself, he had in fact accused her?

'All exactly the same.' Lady Guthrie was looking out of the window. Surely she hadn't expected that the contours of the hills would have altered.

'I want,' she said, 'later on to have a long talk with you.'

It was the familiar phrase and I waited for its corollary—'I think Charlie should do something'—which didn't come.

'Any time you like, as I've told you the house is practically empty of people so we don't have to pick a special hour for conversation.' I moved towards the door, reached it and shut it behind me. Then because my thoughts of the last few minutes had disturbed me so that I felt a great need to be alone I went to my own room. What exactly was it between those two that I didn't understand?

## Chapter Ten

The next morning, sitting on the terrace waiting for Lady Guthrie to come downstairs, I was joined by Sybil.

'Mother, haven't you had a note from Mrs Anderson yet?'

'No, were you expecting one?'

I looked up at my daughter and thought how pretty she looked in her summer dress, fresh and young and at the same time consciously grown up. She sat down in the chair beside me.

'I wasn't exactly expecting a letter but Robert and Geordie did say they would get her to write it as early as possible so that we could get the thing properly started and not have to rush at the last moment.'

'What is it to be this time, an impromptu dance or impromptu theatricals?'

'Impromptu bicycle races followed by a dance.'

'Well, I suppose it will be all right.'

'Hush,' Sybil started up. 'Does that sound like a carriage?'

'You mean does it sound like the Andersons' dogcart?'

I was smiling as I spoke and Sybil immediately accused me of teasing her.

'I wasn't darling, I promise, and when is the great event, if it comes off, to take place?'

'The day after tomorrow and we're going to say it's in honour of Julie because she'll be the only one that they don't all know already.'

Julie Wrottesley, who was due to arrive the following morning, was a girl, rather older than herself, whom Sybil had met in Dresden. I had never been certain that she was an entirely good influence on Sybil who considered her to be very dashing.

'I do hope,' Sybil now said, 'that Julie isn't going to find it frightfully dull, you know, without a party. I know we can always go over to the Andersons and that they're probably going to have this dance, but it isn't the same as having people actually staying in the house. After the twelfth of course it will be all right.'

'But we *have* got people staying and as one of them is a handsome young man I don't think that she will be doing too badly.'

'Oh, you mean Uncle Cecil, but he's quite old.'

'Uncle Cecil is exactly twenty-eight.'

'I suppose to you that really does seem quite young?'

Sybil put the question in perfect good faith, making me aware all over again of the tremendous distance that separates eighteen-year-olds from the rest of the world. I heard a step behind me and looked round to see Cecil followed by a footman coming out on to the terrace.

'Are they waiting for the answer?' Sybil asked, impatiently moving from one foot to the other as the tray holding the expected note was handed to me.

Pausing in opening the envelope, I told her to sit down so that Cecil who had remained standing might do so also.

'But I'm only going to be here a minute because if it's all right I'll have a hundred things to do.' As she spoke she perched herself, like a bird ready for flight, on the edge of a chaise-longue.

Mrs Anderson's note, which I read aloud, explained that the boys had persuaded her into giving a dance and had arranged some entertainment amongst themselves for the afternoon. She hoped that as many of our party as cared to do so would join them.

'I shouldn't think that Uncle Cecil would care about the bicycling part of it and,' Sybil turned towards him, 'as for the dance I doubt if they'll have had time to get a proper band. In fact it may quite well come down to the governess and the piano for the waltzes and just their piper for the reels.'

'I thought we had agreed that now that you are a grown-up young lady you would stop calling me uncle.'

'It's going to be rather difficult to remember when Alistair still does.'

'Then Alistair will have to stop as well.'

After luncheon Lady Guthrie and I, having discussed at some length whether or not we should go for a drive, eventually decided against it and spent most of the afternoon in the rose garden. It is one of my favourite places and just as the boudoir in Berkeley Square always seems to be the best place for confidences so at Kildonan it is undoubtedly the rose garden. Just far enough from the house to make one safe from interruption by people who are just going indoors to change their clothes for lawn tennis, or down to the yard to confer with a ghillie, it is surrounded on all sides by a thick and very high beech hedge.

Lady Guthrie, after all the necessary paraphernalia had been carried out for her by Thompson, had been making a water colour sketch of the statue of Apollo which stood in one corner of the garden while I, sitting on a wrought iron bench close to her camp stool, had been looking through the latest copy of the *Illustrated London News*. At first, while she was still engaged on the intricacies of perspective, we spoke very little but when it was a question of the pink Empress Eugenies that were to be her foreground she began to talk.

She was so happy about the articles of Cecil's that had been published in France. Didn't I think, and she wished I would tell her honestly, that they were really very clever? Some people might think it strange that he chose to write in French rather than English but when one thought that he had known that language, as well as German and Italian, since he was a tiny child there was really nothing very surprising about it.

'And Charlie says,' but of course I didn't tell her in what circumstances the remark had been made, 'that in many ways he thinks as a Frenchman.'

'That is very true,' Lady Guthrie nodded contentedly, 'and he has spent more of his life in that country than in any other. Only,' and paint brush suspended in the air she turned to face me directly, 'I am not completely happy that it is now Paris, and only Paris, where he wishes to be.'

'He tells me that he has an apartment there.'

'That was only for the winter and spring. It was an *apartement meublé* you know, not his own, and he has since given it up.'

'Then he will not be going back?'

'That,' she turned again to her roses, 'is what I'm afraid of.'

'But surely . . . ?'

'It's, I don't know how to explain it, and I wouldn't, naturally, speak of it at all to anyone but you, that I'm frightened.' Putting down her paint-brush she laid her hand on her breast. It was the familiar gesture, used whenever she was agitated or upset. 'It's his friends, the people he mixes with, with whom he seems to spend the greater part of his time. I know that writers have to meet all kinds of people. I am not a prude, or indeed a snob, it goes far deeper than that and I am frightened.'

'But of what?'

'Surely you know, or perhaps you don't for your whole life has been so sheltered, that many people in Paris, especially those who surround artists and writers have habits of life that are very wrong and which inevitably end in the destruction of health?'

Uncertain of what she meant I waited for her to go on.

'I am not saying for one moment that Cecil has acquired these habits but for one who suffers as much as he does, who is so often ill and in pain the temptation must undoubtedly be very great.' The suggestion that Cecil might be in danger of becoming addicted either to alcohol or some kind of drug was extremely disquieting. I looked at Lady Guthrie, wondering if she indeed knew this to be a fact or only feared it as a possibility.

'Have you spoken to him at all on the subject?'

She gave me a long look filled with a meaning which I could not interpret and went on to speak in vague terms of absinthe drinkers and various artists whom she either knew or had heard of who, beginning in an almost innocent way, perhaps merely from curiosity, had ended by dying miserably, their bodies wasted away and their reason gone as a result of the drugs which, once the thing had taken hold of them, they were incapable of giving up.

'But I would not have you believe that such a thing is ever likely to happen to Cecil. His strong sense of right and wrong makes it in the highest degree unlikely, even impossible.'

As Lady Guthrie spoke I had the impression that now that her anxiety on the matter had been relieved by speaking of it she was regretting that she had done so.

'It is so easy, as I'm sure you must know out of your own experience, to fear things for our children long before they are threatened.'

I did not in fact agree with her in regard to myself but thought it perfectly possible that she might very well do so. And wasn't it in her nature always to be frightened for her son, whenever he was away from her immediate neighbourhood or enjoying himself in the company of others? As gently as I could I said that I thought she worried too much on Cecil's account. 'And if what you fear for him is true surely there would be some signs of physical deterioration by which one might know it?' And I thought of Cecil as he had gone off with the children after luncheon, looking as clear eyed and almost as young as they.

'Exactly,' and again Lady Guthrie looked at me searchingly, studying my face as if it were my rather than Cecil's secrets that she sought to discover.

The day was so beautiful that despite Lady Guthrie's misgivings as to the probability of draughts—by which she understood the slightest stirring of the air—I had ordered tea to be laid under the trees which shaded the far end of the terrace. She and I, strolling over there from the rose garden at a little after five o'clock found that the children had not yet returned from the Andersons.

'No point in waiting—they neither of them have any idea of time.'

'You don't think anything can have happened?'

'No of course not, but you know what young people are like when they are all together. I only hope they are not going to put everyone out by being late for dinner.'

The next five minutes were to prove the fear to be groundless for I hardly finished speaking when Sybil, followed by Cecil and Alistair and a strange young man, appeared round the corner of the house. Sybil, quickening her pace but remembering not quite to run, reached us a second or two before the others.

'We've brought you back a surprise and I'm not going to ask you to guess who it is because they're not in the least alike.' She turned to the young man, not so very young after all, for on a closer view he appeared to be something over thirty, who now stood beside her waiting to be introduced. 'Mother, this is Mr Frederic Helbert brother of *our* Mr Helbert and he and Uncle—I mean Cecil—think they once met each other in Paris.'

'Our Mr Helbert' was the tutor whom, as I think I have already mentioned we had had several times for Alistair. Greeting his brother I said that I supposed Mr Helbert had not realized that the Andersons lived so close to us. 'Otherwise I am sure he would have let us know that you were going to be up here.'

'But he isn't staying with the Andersons',' Alistair said. 'He was just over there for the afternoon—he's staying at that horrid hotel next door to the Soames'.'

'Because he's been ill,' Sybil put in.

'And if you're not very careful it will make you much worse,' Alistair said, 'like that man last year who got ptomaine poisoning and diphtheria both at the same time and had to be taken away in an ambulance and operated on in Perth.'

I told Alistair not to be silly and also to go indoors and ring for some more hot water and another cup. I then introduced Mr Helbert to Lady Guthrie, indicating that he should sit next to her. This, for she immediately asked him to help her move her chair further into the shade, resulted in their sitting a little apart from the rest of us.

While I poured out tea I had plenty of time, for Cecil and the children were soon discussing the details of their afternoon, in which to observe Mr Helbert's brother. He was, as Sybil had said, quite unlike the tutor in appearance—in fact very much better looking. Large hazel eyes dominated a thin, somewhat narrow, face and although of only medium height he carried himself so well as to appear to be a good deal taller than was in fact the case.

'It was all right, Mother, wasn't it,' Sybil who was sitting next me asked in an undertone, 'about bringing him back?'

'Of course, darling.'

'I thought that you'd want me to. He's much more, well lively, than Mr Helbert but that's probably because he's in the army instead of being a schoolmaster and he was terribly helpful this afternoon and had the most brilliant ideas about everything, didn't he, Cecil?'

'It is certainly owing to him that the governess and the piano are now in danger of going down before a six-piece band.'

'If only he can get hold of it,' Sybil said, 'and it really is a real band, or part of one anyway who are up here on their holidays and Mr Helbert knows them quite well and is going to see them this evening and make all the arrangements. It was lucky about his happening to be at the Andersons just today.'

'I suppose he's a friend of one of the boys?'

'The twins,' Sybil said. 'It was them that he came over to see and then when he got there he found that they were away and so he joined in with us.'

'The twins!' Lady Guthrie, pausing in the middle of a sentence about something quite different which she had been addressing to Mr Helbert, entered dramatically into the conversation. 'Wasn't it with some Anderson *twins* that Cecil had that dreadful experience in the loch?'

'Oh Mother, you know perfectly well that it wasn't dreadful at all; you merely saw an empty boat on the water and took it into your head that I had been drowned.'

'For me,' Lady Guthrie turned to Mr Helbert, 'it was very dreadful. You can have no idea, no one can have any idea of the state of my feelings.'

'I remember,' Alistair said, 'you were terribly upset and you didn't enjoy the lunch party you were on your way to.'

'How I ever sat through it I don't know,' Lady Guthrie, pointedly ignoring Alistair, continued to address herself to Mr Helbert. 'The fear itself only lasted for a minute or two but it was many many nights before I was able to sleep anything like peacefully or feel myself to be at rest.'

Mr Helbert said that he could well imagine it and that he remembered his own mother telling him how she had gone through very much the same thing after his brother had got into difficulties while swimming at Eastbourne.

There was a second's pause during which I imagined Lady Guthrie to be making the mental effort which would be necessary in order for her to accept the possibility of Mr Helbert's mother undergoing the same emotions as herself. The inward struggle, if there had been one, was evidently successful for she immediately began to express her sympathy with Mrs Helbert.

'Nobody, not even our sons themselves, can know what we undergo. But,' for this was an advantage that undoubtedly she did possess over Mrs Helbert, 'an only child . . . there is, there must be, a great difference. . . .'

'I never was one,' Alistair remarked regretfully, not addressing anyone in particular.

Sybil said that at least until a few months ago he had been an only son.

'And even then Mother didn't agonize over me, or did you,' he turned to me, 'when I wasn't looking?'

I told him that I didn't believe so and then, because I thought the conversation was getting dangerously near the point where it would have to be classified as teasing Aunt Edythe, I suggested that he should talk about something else.

Alistair, stopping just short of giving me a conspiratorial wink, glanced from me to Lady Guthrie and back again. I also had looked in her direction and it was plain to both of us, so deep was she again in conversation with Mr Helbert, that the teasing, even if it had gone a great deal further, would have passed unnoticed.

At dinner that evening there was a great deal of general discussion on the subject of Mr Helbert. Everyone took a part in describing him to Charlie who had not arrived home in time to meet him. It seemed that they had all found him delightful and were hoping to see a great deal more of him during the time he was in Scotland. I think it was Lady Guthrie who first said how much she hated to think of him sitting all alone in that dreadful little hotel—especially when the poor man had been so ill.

Alistair, after an interested enquiry as to what exactly had been the matter with Mr Helbert, and whether he had nearly died of it, information with which no one was able to supply him, said that anyway he wouldn't be sitting alone tonight. 'Probably bicycling about the country in the pouring rain, looking for that beastly band for Sybil and catching his death of pneumonia at the same time.'

From the end of the table Charlie asked why on earth I hadn't asked Mr Helbert to stay at Kildonan.

'Oh Mother, could we?' Sybil was looking at me expectantly and I had the impression that the idea of inviting Mr Helbert had been in her mind for some time.

I hesitated, realizing to my surprise that although I had liked Mr Helbert well enough this afternoon I was not particularly anxious to have him staying in the house. Unable however to offer, or even find, any valid reason for my reluctance to do what everyone seemed to want I said that as soon as dinner was over I would write as Charlie had suggested.

'Dear Mr Helbert, It would give us the greatest pleasure . . .' As I sat down at my writing-table I was feeling a little ashamed. How mean of me to have hung back. Surely having Mr Helbert to stay when he was convalescing from a long and probably expensive illness was the least we could do for the sake of his brother to whom we owed so much gratitude for the way in which he had helped Alistair.

Frederic Helbert and his luggage arrived at Kildonan soon after breakfast on the following morning and from now on, in order to avoid later confusion, I am going to write of him as Captain, rather than Mr. He in fact reached this rank very shortly afterwards and it is as Captain Helbert that I always think of him.

The morning very fortunately had again turned out to be fine and gave every promise that the day would so continue until its end. Just before eleven o'clock, the earliest moment at which the carriage meeting the London train could be hoped for, Sybil and I were sitting on the terrace. It wasn't long before we were joined by Cecil and Captain Helbert.

'I thought you said at breakfast that you were going to fish.' Sybil as she addressed Cecil sounded aggrieved.

'But after breakfast,' Cecil lowered himself into a long chair, and lay back closing his eyes, 'I decided that it was much too bright as well as much too hot and that it would be more amusing anyhow to catch a first sight of your friend.'

'I hope that I haven't made her sound so wonderful that you're going to be disappointed.'

'If we are, you can count on both Helbert and myself not to show it. We are both used to seeing very beautiful women in Paris but are nevertheless prepared to be lenient.'

'You won't have to be as lenient as all that because Julie's very pretty.'

'I'm delighted to hear it and so, only he's too shy to say so, is Helbert.'

Captain Helbert, who had chosen the chair closest to the one occupied by Sybil, said that he had always been told that it was in extremely bad taste to praise one beautiful woman to another.

Sybil, looking I thought rather embarrassed, asked him if he knew Paris well.

'Fairly well, that is I run over whenever I get the chance, which isn't too often.'

Cecil, coming to Sybil's rescue, said that she must surely know by now that although regiments were continually being posted to India for six years they never got sent to Paris for so much as a week.

Before very long we heard the sounds of a carriage as it was driven up to the front door.

'At last,' Sybil got up, 'I was beginning to think that there must have been a breakdown on the line. Either that or that Julie had missed the train.'

The men were already standing and I now got up. We all fell silent, waiting for Julie Wrottesley to step on to the terrace. In another moment she was with us and we were busy exchanging greetings and making introductions. As I presented Captain Helbert I noticed his face light up in admiration. Looking from him to the girl whose hand lay momentarily in his I felt for an instant as if I were seeing her through his eyes. Previously, I had always thought of her as a good-looking girl rather taller than Sybil. I now saw that she was exceedingly handsome and had a really superb figure. Her presence was commanding. Her hair, of which she possessed a great abundance, was as nearly black as it is possible for hair to be and her complexion without a flaw.

My immediate response to all these perfections was to decide more firmly than ever that Julie Wrottesley was not a suitable friend for Sybil. There was nothing, as my conscience constrained me to admit, unbecoming in Julie's manner or *outré* in the cut of her cream-coloured coat and skirt but the overall impression she made on me was not reassuring. A quick glance at Cecil told me that he, as well as Captain Helbert, was much *épris* with the girl's appearance.

By general consent we started to move into the house. In the drawing-room Sybil linked her arm in Julie's.

'Now I'm going to take you upstairs because you'll want to change. I do hope that you're not going to be tired from your journey because we've got a great deal planned for this afternoon and tomorrow evening there's going to be a dance in your honour.'

The girls started to move away. Cecil and Captain Helbert went back to the terrace and I was left alone. As it was nearly time for Lady Guthrie's first appearance of the day I decided that it wasn't worth settling to anything in particular—even another desultory conversation with Cecil and Captain Helbert. I began moving about the room, altering the positions of the objects on the occasional tables and twisting the flowers into what I hoped were more artistic, or anyhow tidier, arrangements. I was wondering whether in my thoughts I hadn't been a little hard on Julie. It wasn't her fault after all if she had blossomed into a positive beauty and I knew her family in its essence to be a perfectly respectable one. True, the father had the reputation of being rather a scamp. It was the old story, so familiar in our class, of a younger son brought up to the solid comforts and luxuries to be found in his father's house, and then when the time came for him to enter the world, being turned loose in it on an inadequate allowance. He had married young, a beautiful girl even poorer than himself and ever since the couple had been hard put to it to provide adequately for themselves and the two children of their marriage. The boy, on an allowance from his uncle, had gone unprofitably into the army and I imagined the whole family must be hoping that Julie would marry well. The fact that at nearly twenty-one she was still a spinster was probably a disappointment to them.

The next few days, of which the Andersons' bicycle races and dance were naturally the highlight, passed very happily. As far as I could see the young people, that is, Captain Helbert, Cecil, Julie and Sybil were getting on well together and seemed to be having a pleasant time. On the morning before Lady Guthrie was due to leave I was, as had become my habit, waiting for her in the drawing-room. As usual it had not seemed worthwhile to engage in any serious activity and I was engaged in alternately opening and shutting the lid of one or another of a family of enamel boxes when she appeared in the room. I write 'appeared' because, in deference I think to her own invalidism, she was accustomed to wearing soft-soled slippers and therefore seldom announced her approach with the sound of footsteps.

'So at last I find you alone.'

As for the past few days we had seldom been anything else I thought the remark a curious one. I said good morning to her and asked, although she very seldom did so, if she would like to come and sit on the terrace.

'I think not,' she had gone over to a window and was peering out of it, 'and in any case I see we have been forestalled by Sybil and Miss Wrottesley.'

She returned to the middle of the room and sat down on a sofa. 'I want to talk to you.'

I didn't think that the drawing-room, which during the summer was used by everyone as an egress to the terrace, was the best place in the house for confidences but I nevertheless sat down and waited to hear what she had to say. It took her, as it always did, a considerable time to come to the point. A great many subjects were touched on and left hanging in the air. I believe, although I do not know if she knew it herself, that she had evolved this oblique method of approach as a form of protection. If she said enough things how was anyone to know which one was really on her mind? And her auditor could thereby be induced to give his or her opinion on something without ever knowing whether or not it was important to her. Today, although with Lady Guthrie one could never be quite certain, I didn't have the impression that Cecil lay at the end of it. The main theme, if there was one, seemed to be concerned with Frederic Helbert. She found him a most interesting young man and, for a soldier, amazingly intelligent.

'I wonder that he didn't enter some other profession but I understand that there was some difficulty about money for the University. I think at the time he felt it very keenly and yet he speaks so charmingly and really unselfishly about the elder brother who did go there. It is really too bad, as my dear one and I have said so often, that the clergy should be so badly paid.'

Still wondering on what subject she really wanted to speak to me I said that I knew the Helberts' father had for many years been the vicar of an East London parish. Although I had never met him I believed him to be a charming man and was sure that he would have done everything which lay in his financial power to give his children as good an education as possible.

'And I'm certain that if Charlie cared to exert himself it could be arranged quite easily. I know that he and Reggie used to be great friends as young men.'

So I had, as happened so often, managed to lose the thread of what she was saying!

'I'm talking about Reggie Cameron, you must have known him yourself at one time.'

'Yes, of course, but . . . ?'

'I wouldn't be suggesting it at all if I didn't believe that ultimately it wouldn't be doing him as well as Captain Helbert a great favour. Intelligent young soldiers with a thorough knowledge of several languages are not to be found as easily as people seem to think. Although, now that the appointment is announced, I'm sure every mother in London who had one dance with him twenty years ago will be harassing someone to put in a word for her son. It's really too disgraceful how these things always seem to go by influence.'

Influence, for I now began to see where all this was leading, was of course what Lady Guthrie was suggesting Charlie should exercise on Captain Helbert's behalf.

'My dear one, naturally, would never allow of it. As ambassador he was for ever being besieged by the sisters, cousins and aunts of place-seekers but he never let himself be influenced and always took an immense amount of trouble over finding suitable men to be on his staff—merit, it goes without saying, was ever the criterion.'

I nodded approvingly. It was now clear to me that she intended Charlie to persuade his old friend General Cameron, who had just been appointed British military attaché in Paris, to ask for Captain Helbert as one of his aides. She herself, as she now explained, had this morning written a letter to the ambassador.

'It does seem so hard when a charming and *really* intelligent man of that kind has no one to put in a word for him. They get overlooked merely because no one has ever heard of them and the places they should have had are given to nincompoops who can't put one word of French, let alone German or Italian, in front of the other.' I said that our being so fond of Mr Helbert would naturally incline Charlie, if he thought the idea a good one, to do what he could for the brother. I knew that it would do no good to ask her the reason why she was suddenly so anxious to be of use to the captain. A natural taste for dispensing patronage? Simple charity—of which, when the thing didn't go against her own interests, she possessed more than a fair share? Either reason was a possibility, or was it that the captain had somehow managed, as the children say, to 'get round her'? The idea, for he was after all a guest in our house, made me a little uneasy.

## Chapter Eleven

In the following year, on June 3rd 1895, Sir David died in Baden. Immediately after the event Lady Guthrie and Cecil accompanied the body to England and themselves stayed for several weeks at The Manor.

During most of that time Lady Guthrie, reported to be prostrate with grief, remained in seclusion, but just before she and Cecil returned to Cannes, where they were to pass the remainder of the summer, Charlie and I spent an afternoon at Windsor. The meeting was a sad one, Lady Guthrie was extremely low-spirited and Cecil, although he made some effort to rouse himself for our sakes, was obviously very depressed and unhappy. He had been ill for some months during the spring and although he assured me that he was now fully recovered I thought that he was looking very far from well.

At the end of September I had a letter from Lady Guthrie saying that Cecil had started for Italy, begging me to go to her. When the letter arrived we were up at Kildonan. We had a house full of people and my leaving at that particular moment was far from convenient. Directly breakfast was over I caught Charlie alone, showed him the letter and we reluctantly agreed that it was probably my duty to do as she asked. The thought of it depressed me and Sybil, who happened to come into the room while we were discussing it, was loud in her protests, wanting to know why Aunt Edythe, if she was lonely, didn't come here instead of dragging me out to Cannes.

'You forget that she is in mourning and in any case is not well enough to travel.'

'She's always said that, ever since I can remember. But it never seems to stop her doing anything if she really wants to.'

Charlie, because he himself was annoyed, rebuked Sybil for speaking disrespectfully and for giving her opinion about something which was no concern of hers.

Sybil's face flamed red and she went out of the room without saying anything further. Charlie announced that everything was intolerable and said he couldn't understand why Cecil, who had nothing whatever to do, couldn't stay at home and look after his mother himself. He then went off to join the men who were going to spend the day on the moor and I sat down to write to Lady Guthrie.

'Mother, did you know that when we were all up here last summer Cecil fell in love with Julie and asked her to marry him?'

After I had finished my letter I had gone to look for Sybil and had found her sitting alone in the room which used to be the schoolroom.

'No I didn't. What an extraordinary thing.' Wondering why Sybil had chosen this particular moment to tell me I sat down at the table.

'I don't see it was extraordinary at all and I rather think Captain Helbert was in love with her at the same time, but of course that didn't come to anything.'

As Sybil spoke I remembered the captain's eyes as they had rested on Julie at the moment I introduced them to each other.

'And what about Julie?'

'Well at first she didn't know what to do, about Cecil proposing, you know. He asked her the same evening that he came back from taking Aunt Edythe to Dover. They had only known each other for a week and I thought it was one of the most romantic things I had ever heard of. I was terribly sentimental in those days, wasn't I, Mother?'

'Were you, darling?' I wondered if she had wanted me to deny it.

'They went for a walk after dinner and then sat on a seat in the rose garden and he asked her to marry him.'

'The rose garden! That's where Cousin Nealie was so anxious he should propose to Lydia.'

'And when she heard that he had chosen the croquet lawn instead she was quite cross about it. I remember you telling me.'

I said that I didn't remember telling her anything of the kind and that if I had it had been most indiscreet of me.

'Anyhow with Julie it truly was the rose garden.'

'But she refused him?'

'Well not exactly. She wanted to accept but then of course she knew that her parents weren't very likely to approve, and would probably do everything they could to prevent her marrying him.'

The last I could well imagine. It was obvious that the impoverished Wrottesleys would expect much more for their beautiful daughter than Cecil, a commoner possessed of no landed estates and having only a moderate income, was able to offer. If his delicate health and dilettante way of life were taken into account his prospects of being favourably received as their son-in-law became almost negligible.

'But if Julie didn't say yes or no what did happen?'

'In the end she agreed to their being secretly engaged. But what I don't understand,' Sybil looked at me suddenly, 'is how you didn't know anything about it. Surely, when Julie went to stay at the Villa you must have guessed there was something?'

'But I didn't know that she did go there.'

Sybil, expressing surprise, said that at the time she had promised not to say anything about it but thought that by now I would have heard of it from Aunt Edythe.

'She has never said anything.'

'How extraordinary. I thought she was always talking to you about Cecil and what was the best thing to do.'

I asked Sybil if Lady Guthrie had known about the secret engagement.

'Oh yes, because Cecil told her about it when he went back to France in October—he thought, you know, that it would be too cruel not to, and she wrote Julie a very nice letter saying how anxious she was that Cecil should settle down and marry and she didn't seem to mind a bit about Julie not having any money. By that time Julie and Cecil had decided,' and Sybil's eyes glowed with the remembered excitement, 'that if necessary they would just make a dash for it.'

'You mean elope, but they didn't do so?'

'No, because Aunt Edythe was being so nice about it all that there didn't seem any point. She said that as there was nothing, legally, you know, to prevent Julie from marrying whenever she wanted it was much better to have the thing properly arranged. She said that she was sure that Grandfather, after he had met Julie, would be quite willing to make Cecil a larger allowance. Aunt Edythe begged Julie not to do anything foolish because if she and Cecil rushed off and married in a hole-and-corner fashion it would only make everything much more difficult later on.'

As I listened I recognized, or thought I did, the old tactics of 'playing for time'.

'So then in her next letter Aunt Edythe invited Julie to go out to Cannes for Christmas so that they could talk the whole thing over sensibly.'

'And Julie thought that was a good idea?'

'Yes, because she didn't see, unless Grandfather did do something for them, what she and Cecil were going to five on. Cecil had told her that they could manage quite easily, especially if they lived in Paris, on what he had already but Julie thought that if Grandfather was willing to give them more it would probably be quite useful.'

'But didn't her parents, although I gather that she still hadn't told them anything about her engagement, raise any objections to her going to stay with the Guthries?'

'Oh no, and I must say that Aunt Edythe was really awfully clever about that. She managed it so that the Wrottesleys never guessed that there was anything "in the wind". In fact,' Sybil giggled, 'I believe she sort of gave Mrs Wrottesley to understand that she was filling the house up with eldest sons and two or three American millionaires especially so that Julie should have an opportunity of meeting them and choosing the one she liked best.'

'And Mrs Wrottesley believed her?'

'She must have, because even before Aunt Edythe had written again, sending the money for the fare, she had decided that Julie was to go.'

'But in fact it wasn't true?'

'In actual *fact* their only other guest was Captain Helbert who had come down from Paris with Cecil. It was just after Aunt Edythe had got him the appointment at the Embassy. I wonder how she arranged that because I'm sure they can't have wanted him.'

'They had to have somebody and secretary to the military attaché's secretary doesn't sound like a very important position. Anyhow I don't think you ought to insinuate that the head of the Foreign Office allows himself to be influenced over the appointment of Embassy staff.'

'I expect he is, all the same, and it must be quite nice, when it doesn't matter one way or the other, to oblige people sometimes. What I don't understand is *why* Aunt Edythe wanted them to oblige over Captain Helbert. There must have been something at the back of it but I can't think what.'

I said that I didn't think it was necessary to try and find a disagreeable reason for everything that Lady Guthrie did.

'All the same there usually is one.'

I reminded Sybil that it was our duty at least to make the attempt of loving our neighbours or, in cases where such a thing seemed to be really impossible, anyhow to refrain from ceaseless criticism.

'I know and I do try but I have always thought of Aunt Edythe as being the test case. The sort of test, *bien entendu*, that nobody's expected to pass.'

Half inclined to agree I said nothing more on the subject but asked Sybil what had happened, for I didn't suppose them to be still engaged, to prevent Julie and Cecil from marrying.

Sybil hesitated, said something about not knowing all the details and then told me what she *did* know of the pathetic story. From her recital and from things which have since come to my knowledge I think I have been able more or less to make out the way of it.

It seems that when Julie first arrived in Cannes there was a great deal of talk as to where the young people were to live and how they were to be provided with a sufficient income on which to marry. The discussions, on one pretext and another, dragged themselves on and the actual date for the wedding, which Julie had at first thought would be quite soon, was somehow always receding. I have an idea—although it is no more than that—that at some time during those long weeks Julie allowed Cecil to anticipate the wedding night. He now felt more than ever that he should marry her but it is possible that he no longer felt a great sense of urgency.

At the beginning of February he contracted scarlet fever and Lady Guthrie arranged that instead of being nursed at home he should enter a clinic. When he was a little better he went to stay with some friends in Spain. In the meantime Julie, who had remained with the Guthries throughout Cecil's illness, was being paid a great deal of attention by a Frenchman. I do not think, for he is still alive, that there is any point in mentioning his name but he was a great *parti*, possessed of one of the oldest names in France and a marriage between him and their daughter would have been an unbelievable catch for the Wrottesleys. As soon as Cecil was declared to be out of danger Julie returned to England. The *Duc* followed her there and foolishly, without making any proper enquiries as to his intentions, her parents encouraged him and allowed Julie to be continually in his company. The fact that the *Duc* was paying her so much attention became public property and, inevitably, Cecil came to hear of it. He thereupon wrote to Julie accusing her of being untrue to him. As she had been capable of giving way to him I suppose he suspected that the same thing had happened with the other man. Indignantly Julie wrote back denying it, telling him that if that was what he thought of her she would not dream of becoming his wife. It would not be surprising if by that time she had begun to waver over Cecil. So many difficulties had seemed to stand in the way of a marriage to him that the idea of becoming the *Duchesse de* —, living in luxury and being looked up to and respected for the rest of her fife may well have seemed a more tempting *avenir*. However it was; Cecil decided to take her letter as breaking off their engagement. Very soon afterwards a formal announcement was made of the *Duc*'s forthcoming marriage to a partner of his parents' choosing. In France, as everyone knows, marriages are usually arranged and I believe that that of the *Duc* and *Duchesse de* —, had been on the *tapis* for some considerable time.

The Wrottesleys, disappointed in their ambition, had turned on their daughter who had been sent to stay, as Sybil now told me, in the capacity of a kind of unpaid nursery governess with some cousins in Ireland.

'I have not heard from her for some time but when she last wrote she was very unhappy.'

Sybil came to an end—as I have said, not all of the story was known to her—and we looked at each other for some moments in silence. I broke it to ask Sybil if she, or rather Julie, truly believed that Lady Guthrie had ever really wanted Cecil and Julie to marry.

Sybil wrinkled her forehead, considering. 'It's difficult to be sure. Julie believes that she did and it certainly looked as if she was doing everything she could to bring it about and yet it was she, after all, who introduced the *Duc* to Julie and kept on inviting him to the house even after Cecil was no longer there. But that may have been only because they were near neighbours and she didn't want Julie to be bored with only herself and Grandfather. It's all very odd because although Aunt Edythe seemed to be helping I can't put it out of my head that she was really working against it.'

'But Julie doesn't believe that to be so?' I was thinking that if Lady Guthrie had really planned the thing it was a diabolical trick to have played on the girl. I wondered if something of the kind had been in her mind from the moment she realized that Julie was a threat to the *status quo*? Alternatively it was possible that she had only been trying to put off the evil hour and that the advent of the Frenchman was entirely fortuitous. If so, fate had played into her hands in the most obliging manner.

'If I were not going away we might have asked Julie up here to stay. Perhaps in any case you would like to invite her?'

As I spoke I realized that once again I was trying to mend broken hearts with picnics and days on the moor and said something about it to Sybil. At that moment the door opened to admit Nealie.

'So here you are. I have been searching for you all over the house and now you look as if you were in a deep conference about something important.'

Nealie sat down at the table and looked enquiringly from me to Sybil whose eyes flashed me a warning to say nothing of what we had been talking. I had not had any intention of doing so and instead told Nealie about Lady Guthrie's letter saying that Charlie and I had decided that I must go to her.

Nealie, although she herself would have travelled half across the world to help any human being who had turned to her in distress, declared the idea of my going to Lady Guthrie to be quite ridiculous. 'It's more than understandable that Cecil, who has been continually with her since his father's death, should now have run away to Italy but that's no reason why you should be sacrificed in his place.'

'But if she is alone?'

'I don't believe for a moment that she is. In fact I have an idea that Margot's girl who I know was there earlier is still with her. Anyhow she has at least four sisters as well as a mother left alive, why aren't some of them doing their duty, as you call it?'

'The only one she cares for is Margot who is too ill to travel.'

'Very convenient for her.' And then with a sudden change Nealie said that if I was really determined to go, which she saw I was, she would travel with me to Cannes.

'Not to stay with Edythe, Heaven forbid, and anyhow she wouldn't want me, but I could find some way of going on from there to Pau—I really do owe my sister Nannie a visit. I think too that I shall arrange for Willie to come with us. It will be less dismal than if we travel alone and have to spend the whole journey in translating to Copley what the French porters have just said to her.'

Evidently, having decided to accompany me on an errand of mercy—of which she thoroughly disapproved—Nealie was now intent upon turning it into a pleasure party in which as many people as possible should be included.

The next day she departed for the South. In an obviously hastily scrawled letter which I received two days later she told me that I had nothing at all to worry about as all her plans for our journey were *en train*.

The following week I met her and Willie at Victoria. As soon as we were settled in our carriage Nealie told me that Willie fully agreed with her in thinking it most selfish of Lady Guthrie to be dragging me away from my family when she must know that I would rather be with them than with her.

Willie protested that he had not said any such thing.

'Didn't you, I thought that you had. Anyhow,' she turned to me, **'I think it's selfish and I'm very glad for your sake that we are not going to be *too far away because a foreign land with no one in it but Edythe would be intolerable.'

## Chapter Twelve

'Arrived safely good journey my love to you all Anne.' I finished writing my telegram to Charlie and handed it to Thompson.

Holding out the salver for its reception he said that Lady Guthrie had been very anxious that the matter should be attended to the moment I arrived. 'She sets great store by them you know. For that matter so do the whole family. During the last twenty years I must have sent off thousands of them. Rowing ashore for Sir David and Mr Cecil at all those ports along the Mediterranean.' His face changed. 'Of course with Sir David gone there will be fewer of them. It's very sad and the end coming so suddenly—it took us all by surprise.'

I said that I could quite understand that and I was sure Thompson had done everything for Lady Guthrie and Cecil that it was possible for anyone to do. 'It must have been a great comfort to them both to have had you with them.'

As I spoke I was looking round the large dim *salon* into which at the moment of setting foot in the house I had been conducted. The jalousies prevented the smallest ray of sunshine from penetrating into the room which was indeed so dark that in looking over the few words I had written on the telegraph form I had had some difficulty in making them out.

'Would you perhaps like to be shown your rooms or would you rather wait until the maid has finished unpacking?'

Making no immediate decision on the point I again asked him—as I had already done when he met me at the station—how ill he thought Lady Guthrie to be.

'It's difficult to say, my lady. She took Sir David's death very hard at the time and now her grief seems as you might say to come over her in waves. One day she will be all right and the next she stays in her room and it's as if we were back at the beginning.'

'I suppose it's to be expected.'

Thompson, fidgeting a little, said that it wasn't to be wondered at but that it was unfortunate that today had turned out to be one of her bad ones.

'She's had her ups and downs for years, we all know that, but last night she was almost what Mr Cecil calls "chipper". So much so in fact that when Mademoiselle came down this morning and said that her ladyship wasn't so well I was quite surprised.'

Gathering from the reference to 'Mademoiselle' that Nealie had been right in believing Lilian still to be in the house I wondered a little that the girl had done nothing about coming downstairs to greet me. I did not mention the matter to Thompson or, being rather piqued by what I considered to be her off-hand behaviour towards myself, take the trouble to enquire after her.

'You think that Lady Guthrie really will be well enough to see me this evening?'

'That was the message I was given my lady.'

He didn't seem inclined to say anything further and I got up saying that I would now be glad to be shown my room.

'If you will follow me.' Thompson bowed me into the hall and then led the way towards the staircase. He told me that I had been put in the 'new wing' which I should have to myself.

'It was built at the time Mr Cecil was to have been married to Miss Lydia.'

The remark reminded me of the time when Cecil had been so happily busy preparing The Manor for the reception of his bride while Lady Guthrie made even more elaborate preparations to receive the couple at the Villa Victoria. How, if Cecil and Lydia had married, would it all have ended? How many months in every year would they have been permitted to spend in their own home? Was it possible that Lydia would ever have developed a will strong enough to prevail on Cecil to stand up to the one before whom he had always been accustomed to give way?

On reaching the top of the staircase Thompson turned to the left and after passing several other rooms opened the door of a little saloon. It was a pretty room decorated in *toile de Jouy* and a second door, which stood open, led into a bedroom.

If there is anything you would care to have brought to you ...?'

I said that at the moment there was nothing. Thompson withdrew and I stood looking out of one of the windows. It commanded a distant view of the sea on which the sun was sparkling and I thought I could make out a little cloud of white sails. I imagined, although it was all too far away to be certain, a sailing race must be in progress and thought of the many letters in which Lady Guthrie had described the yachts skimming over the water and the sadness which always overcame her when Cecil was not amongst those who sailed them. I wondered why he had now taken himself off to Venice; I thought it probable that over four months of Lady Guthrie's particular brand of sorrow had proved too much even for his devotion; and queried, with a slight sinking of the heart, if the fortnight I had promised to stay here was going to be too much for my own endurance. With all my heart I wished that Nealie was not already travelling away from me and took comfort from the fact that at Pau she would not, after all, be impossibly far off.

There was a gentle tap at the door. So deep had I been in my own thoughts that it startled me. I spun round from the window calling to whoever it was to enter. The door opened and to my utter astonishment Julie Wrottesley came into the room.

'My dear child, what on earth are you doing here?'

The next moment I was wondering what on earth had induced me to address the girl in such a manner. I had never, even when she was sixteen or seventeen years old, thought of her as anything but a grown woman.

Julie, advancing into the room with her usual assurance, in her turn expressed surprise at my not knowing that she was staying at the Villa.

'And you must please forgive me for not coming to you sooner but Edythe was so prostrated just now that it was impossible to leave her. Fortunately she has become calmer and I have called for Louise to sit with her.'

'I am glad that Lady Guthrie is better.' It was all I could think of to say and even to me the words sounded cold and unnatural.

'A *crise de nerfs* only, I think, but they upset her terribly at the time.'

Julie then asked me if there was anything I wanted in the way of refreshment and I told her that I had thought that before I did anything else I would like to have a bath. 'One gets so dirty with travelling and the arrangements for washing on the trains are not really satisfactory.'

'Then I will wait for you downstairs. I shall be in the *grand salon* as it is much too hot to sit out of doors. I hope that by the time you are ready to come down Edythe will be well enough to join us or at least to receive you in her room. Once these *crises* are over she seems to recover from them very quickly.'

Julie smiled at me in the kindest manner and left the room. I was left standing in the middle of it, stupidly looking at the door which had closed behind her. What on earth *was* she doing here, calling Lady Guthrie by her first name and behaving generally as if the house belonged to her and I was her guest?

Just as I was ready to go down there was a message from Lady Guthrie. She was feeling somewhat better and would I give her the joy—if I was neither asleep nor resting—of going to her room?

I was conducted there by her maid and then ushered with an air of tremendous ceremony into her presence.

'So very good of you to come.'

The voice came from the bed where she lay back against the many pillows. As usual she emanated a great air of luxury; a cherished wife and an inconsolable widow co-existed in one form; the room was heavy with the scent of roses mixed with the more sophisticated smell of her scent. The braided hair—how often have I seen it dressed in that way—lay on her neck, the arms in the billowing lace sleeves were held out to me. I went over and kissed her and then stood back looking into the still beautiful and always inscrutable face.

'I am glad you are a little better.' I was afraid that I sounded cold and somewhat unnatural.

'As to being better,' she shrugged her shoulders, 'for me the words can never be more than a form, a way of speaking; they will probably still be saying them when I am lying in my coffin, but then, at last, they will be true.'

She shook her head sadly, her eyes turned away from me to the photograph of Sir David which, with a prayer book, an open Bible and two pictures of Cecil, stood on the table beside the bed. 'I can still hardly believe that I will never in this world see my dear one again, hear the sound of his beautiful voice, feel the touch of his hand.'

It was the kind of remark to which there can be no possible answer. My glance followed hers to the photograph and we remained for what seemed like a full minute in complete silence.

A deep, long-drawn-out sigh came from the bed and I looked back at Lady Guthrie. She shifted restlessly against the pillows asking me plaintively, almost querulously, why I was still standing. She pointed to a chair placed near the bed and told me to sit down.

'Louise is going to bring us some chocolate, but perhaps you would prefer tea or *limonade*. It's so hot, I don't know, perhaps soon there will be a storm and it will be better.'

The maid came in with a tray and poured out the chocolate. I refused the offers of tea and *limonade*, also of the small sticky cakes, a kind of *petit fours* which were passed by Louise. Lady Guthrie motioned to her to put the plate containing them down on the bed and continued to help herself to them while we talked.

As soon as we were alone I turned to her eagerly. 'I was so surprised to find Julie here, I understood you had only Lilian.'

'But surely,' Lady Guthrie's eyes widened in what may have been surprise, 'I must have mentioned in one of my letters . . . As for little Lilian I had her for a week or two to oblige my sister. But finally it became too much and I thought it wiser to send her home. My sister, that is Margot, understood perfectly. You don't,' the voice had taken on an admonitory tone, 'think that there's anything peculiar about Julie being here?'

'No of course not.'

'It was after all in your house that we first met her. A friend of dear little Sybil's, although I wouldn't have thought that the two had much in common. Julie seems so much older, almost— although that of course is ridiculous—of one's own generation. She was with us for a long time last winter and my dear one and I hoped so much that she and Cecil would marry; unfortunately, owing to an indiscretion on her part, quite an innocent one, I am sure, nothing came of it.'

'But I thought, in fact I know, that she and Cecil were engaged. Isn't it rather awkward?'

'Poor Julie—I don't know how her parents could have been so unkind—had been sent to stay with some quite dreadful cousins in Ireland. I had such pathetic accounts of her that I felt the very least one could do in common humanity was to invite her here.'

'But Cecil . . . ?'

'Cecil,' Lady Guthrie said in tones that brooked of no further questions, 'is in Italy.'

So Julie had only arrived in Cannes after he had left. But why, if she had Julie, had she invited me?

'So kind and gentle. How I wish that things had fallen out otherwise and that she were now my daughter.'

But Lady Guthrie in her last letter had surely stated quite clearly that she was not only unhappy but also lonely. The fact of Julie being here, or at least expected, had been concealed from me, nor—no matter how long and vague her sentences became—was I to be persuaded that it was otherwise.

'So very kind, but one feels a great need in the midst of sorrow to have one's own people around one; that is why, selfishly perhaps, I begged you to come to me.' She held out her hand.

I decided that she must have written to Julie and me at the same time; not being sure if either of us would accept but determined not to be left alone.

'Dear Anne, I have always felt, without knowing exactly why, that you were very close to me. I am in very deep trouble, very disturbed.'

I thought that she was going to speak of her husband. I was in error for it was Cecil who, as he had done since the day he was born, occupied all her thoughts. She spoke of him now as lovingly as she had always done but, and this I noticed only after she had been talking for several minutes, there was for the first time a difference. In the past she had always seemed certain that in no matter what crisis of his life she alone knew what was best for him to do. She had seen herself not only as his mother but as his guardian angel and omniscient counsellor. Now all that was changed and she was uncertain and bewildered.

'It has come to the point where I absolutely have to speak to someone of the things that are on my mind.'

Lady Guthrie hesitated, made a great to do over pressing me to have one of her cakes, of changing her position in the bed and at last, in the midst of much that was irrelevant, managed to tell me what was troubling her. The gist of the matter was that Cecil had got himself entangled with a woman of bad character.

'I do not know how much of it has to do with the disappointment he suffered over Julie. Anyhow, in the spring of this year he was in Paris—where he remained until two days before his father's death—and it was there that he met the creature. It seems that he is absolutely enamoured of her and she has obtained an influence over him which none of his friends can understand.

They believe indeed that it is only the fact of her having a husband already that prevents him from marrying her.'

I started to say the obvious things about young unmarried men but she cut me short.

I surely didn't believe her to be so stupid as to think he should lead the life of a monk or a convent schoolgirl. He was, or had been, a normal healthy young man. He had had mistresses from the time he was seventeen but this was something entirely different. The woman had him completely in her power.

'He has corresponded with her daily during the months he has been with me and for all I know, although he says he is alone, she may now be with him in Venice. I don't know because I can't be sure any longer that he tells me the truth.'

Her voice broke on the last words, for this to her was the most terrible part of it. Every act and thought of her daily life had had for its basis a complete understanding with her son; take that away and her whole world was overturned. She had been accustomed to pride herself on knowing all his thoughts, of being the confidante, the twin soul from whom he had never wanted to hide anything. She had lived with him in an intimacy of spirit closer than that which exists between the most impassioned lovers. An intimacy from which most people would have shrunk, which any impartial person must have found repugnant.

'Is it not very dreadful?' Lady Guthrie's voice had resumed its usual conversational tones. 'The creature must be completely abandoned—if I could only get near her I would strangle her with my naked hands.'

She raised the small well-nourished hands to the level of her face. The fingers curled inwards, one could imagine a white throat—which would later be found to have purple bruises—lying between them. One could imagine the vacuous face, the pretty but undistinguished features, the fair hair becoming unpinned and tumbling about the woman's shoulders.

'How he could have let himself be so far led astray. And yet,' the smile of conscious, loving understanding was even now playing about Lady Guthrie's lips, 'it is very easy to understand his temptation. The terrible pain he suffered after his last illness.

The lack of sleep and the dreadful headaches for which the doctors could do nothing. You remember,' she looked at me to see if I had understood, 'the thing of which I once spoke to you at Kildonan. At that time I only feared it as a possibility but now. . . .'

In the pause that followed I thought of the conversation in the rose garden; Lady Guthrie sketching the Apollo statue while she talked about Cecil and now that which had been a shadow was reality and he had become addicted to narcotics.

'. . . and it is that woman I am sure who is responsible. I am told that she herself has long had the habit. She has taken him down with her into the pit and there can be only one ending. I shall live to see my son lying on his death-bed.'

'But surely . . . I had understood that, taken in time, such addictions can be cured, that doctors nowadays. . . .'

'What do they know about it?' Lady Guthrie spoke contemptuously. 'They give drugs to prevent their patients from taking other drugs, and all the time the will and the intellect continue to weaken. The only cure is to get him away from that creature—unspeakable, degraded.'

'You believe that you will be able to do that?'

'If it takes all of the little strength I have left in this poor weak body it will be managed.' The fingers curled further inwards, almost touching the palms. 'That horrible woman shall never be allowed to destroy the one beautiful thing in my life. She who is more unworthy of his love than . . . but there are no comparisons.' She allowed the hands to drop on to the coverlet where they lay inert, obviously harmless. Suddenly she looked up. The burning eyes looked directly into mine.

'I do not know any more how to help him.'

They were words of defeat, an appeal for help which I did not know how to give. 'I cannot be sure any longer that he tells me the truth'—so it had taken her all these years to discover that he had ceased to trust her. Never since the ending of his engagement to Lydia had she had his full confidence yet, for that was Cecil's tragedy, she had retained her power. She was uncertain of it at the moment but it was there, lying in those small plump hands which gave no indication of the bones which lay beneath the white flesh.

To Cecil the woman in Paris would seem for a little while to be an ally; someone who would help him to escape. But ultimately, and I was terribly sure of it, she would not prevail against the mother whose love must always end by overpowering every other.

For a moment, sitting in Lady Guthrie's room on that September day in 1895, I felt as if it was I who sought desperately for a door of escape—only to find that all doors were locked against me. There was no escape; only the drugs—they at least would give me the illusion that I was free; lead to a place where no one loving or hating could reach me.

## Chapter Thirteen

THE CABLE CAME early in the afternoon of June 10th 1896. Cecil was dead and had been buried at sea. The news was softened by no details as to the manner of his death.

'Dead!'

Charlie and I looked at each other in horror.

'And Lady Guthrie?' It was, it had to be, one's first thought.

'The same message,' Charlie looked down at the piece of crumpled paper, 'has been sent to Cannes. We can only hope that Helbert had the sense not to address it directly to my stepmother.'

'However she hears it can make little difference.'

I sat looking towards the window, at the vague shapes made by the buildings in the mews as they appeared through the obliterating curtains. Impossible to realize that it had happened and yet all through the preceding winter and spring, and despite the often cheerful news contained in Lady Guthrie's letters, I had had a premonition of something terrible overshadowing our lives.

Cecil had spent the winter in Paris, working, so his mother wrote, on a novel. She seemed very happy about it and reported his editor, Monsieur Lucien, as having said that Cecil was working steadily and quietly and that if he continued to do so a great future assuredly awaited him in literature. In none of the letters did she make any reference either to the taking of drugs or the woman who, so she had declared to me in Cannes, was wrecking his fife. The fact of Cecil's never visiting her during all those months was explained by her saying that she herself had insisted that he should not do so.

'He was so anxious to come for a short visit at Christmas; but it would only have the effect of putting everything back if he were now to place his work on one side. In Paris he has Lucien to guide him and that is everything. My own sacrifice in loneliness; the heartbreak that his absence brings me; is the contribution that I willingly make to his success. How proud my dear one would have been if he could only have lived to see the day—so very proud and what bitterness for me that it will come too late for his father to know of it.'

In March she told of the book being finished: 'there will be necessary revisions but the first draft is completed.' Now at last, I thought, Cecil will go to her, but once again the visit was postponed, this time on account of his health. Lady Guthrie wrote that Cecil was very far from well: 'You will not have much difficulty in guessing the cause, it is the old trouble. Knowing how much it must distress me he has tried to keep it concealed but I know it on the authority of Frederic Helbert—what a good friend he is. He is now constantly with my dearest boy. He tells me that the doctor wants to place Cecil in a hospital but this, *I am determined to avoid at all costs if possible.*'

In her next letter Lady Guthrie said it had been decided that Cecil was to go for a short while to America travelling with Captain Helbert. 'The change of scene can but do him good and away from his old associates I am sure that his habit of taking morphia will be easily broken. The journey I am convinced, and am supported in my conviction by medical opinion, will serve to set up my darling's health—I pray permanently. Fortunately, for he at first wanted to travel either alone or with Thompson, I have succeeded in persuading him to accept Frederic Helbert, who has his welfare so very much at heart, as a companion. I am sure that it will be only a matter of weeks before he is cured. He and I will then spend the rest of this summer at The Manor and in the autumn will travel to India and Ceylon. What a joy it will be to both of us to be uninterruptedly together again. My dearest boy writes that he can hardly wait for that time. In the meanwhile I continue in this sad villa, filled with memories and soon, I hope, to be sold. I have Julie as my only companion. She is very sweet and patient and much closer to me than any of my sisters or nieces could ever be. I really love her and what I should have done without her during all these sad months I do not know.'

Lady Guthrie's most recent letter, received only a day or two before, had contained the intelligence that Cecil and Captain Helbert had embarked on the S.S. *St Paul* on Saturday May 30th. Very sad to think of her darling boy going so far away from her but every day that passed was bringing them closer to the time when they would be reunited.

And four days after the ship had sailed, on June 3rd 1896, the first anniversary of his father's death, Cecil had died.

I looked across at Charlie; he also, I am certain, had been thinking on the past.

'What on earth can have happened?'

'How can we possibly know?'

That was the most terrible thing, not knowing, and it was a full ten days before anything essential was added to our knowledge. In the meantime Lady Guthrie steadily refused, through the medium of telegrams and letters written by Julie, to allow any notice of .the death to be inserted in *The Times*.

Ten days after the reception of the cable Charlie went down to Southampton to meet the boat in which Frederic Helbert was returning from New York. He had to leave very early in the morning and when he came into my room to say good-bye I asked him, for perhaps the thousandth time, what he thought could have happened.

'He was, or so Edythe has said, in a bad state of health before he left.'

'The drugs? Oh, I do so hope that it wasn't that.'

'Later on today we shall probably know.'

There had been a second cable mentioning an accident but it had told us little more than we knew already.

'I should be back early in the afternoon and will try and bring Helbert with me.'

The door shut behind Charlie. It was nearly six o'clock before he returned and came straight up to the boudoir where I was sitting with Nealie.

'We thought you would never come. Was the liner delayed?'

'I have been in London since two o'clock and have spent the last three hours in Willie's office.'

'With *Willie!*' Charlie's words had conveyed nothing to me beyond their surface meaning.

'With him and Sir Terrence.'

'Oh my God!'

I had never heard Nealie swear in that manner before and looked at her in surprise.

'There is nothing that can be proved in law.' Charlie sat down heavily. 'I can tell you as much as I know myself which is very little.'

He then said that he had met Helbert, as had been arranged, as he came off the boat and that the two of them, alone in a reserved carriage, had travelled up to London together.

'At first there didn't seem to be anything wrong with his story. He told me that Cecil, during the first three days of the voyage, had been in excellent health and spirits, and looking forward to visiting America. He didn't refer to the drugs, by the way, except to mention in passing that he thought Edythe was apt to exaggerate anything which related to her son.'

Charlie went on to say that the fourth night out from Southampton had been spent by the two men in the smoking-room in the company of some acquaintance whom they had made on board the ship. At one o'clock in the morning the party had broken up and Helbert and Cecil had gone to their cabins which had a communicating door which Helbert, after he had seen Cecil into bed, had shut before himself retiring for the night.

## 137 | CECIL

'He gave me to understand that Cecil was somewhat the worse for drink and he had had to help him to undress and get into his bunk.'

'But he never did drink,' Nealie said. 'I don't understand it.'

Charlie reminded her that he was only repeating the story as it had been told to him.

'Helbert said that about five o'clock he woke up and heard groans coming from the adjoining cabin. He went in and found Cecil in a state of great distress. He had been violently sick and appeared to be suffering from acute pains in his stomach. Helbert said he noticed that a glass containing a small amount of darkish liquid was beside the bed. Thoroughly alarmed he summoned a steward and directed that the doctor should be sent for immediately. The doctor did not arrive for some time. When he did he was, according to Helbert, in a thoroughly bad temper and inclined to put Cecil's troubles down to his having drunk a great deal too much whisky on the previous evening. Helbert showed the doctor the glass and drew his attention to the bitter smell of its contents. At which point Cecil, who was still conscious, pointed to a medicine bottle, or Helbert said he did, which stood amongst several others on a shelf by the wash basin. It contained a tonic which he had brought on board with him and which had been prescribed by his Paris doctor. The ship's surgeon, who was still of the opinion that Cecil's condition was due to alcohol, seemed uninterested. Later, after Helbert had insisted that he should do so, he took charge of the bottle. Cecil's pain appeared to be momentarily increasing and the doctor, with the idea, Helbert believed, of keeping him quiet and in order to avoid disturbing the people in the adjoining cabins, said that he would give him a morphia injection. He went to fetch it and was away for some ten minutes during which time Helbert was alone in the cabin with Cecil.

'Helbert told me that at first he was occupied in trying to comfort my brother and hold him in his bunk. The pain was apparently so great that Cecil was throwing himself from side to side, crying aloud and attempting to beat his head against a bulkhead. After a few minutes he became quieter and it was then that Helbert, while he still held my brother in his arms, said he noticed the half-empty bottle of the mixture which Cecil used to develop his photographs.

I thought of the letters written on board the *Thalassa*—'Oran, December 10th 1893: Although we are delayed by the weather and there is little or nothing of any interest here I do not find time lying heavy on my hands, for I hardly know how to get through the photographic developing that must be done—In Algiers I was able to take one or two snapshots but fear the weather's gloom.'

'Helbert said that the bottle had been full when it was brought onboard and professed himself to be certain that Cecil had not done any developing during the voyage.'

So one bottle had been mistaken for another. Cecil had taken the photographic mixture, believing it to be his medicine. The error, if that is what it was, had resulted in his death which took place later in the morning of June 3rd 1896. Mercifully, some time before the end Cecil, probably as a result of the injection, fell into a coma so that the passing itself was without pain. The doctor had professed himself as being satisfied that death was due to a quantity of photographic mixture being introduced into the body, self-administered as a result of an error by the victim and the death was entered in the ship's log as having been accidental. The month was June and the body was accordingly committed to the sea early on the following morning, the burial service being read by the captain of the vessel.

Charlie paused and then repeated that at first there didn't seem to anything wrong with Helbert's account of what had happened. 'He told it all quite straightforwardly and showed me the doctor's report. The same I believe as is recorded in the ship's log and there seemed to be no reason to doubt the truth of any of it.'

'And then?'

'And then we didn't talk for a while. I was thinking about the manner of my brother's death; thinking how unnecessary it had all been. Thinking of his mother and the terrible effect it is bound to have on her. The possibility of suicide did, as it was bound to, enter my mind only to be instantly dismissed. There was no reason that I could think of for Cecil to take his life. Even if he had decided upon such a course, that was decidedly not the method that he nor anyone who knew the nature and effect of the poison administered, would have chosen. I accepted the thing for what it appeared to be—a tragic accident. I remember feeling sorry for Helbert; thinking how well he had acquitted himself of the painful duty of going over the last hours of Cecil's life for my benefit. I thought what a terrible experience the death of his friend must have been for him and of how helpless and alone he must have felt on that ship; unable to communicate with any of the family and quite alone with people whom, until a few days before, he had never met. I was grateful for the little he had been able to do for Cecil and for the suggestion he had made about going directly to Cannes in case Edythe should wish to see him.

'I had fallen I suppose into a kind of unhappy reverie from which I was roused by the sound of Helbert's voice. It was the sound of the voice, not what he at first said—for I don't even remember what it was—which caught my attention. The tones were quite different from what they had been earlier. I don't mean that they were harsher or louder or anything of that kind, but so different that I knew immediately that what was to follow would be something terrible. What he in fact said was, and now I am going to quote his exact words: "I have to tell you that before Cecil left Paris he made a Will leaving his entire fortune to me." That is what he said and before he had finished speaking I knew that my brother had been murdered. Knew, too, without any possibility of doubt that I was looking at his murderer, sitting opposite him, his foot almost touching mine. I might have killed Helbert at that moment and I still don't know why I didn't. As it was I got up and went and sat in the furthest corner of the carriage. I couldn't bring myself to speak to him or look at him again and when we reached London I got a cab and drove straight to Sir Terrence's office.'

## Chapter Fourteen

Sir Terrence Lucas was, as I have mentioned and indeed as everyone knows, the greatest lawyer of his day. He died in somewhat sad circumstances just before the war and it is only now when his wife and his only son, who fell at the battle of the Marne, are also dead that I feel free to tell the next part of my story.

There was, as Sir Terrence said to Charlie during their interview on that June day in 1896, no possible way of bringing Helbert to justice. The murder would go unpunished. As regards the inheritance there was nothing, if the will proved to be in order, to prevent the murderer from receiving the money for which he had killed the man who had supposed him to be his friend.

'Legally you haven't a leg to stand on but leave it to me,' had been Sir Terrence's words when the case was first put before him and, as Charlie told us, nothing further was to be had from him during that first interview.

'But he must,' Nealie urged, 'have said *something* more than that.'

Charlie assured her that we now knew as much as to what had passed between him and the lawyer as he did himself.

'Our present problem,' he looked from one to the other of us, 'is to decide what to do about Edythe.'

'Will she have to be told about the will?'

'Naturally. The thing that is worrying me at the moment is that Helbert will probably try and see her.'

'He can't,' Nealie said, 'it would be too horrible.'

I agreed that it was unthinkable that Helbert should ever again be in the same room with Lady Guthrie.

'Do you think,' Nealie asked Charlie, 'that that horrible man will have decided to travel straight on to Cannes? Did he say anything to you before you parted at the station?'

'I've already told you that after he made the announcement about the will we never spoke again. I might, I suppose, have got him to promise me *not* to go to her but what chance was there of his keeping his word? The very fact of knowing that I did not wish him to see her would probably have had the effect of sending him out there all the sooner.'

'Do you,' I said, 'think that one of us should go to her or would a letter to Julie explaining what has happened and that you have seen Sir Terrence . . . there is nothing is there that can be said in a telegram; no way in which we can warn Julie?'

'If Helbert does go there,' Nealie said, 'Edythe is sure to see him. She will be as anxious as we were to know the details of what she believes to have been a tragic accident; to talk to the last person to see her son alive.'

'I suppose,' Charlie got up, 'I could telegraph to Julie, begging her not to receive Helbert and at all costs to keep him away from Edythe until she receives my letter.'

'You have already written?'

'No, but I am going to do so now and if you think it is a good idea send a telegram to Julie. Whether, if Helbert arrives there before they get my letter, it will do any good or not we can't tell.'

Charlie was moving towards the door. Just before he reached it it was thrown open.

'Lady Guthrie, my lady.'

It was the only time in all the years he was with us that I ever heard astonishment in Purvis's official voice or knew it to betray by so much as a semi-tone that he was after all subject to any other human emotion.

'Edythe!' Charlie, recovering from his amazement, took both Lady Guthrie's hands in his.

Nealie and I got up, each of us murmuring words indicating sympathy mingled with surprise. We had had no idea that she was in England, that she whom we had imagined as being prostrated with grief in Cannes should have found the strength to make a long journey; that, having decided to do so, she should not have let us know that she was coming.

'Where is he?' She looked round the room as if she had expected that someone else would be there.

It was a terrible moment for all of us for it was clear that the person she had expected to see was Frederic Helbert.

Helplessly, I looked from Charlie to Nealie. It was a question which of us was to tell her; how much of the knowledge that was already ours was to be imparted to her.

'He isn't here.' Charlie led Lady Guthrie to the sofa where she sat bolt upright as if ready to take off again as soon as she knew where Helbert was to be found.

'When I got the cable saying he was to be in England today I couldn't rest. I felt that I had to hear at the first possible moment everything but everything, that concerned my darling. He did arrive, didn't he?' She looked at Charlie and there was anxiety in her voice. 'Nothing happened to prevent him? The cable from New York was sent off just as he was about to sail.'

'Yes, he arrived this morning,' Charlie sat down on the sofa beside Lady Guthrie, 'and I met him at Southampton as I told you I was going to. And now,' he paused for a brief moment, 'there is something very terrible that I am going to have to tell you.'

'More terrible than that which has happened already?' She still sat upright as if poised for flight; the quality of her voice was oddly theatrical. I wondered if perhaps she might not have some premonition of what was to follow.

Charlie, speaking very gently, told her as quickly as he could. 'You know that Helbert was quite alone with Cecil when he was taken ill and, for reasons which I will explain later, we believe and I'm afraid that there can be no doubt but that my brother was murdered.'

'I see.'

She accepted the statement without any question; without any of the lamentations or tears which might have been expected. I had moved forward with the idea I think of taking her in my arms, of offering her my shoulder on which to cry and the comfort that is supposed to exist in ineffectual pattings and claspings of the hands.

'Please tell me what has happened or what you know for I suppose it cannot be everything?'

Charlie started to repeat in more or less the same words the things he had already said to Nealie and me—the moment in the railway carriage when Helbert had told him about the will and his subsequent interview with Sir Terrence. Lady Guthrie heard him out without interruption. Her position remained unaltered; the calm which had fallen upon her earlier to all outward appearances undisturbed.

So unusual, so totally unexpected was her demeanour that I found myself watching her almost without pity. Here was a woman in the process of learning that she had sent her son, the being who for the past thirty years she had loved to the point of folly, to his death and yet the terrible knowledge was producing no sign of anguish. Could it be possible that she did not realize that it was only in the circumstances provided by the voyage that Helbert would have dared make any attempt on Cecil's life; or in which he could have had the least hope, if he had been mad enough even to contemplate it, of the crime going undetected?

As I watched her I was thinking that it was she who had induced Cecil to undertake the journey and had arranged for Helbert to accompany him. Unwittingly she had played directly into the hands of her son's murderer to whom perhaps the very idea of murder had not occurred until she had presented him with the opportunity of committing it.

'How wicked, how dreadfully dreadfully wicked!'

Charlie had come to the end of his recital and Lady Guthrie's words fell into the momentary silence of the room.

'And there is really no way,' she went on, 'in which, except through the medium of his conscience, he can be punished?'

'Apparently not.'

'Perhaps it is better so. I do not believe that we should seek for vengeance. I know my darling would not want it for himself, that he doesn't want it, that he is at peace.'

'I don't know how you can talk like that,' Nealie's voice was raised in indignation.

Charlie got up abruptly. 'You will let me know Edythe if there is anything I can do for you. In the meantime I suppose you agree to our being guided by Sir Terrence?'

'There is nothing he can do that will bring back my son.'

'He may at least be able to do *something* to prevent Helbert from getting hold of the money.'

'As to that you must do as you think best.'

Charlie, obviously thoroughly exasperated, went out of the room. Nealie and I, who would also have been glad to escape if it had been decently possible, were left alone with Lady Guthrie. She continued to sit on the sofa, a smile of saintly, infuriating resignation playing round the corners of her mouth. I realized that for me she had lost all reality. She was no longer a woman in a terrible situation but rather an actress whose role demanded that she should be 'no longer of this world'. Her audience was to understand that her son's death had translated her to a higher state of being; that already she walked with the angels; that human concerns, sorrow or a desire for vengeance, were no longer a part of her. But even those who deem their souls to be already ethereal have, as they still demonstrably possess human bodies, to be dealt with in the ordinary way by other people. Lady Guthrie, unexpectedly arrived in England, would have to have somewhere to sleep and might be presumed later on to be in need of dinner.

I asked her if she was already at an hotel and suggested that she might prefer to come and stay with us. The wide beautiful eyes were turned on me and, as if it were taking her some little time to return to us, there was an appreciable pause before she answered.

'I am staying at the Coburg and I have Julie with me as well as Thompson and Louise.'

Quickly, feeling that I was being a little mean in doing so, I accepted the statement as a refusal. 'But perhaps you and Julie, if you are not too tired after your journey, that is, would like to come to dinner?'

'I am not tired but I have things to do.'

The fact of Lady Guthrie admitting to not being tired was as surprising, as out of her character as we had hitherto known it, as everything else she was now saying and doing.

'And that reminds me. I left Julie to wait in the carriage and should not perhaps keep her waiting any longer.' Lady Guthrie rose to her feet.

I begged her to let me send a message for Julie to be brought in.

I was thinking that as the Coburg was only one minute away, and as Julie must have been sitting outside our door for a considerable time, Lady Guthrie had, if changed in all else, nevertheless managed to retain her selfishness intact.

'It is kind of you but there will not be time. I have to reflect upon what Charlie has just told me. It must alter, I suppose, what I had intended to do for Helbert.'

'Of course it must,' Nealie said. 'Haven't you understood that he actually *killed* Cecil?'

The all-forgiving glance was turned in Nealie's direction. 'I have understood that Charlie and Sir Terrence Lucas say that he did and it is for that reason that I must reflect.'

The footman came to conduct her downstairs and after embracing me and bowing somewhat coldly to Nealie Lady Guthrie went slowly out of the room. The door shut behind her. Nealie, as soon as she judged Lady Guthrie to be unquestionably out of earshot, started to speak.

'Poor foolish woman, she sends her son to his death and doesn't even know it. "Cecil is at peace and Helbert is dreadfully, dreadfully wicked". Is she really too stupid to understand that if it hadn't been for her interference Cecil would still be alive; living in Paris with his mistress and refusing, as he did all through the winter and spring, to go and incarcerate himself in Cannes? That's what Edythe couldn't bear, of course—the fact that he could be happy away from her; that he had escaped to some other woman. Well now at least she hasn't got that to worry about. He's dead and she's got him to herself.'

'Oh Nealie, you talk as if she had somehow done it on purpose, as if it had all been planned.'

'Of course it wasn't planned. I don't believe even Edythe is wicked enough to have intended his death. But now that it's happened she's not going to admit that she herself was in any way to blame. I can't bear the dishonesty of it and I hope I shall never have to see her again in my whole life.'

'Don't you think,' I said, 'that it is herself, not only other people, whom she is intending to deceive?'

'Anyone else,' Nealie went on, without paying any attention to my interruption, 'would never have stopped blaming themselves from the first moment they heard he was dead. Even before they knew that Helbert had killed him they'd have gone on and on turning the thing over in their minds, thinking, if only I hadn't sent him abroad it would never have happened. And that's quite true. I mean it's only in a small cabin that the tonic and the photographic mixture would have been anywhere near each other. In a house, in Paris in fact, they wouldn't have been. For one thing Thompson wouldn't have allowed it.'

That's all perfectly true but to be fair to her she didn't know, until Charlie told her just now, that that was the way in which it was supposed to have happened. And we don't really know, do we, if there ever *was* any mistake about the bottles. Obviously, if Helbert murdered him there wasn't.'

'It probably wasn't the photographic mixture anyhow,' Nealie said, 'but that of course no one will ever be able to find out.'

'I suppose the doctor must have been satisfied at the time that it was, otherwise he'd have made some sort of fuss about it.'

'At the time there was nothing for the doctor to be suspicious about. After all, why should anybody be, until they knew about the will?'

'If only Thompson had been with them! I wonder how Helbert arranged that he shouldn't be. Cecil hardly ever travelled without him.'

'I expect,' Nealie said shrewdly, 'that this time it was fairly easy to persuade him to leave Thompson behind. Cecil knew perfectly well that if he managed to smuggle any morphia on board with him Thompson would have gone through that cabin like a ferret until he found it. Helbert's too, if he'd thought Cecil was receiving it from him.'

'I do wish we knew what Sir Terrence is going to do, what he *can* do!'

'I suppose Willie would be able to tell us about that. He's dining with me this evening and I intend for him to tell me *everything*.'

I was just going to suggest that Nealie should bring Willie round after dinner when Charlie, who had waited until after Lady Guthrie's departure to do so, came back into the room.

'I must say you got rid of Edythe pretty quickly. You didn't,' he looked at me apprehensively, 'invite her to come back for dinner or anything, did you?'

'I did but fortunately she refused.'

'Thank goodness for that at any rate. Do you think it possible that she has gone out of her mind?'

I said that I didn't know. 'If she had been hysterical it might have been worse, worse for us that is.'

'It would have been more natural.' Charlie sat down.

'I always told you she was odious,' Nealie said 'and you never would believe me.'

'I believed you,' Charlie said, 'in fact you didn't have to tell me.'

I said that I couldn't imagine what Lady Guthrie's life would be without Cecil, or even, with the Villa Victoria as good as sold, where she would decide to live.

Nealie, getting up to go, said that she supposed that Edythe would either try and buy back the villa or, more probably, move to Paris.

'Why Paris? She and Cecil were to have settled at The Manor.'

'Because Paris was the last place in which Cecil lived.'

'What an extraordinary idea,' Charlie said, 'but I shouldn't be surprised if you're not right.'

After dinner that evening Charlie and I sat in the library. We were both reading, for if we talked we found that our conversation came back inevitably to the tragedy, when the footman came in to say that Mr Cecil's man was here and asking to see Mr Guthrie.

'Thompson . . . what on earth!'

I said that Lady Guthrie had brought him over with her from France.

'Yes, I suppose she would have done. Tell him,' Charlie said to the footman, 'that I'll be with him in a moment.'

'Wouldn't you rather see him in here? I expect he only wants to offer his condolences, but if it was anything private I could leave you.'

'If you're sure you don't mind?'

'I should rather like to see him in any case. I shall never forget how good he was that time when we had Cecil here when he was ill. His death must have been a terrible shock to Thompson.'

Thompson was shown into the library. Charlie made him sit down with us and after the first painful minutes of the condolences were over, insisted upon his having a glass of port.

'A terrible business indeed. When the cable came I couldn't believe it. I'd been certain, of course, that it would be from him letting her ladyship know that he'd arrived safely.'

Charlie asked to whom the cable had been addressed.

'To her ladyship herself. That devil, I beg your pardon, Captain Helbert, hadn't even thought to send it to Miss Wrottesley. Fortunately though, for her ladyship was out at the time, it was me that opened it.'

Charlie said that that at least was something to be thankful for.

I said that Lady Guthrie seemed to have withstood the shock of Cecil's death better than one would have expected.

'Yes.' The man's face was expressionless and he made no attempt to add anything further. Then, and with a complete change of manner, he turned to Charlie: 'When her ladyship came back to the hotel she told me that Mr Cecil died because of drinking some of that photographic mixture. She said that he'd taken it in mistake for that tonic Dr Marbon ordered him before he left Paris.'

'That was what it said in the report written out by the doctor on board the ship,' Charlie said carefully. 'Captain Helbert showed it to me in the train this morning and I told Lady Guthrie about it when she was here.'

'And it's exactly that, sir, that I wanted to see you about.' Thompson glanced uneasily in my direction. He was obviously apprehensive as to what effect the disclosure he was about to make was going to have on me.

'You can go on,' Charlie said, 'and I think I know what you are going to say.'

'Well, it's this. It can't possibly be true because the bottles weren't the least bit alike. They weren't the same shape for one thing and the one that had the photographic stuff in it was about four times the size of the others. I packed them myself and I ought to know.'

'So,' Charlie said, 'there was more than one bottle of tonic?'

'That was so there should be enough to last him while he was away.'

'It certainly made things simpler for Captain Helbert when the time came.'

'So,' Thompson said, 'you think the same as I do, you think he murdered Mr Cecil?'

'Frankly, I do. But I don't think it's a good thing to go round saying so when we can't prove it.'

'But we can,' Thompson insisted, 'I can tell them what I've just told you. And that's enough to show anyone that Mr Cecil, even if he wasn't quite himself at the time it was supposed to have happened, couldn't have made a mistake.'

'The surgeon's report said distinctly that the medicine and the photographic mixture were in almost identical bottles.'

'They couldn't have been.'

'When the doctor was there they were. And I've no doubt that Captain Helbert, if he was ever in a position where he could be questioned about it, would say that it was Mr Cecil himself who poured a quantity of the mixture into an empty medicine bottle.'

'Why would he have done that?'

'You and I don't believe that he did but Captain Helbert's answer would probably be that it was for easy handling or something of that sort.'

'You mean that he's going to get away with it?'

'I'm afraid it looks very much as if he will.'

Thompson expressed his indignation that such a thing should be possible; refused to believe that British justice should fall so far short of what was *right*. He then said that it wouldn't surprise him if it didn't turn out that Mr Cecil had left the captain a good bit of money. 'Anyhow he must have thought he was going to, or there wouldn't have been any point in killing him, would there?'

Charlie, without going into any details, said that it was possible that that had been Captain Helbert's motive.

'And when I think of everything he got out of him while he was alive! Always did, if you ask me, but for these past three or four months he's been as good as living off him. You know what Mr Cecil was for helping any one he thought was in any kind of trouble.'

'What kind of trouble was Captain Helbert in?'

'Well he wasn't at the Embassy any more and then in April, I don't expect you noticed it but it was in the paper, he resigned from the army. So he wouldn't have been getting any money from anywhere would he?'

'Except from my brother?'

Thompson said that that was about the way of it; or at least what he had a pretty shrewd idea of, for of course nothing had ever been said about it directly. And even then, with all that he was being given, it wasn't safe, if Charlie and I would believe it, to leave Captain Helbert and any money, French *or* English, alone in a room together.

'Did you ever tell my brother that?'

Thompson said that he'd hinted at it more than once, but that Mr Cecil wouldn't have it.

'So he trusted Captain Helbert completely?'

'I suppose he did.' There was a certain hesitancy in the way Thompson spoke. 'But *I* didn't and no more would anyone else if they'd been with us in Paris and seen what was going on.'

'Obviously, he was pretty clever about it all.'

'He was clever all right when it came to looking out for himself and then he had her ladyship twisted round his little finger. He could do what he liked with her. There was a lot she didn't know too and it wasn't any use anyone trying to warn her.'

Thompson paused and then after reminding us that he had been with the family for twenty years and would have done anything for any of them, especially, I gathered, for Sir David or Cecil, went on with his story.

It went back to Cecil's long illness in the spring of 1895 which was when the doctors, who Thompson supposed couldn't help themselves, really put him on to morphia.

'And once on it, as I expect you know, it'd be difficult to get off it again. It came to a head I should say a few months after Sir David's death. That,' Thompson turned to me, 'was when Mr Cecil went off to Venice on his own and you came over to France to stay with her ladyship.'

I nodded, remembering that painful visit. Once again seeing Lady Guthrie lying back against her pillows while she told me about 'the dreadful abandoned woman' who was encouraging Cecil to take drugs and, incidentally, trying, perhaps successfully, to estrange him from his mother.

'Well he came back to the Villa, at the end of October it must have been, but after two days he was off again to Paris, only this time he took me with him. Whether or not it was her ladyship who persuaded him to it I don't know, but that was the way it was arranged.'

'He was in pretty bad shape then, was he?' Charlie interrupted to ask.

Thompson, after considering for a moment, said that he supposed that he was; that Lady Guthrie, before they left, had begged Thompson to keep an eye on Mr Cecil and had explained that he would be seeing a very clever doctor in Paris who was going to cure him. 'She said that she knew that Mr Cecil was going to be cured, because *they*,' Thompson paused significantly, 'had told her that he would be.'

'They?'

'You know,' Thompson said, 'the spirits that she thinks come and spell things out to her when she's pushing that board about. She thinks that Sir David talks to her through that; only it works better when there's a medium there to help and they don't have to use the board at all. That's called "the direct voice" and of course it's easier to understand.'

Charlie made a noise denoting extreme disapproval of any such goings on and asked about the Paris doctor. Had Cecil been to see him and had he in fact been able to do any good?

'Oh yes,' Thompson said, 'we were doing very nicely.'

By Christmas in fact Cecil, in Thompson's opinion, was quite himself again and working very hard at his book. Really working that was, not just doing a little bit in the evening and then putting it aside and not looking at it again for months. And Monsieur Lucien, the gentleman who was going to see about having the book printed as soon as it was finished, had said that he was delighted with it. 'Mr Cecil had moved from the hotel by then and was living in that little apartment he'd found and I had a room close by and used to go in every day. Just to valet him, you know, because everything else was arranged for.'

I took the last sentence to be a delicate way of saying that Cecil's mistress, if not actually living in the apartment, had made herself responsible for its domestic maintenance.

Charlie asked Thompson if he thought the morphia habit had been given up completely.

Thompson said that at the beginning of January Dr Marbon had told him that he was no longer having to give Cecil any injections at all. 'They have to do it little by little you know, because if a person's been used to it and then stops all of a sudden it makes him worse than he was before. It isn't easy for the doctor either if the person isn't somewhere where he can be watched, because quite often they give it to themselves on the sly. That's why Dr Marbon used to confide in me; so that I could keep a look out, discreetly you know, and let him know if I found anything.'

'But you never did?'

Thompson said that for a long time he hadn't. Cecil had continued in good health and there had been no reason to suspect that he was taking any drugs other than those ordered him by the doctor. Then in March, soon after he started seeing so much of Captain Helbert, there were signs that he might be reverting to the habit. 'And I'd take my oath that it was the captain that was getting the stuff for him and encouraging him to take it.'

'What made you think that?'

Thompson said that he couldn't really put a finger on it. It was more a feeling, he supposed, than anything else and it was always after the captain had been to the apartment that Cecil seemed to be worse. 'Excited you know and not knowing properly what he was saying. And then he seemed, although it's difficult to describe, to depend on the captain in a way he never had on anybody else. And he was giving him more money all the time—that I know for a fact.'

Charlie said that he had understood that at one time Lady Guthrie had believed that it was some other person who had been responsible for encouraging Cecil in his addiction and had indeed introduced him to the habit.

'You mean perhaps,' Thompson glanced at me and automatically dropped his voice, 'a lady?'

'Exactly.'

'Well, it wasn't her this time because after she'd seen the effect it had on Mr Cecil and how much better he was without it she was dead against it. As a matter of fact, she was the one who found the hypodermic and brought it to me and I took it to Dr Marbon.'

'What happened then?'

'Well then we were sure of course and the doctor was all for Mr Cecil going into some kind of a home and it was all arranged. And then suddenly, Mr Cecil changed his mind. He'd had a letter from her ladyship, though how she knew anything about him being worse again, I don't know. Anyhow, her ladyship wrote to Mr Cecil telling him that she'd read, in the encyclopedia I believe it was, about it being a better idea for a person to go on a long sea voyage.'

'So that, in preference to taking the doctor's advice, was what was decided upon?'

'It got him away from Paris which I believe is what her ladyship had been wanting for a long time. She knew all about the lady being there with him and she didn't like it. And then Captain Helbert was all for it and by that time Mr Cecil was doing pretty well everything the captain told him to.'

'It seems extraordinary,' Charlie said, 'the way everything fell out in the way Captain Helbert must have wanted it to. I mean Lady Guthrie being the first to suggest the journey and all that.'

'Very odd indeed, sir, except, and this I've only just thought of, that in the last month or so, so Louise was telling me today, her ladyship had been getting a lot of letters from Captain Helbert. What was in them of course we don't know; but nobody,' Thompson was quick to exonerate his fellow servant, 'could help noticing the captain's handwriting. It was different from anyone else's, not a gentleman's writing, if you understand me.'

## Chapter Fifteen

THERE WAS NEVER any doubt in the minds of those who knew, so far as it was possible to do so, the full facts of the case but that Cecil Guthrie was murdered on board the S.S. *St Paul* on the night of June 13th 1896: that the murderer who, under the terms of his victim's will, stood to gain fifteen thousand pounds was his travelling companion Frederic Charles Helbert, lately third secretary to the British Military Attaché in Paris.

To have no doubt of a thing is however a different matter from being able to prove it in law. Helbert could not be brought to trial and under the law stood to receive a substantial profit from a calculated and cold-blooded murder. Sir Terrence Lucas nevertheless determined that he should not do so. Several days after their first interview he sent for Charlie and told him that he had decided to prepare a case against Helbert in which he would seek to show that undue influence had been exercised in regard to the will.

There was, as Sir Terrence warned, no certainty that such a case would succeed. The terms of the will were not demonstrably unreasonable. Cecil had no dependants for whom it could be shown that provision should have been made. The capital involved had brought him in an income which probably represented only about half of his annual expenditure, the rest of which was met out of an allowance provided by his mother. She therefore was rendered financially better off as a result of his death and it could not be claimed that the money being left away from her constituted any hardship.

In fact, but this is incidental, a paper was found at Mr Goodenough's, our family lawyer, in which Cecil had previously directed that in the event of his death his money and The Manor, Old Windsor, was to pass to our younger son. Typically, Lady Guthrie, when this memorandum was shown to her, immediately pointed out that Cecil had of course never had any idea that he might predecease his always ailing mother.

Cases of 'undue influence' most often turn upon the point of the testator having been, at the time he signed the will, either of unsound mind or, alternatively, too ill or too under the influence of drugs to have a full understanding of what he was doing. The plea is usually accompanied by the suggestion that the person named as the beneficiary was able to exercise such an influence because he or she had some kind of power over the testator, or that the testator stood in fear of him. It may then be assumed that the terms of the will were dictated as the result of threats uttered by the beneficiary and the court may decide that the will cannot go forward for probate. If this happens, and if there is no earlier will in existence, the estate is then dealt with as it would be in a case of intestacy.

In Cecil's case there was his known addiction to drugs and Sir Terrence now told Charlie that the lawyer in Paris who had prepared the will had announced himself as being ready to swear that Mr Guthrie, when he gave his instructions, was in a dazed condition. The man's own reputation, in so far as he had one, was to be safeguarded by the additional statement that he had strongly urged Mr Guthrie—whom he had never previously met—to wait for a more propitious moment and had been roundly abused by Mr Guthrie for his trouble.

The whole story of the signing of the will was, as it appeared in Sir Terrence's indictment, extremely damaging to Helbert.

How much truth there was in it all I do not know but it is my opinion, although even at this distance of time one hesitates to write it, that the evidence of the French lawyer was paid for. Its price being conveniently lost in the general costs of preparing the case which, as may be imagined, were enormous. If it were not so I do not see any reason why the lawyer, who admitted that Cecil had been introduced to him by Helbert, should have decided—for that is what it amounted to—to change sides.

The testimony to be offered by the lawyer, although it would undoubtedly arouse strong suspicions against Helbert, would hardly by itself have been enough to induce any court to consider setting the will aside. Fortunately it was possible to reinforce our case with the evidence of two men whose positions in society and unquestionable integrity made it well-nigh impossible for anyone to doubt their word. It was inconceivable that either of them would have agreed to bear witness to something that they themselves did not believe to be true.

The first intimation we had that such testimony was to be available to us was when Charlie met Reggie Cameron in the club. General Cameron was the British Military Attaché in Paris. Eighteen months before Lady Guthrie—although without the assistance from Charlie upon which she had evidently counted—had steam-rollered him into taking Helbert into his office.

Most people, naturally, had said how sorry they were for Helbert; imagined how terrible it must be for him to feel that, if only he had happened to go into the cabin earlier, he might have been the means of saving Cecil's life. General Cameron said none of these things. He referred to his erstwhile subordinate as 'that scoundrel', adding that if anybody was going to take a poison instead of a medicine it was a great pity that it couldn't have been Helbert.

'You didn't have much use for him?' Charlie put the question in the hope of hearing more in the same vein. 'He left the Embassy some time ago, didn't he, and now I hear he's resigned from the army.'

General Cameron said that Helbert had been requested to relinquish his commission. The reason for it, which was never made public, being that certain papers to which he had access had disappeared. Helbert, who was heavily in debt, had hoped to sell them but in this he had been unsuccessful.

'After we kicked him out he remained on in Paris and, as you can imagine, we were keeping a pretty sharp eye on him, which is why we knew he was seeing so much of your brother. He hadn't bothered too much about him when everything was going well—although of course he owed his appointment entirely to your family. I tried through one of the other secretaries to warn Cecil that there was something wrong about Helbert, but it seems he wouldn't hear a word against him. Of course owing to the secrecy that was being maintained it wasn't possible to be very specific.'

Charlie said that if the Embassy officials had told Cecil exactly what was in their minds it was probable that the only effect it would have had would he to make him all the more anxious to befriend Helbert. 'He was a great righter of wrongs, you know, and if Helbert wasn't going to be accused openly and given the chance of defending himself Cecil would certainly have seen him as a victim of bureaucratic injustice. I am sure that he waxed exceedingly indignant on the fellow's behalf, and if you had but known it, the two of them were probably hatching a plot to get Helbert reinstated and the rest of you sent to perdition.'

General Cameron said that they wouldn't have been likely to get very far with that one.

'To be perfectly fair to Cecil I don't believe that he would have had anything to do with it, or with Helbert at all for that matter, unless he had believed him to be innocent. Helbert could be pretty plausible as I, and I suppose all of you, now know to our cost. He stayed with us in Scotland two years ago and if anything I rather liked him. One sees now that there was something altogether too smooth about him but I have to admit that at the time I was completely taken in.'

General Cameron agreed that Helbert was certainly plausible and said that no one at the Embassy had, until the last moment, entertained doubts as to his loyalty. 'I can well imagine how, when he found himself out on his ear and with his debts still unsettled, he managed to work on your brother's feelings. Once having decided, as I suppose he did, that Cecil was his best, if not only, chance of getting hold of some money, I bet he played on the "dastardly treatment" he had received from us for all he was worth. I've no doubt either that he found ways of making himself useful.'

'You knew that during the last year or so of his life Cecil was addicted to morphia?'

General Cameron admitted that the thing had been more or less common knowledge: 'And I'm sure Helbert didn't hesitate to exploit it. It was something which would have made Cecil all the easier to influence, but from what I hear Helbert never got him to settle his debts in full, for his creditors are still after him.'

It was at that point that Charlie decided to tell General Cameron about the contents of the will. 'It all fits in much too well, doesn't it? Helbert persuades Cecil to leave him his money, possibly as a purely temporary expedient in case something should happen to him while he is abroad; because, for all we know, he may have had some sort of promise from Cecil as to the debts being paid off at a future date. Probably, if I'm right about the promise, it would have been fulfilled when Cecil received his share of the purchase price of the Villa Victoria. Helbert, with the will safely signed, then poisons Cecil in mid-Atlantic, knowing full well that the body, in the month of June and with the ship still six days out from New York, will have to be buried at sea. Odd too, wasn't it, that that particular boat should have been chosen when the Cunarders make the crossing in five days?'

General Cameron, on hearing about the will, was naturally horrified and I think then and there offered, if a case was eventually brought into court, to give evidence against Helbert.

Talking it over with me later Charlie said that he hoped that when it came to the sticking point Reggie wouldn't try and back down. 'It will be very awkward for him to handle the part about the reason for Helbert's dismissal without either giving away government secrets or rendering himself open to a libel suit. What he is going to say is that Helbert was in desperate need of money and failed to get it because the foreign power to whom he offered secret information weren't prepared to buy. And Reggie, or so I assume, will not be in a position to offer any proof in support of his statement.'

'But surely, even if he wanted to, he can't refuse to give evidence?'

'Helbert will not be appearing on a criminal charge. Reggie, on thinking the matter over and after discussing it with his superiors, may well feel that it is not in the interests of Her Majesty's Government to disclose an affair which it has already been decided shall be kept secret. There may be all sorts of difficulties that we don't know anything about. The German ambassador, for instance, although I am only assuming that Germany is the country concerned, may have been a party to the original decision. If that were so it might have serious repercussions if the British, after having agreed or even requested that the thing should be—shall we say "hushed up"—were suddenly to turn round and allow it to be made public.'

'And if that were to be left out, our case would be a great deal weaker? It wouldn't be enough just to show that Helbert was in need of money?'

'Don't you see that the other would do more than anything else to discredit Helbert as a witness? It shows him to be untrustworthy to the point where he is capable of committing a treasonable act in order to gain his own ends. From that you, as the court, do not have to assume that having failed to gain them in one thoroughly disgraceful manner he immediately turns to murder. All you are asked to believe is that he used undue influence when he persuaded Cecil to make out a will in his favour. Nothing very much really compared with treason.'

'So General Cameron's evidence is very important?'

'It will be more telling than anything else we have to offer. You see the case, or so I imagine, is going to be largely a question of Helbert's word against that of other witnesses. If, at the outset, he is shown to be a thorough blackguard it is highly unlikely that anything he says—that is not corroborated by others—will be believed.'

I asked Charlie, for the matter had been much on my mind, how much of the details of the case would have to be explained before-hand to Lady Guthrie.

'As little as possible,' Charlie said grimly. 'We have her general permission, although whether she realized she was giving it I don't know, to go ahead with Sir Terrence. And neither he nor I want any interference from her until the thing is in the bag.'

'You do think that we are going to win?'

'If Reggie doesn't back down and Edythe doesn't meddle I do. Thank goodness she decided to go down to The Manor. At least she can no longer come round at every hour of the day to give helpful advice and tell us utterly irrelevant things that have just come into her mind. It's fortunate too that we aren't going to have to call her as a witness. Edythe on the stand being maudlin about her dearest boy would probably just about finish us.'

I was sorry, although I understood his feelings very well and to a large extent shared them myself, that Charlie should feel so bitterly about the wretched Lady Guthrie. I thought of her now living alone at The Manor. She had made such happy plans for the time she would spend there this summer with Cecil before they started on the voyage which would have taken them to India and Ceylon.

'I wonder if Helbert has made any attempt to see her?'

The words breaking in on my thoughts startled me considerably.

'Oh Charlie, not now, he couldn't possibly.'

'You think not. I only hope you are right, but I wouldn't put it past him. It would after all, for he must at least guess that we are not likely to let the thing drop without putting up some kind of a fight, be in his interests to try and bring her round to his side.'

'How could he possibly do that when she knows that he murdered him?'

'Helbert may have persuaded her that he didn't. She made every possible mistake while Cecil was alive, why shouldn't she go on doing it after he's dead?'

'I must go to her, I must *make* her see. Tell her all the things over again that you have told her already. And why did you say "*may* have persuaded"? You don't think he's been there already, do you? I thought he went back to Paris the day after he landed here.'

'That is what we suppose. We don't know it for certain.'

'Then I *must* go to her. It would be so horrible . . . I don't mean only because of the case.' I was stumbling over my words now. There was something so utterly repugnant, even obscene, in the mere possibility of Lady Guthrie being deceived yet again by the traitor who had murdered her son. And it could happen, Charlie was right about that. She would want, wouldn't she, to believe in Helbert's innocence. It was the only belief in the world which took away even so little of her own guilt.

## Chapter Sixteen

It wasn't in fact until several days later that I went down to The Manor. After eight hours of sound sleep I had awoken to find that the feeling of urgency which had prompted me, when talking to Charlie, to rush down to Windsor immediately had passed. Feeling myself to be now in a more sensible frame of mind I wrote to Lady Guthrie asking if she would like to see me. She replied in the affirmative and I then set off for The Manor, not as I had suggested and would have preferred, just for the day but for a visit of several nights.

On the way down in the train I speculated, to the exclusion of any other thoughts, upon what I was likely to find at the end of my journey. Would the strange mood which had been upon Lady Guthrie during the time she remained in London have persisted? Would the, for her, unnatural calm not by now have given way to querulous tears?

I arrived, the door of The Manor was opened by Thompson and I stepped into the long hall. No fires today, of course, to greet one as one entered. In their place, with the sunlight reflected on their sides of dark polished wood, hooped with brass, great tubs filled with blue hydrangeas stood before the grates.

I smiled at Thompson noticing as I did so that his manner had returned to the formality of every day. There was nothing to recall the intimacy of the hour he had spent with us in Berkeley Square. Nothing, either, to remind one of the bright cheerfulness that had been his when, nine years ago now, we had come here with Cecil and the Marsdens.

'Her ladyship is upstairs. She wishes you to have tea with her there as soon as you are ready.'

Thompson turned, unexpectedly—for from his words I had imagined that I was to be taken straight up to my room—towards the door of the drawing-room, opened it and announced my arrival. Julie, who had been sitting at the far end of the room, jumped up immediately and came towards me.

She was as handsome looking as ever. The black dress she was wearing, although black does not always suit very dark people, becoming her extremely well.

'Edythe is so delighted that you should have asked to come. I don't know whether Thompson told you, but she wants you to have tea with her upstairs. She thought it might be more restful . . . after your journey . . . and I . . .' Julie was becoming increasingly embarrassed . . . 'that is Edythe, thought that you might not wish to meet Captain Helbert.'

'Helbert, in this house!' I sprang up looking round, for that was my first thought, for a means of escape.

'He isn't staying here,' Julie hastened to assure me. 'He is staying in Windsor, at least I think so, and came in to tea yesterday and is coming again today. He didn't arrive until after your letter had been answered . . . otherwise of course . . . But Edythe didn't like to tell him not to come back today. He was, after all, the last person to see Cecil alive. It gives her some little comfort to learn about those last days. But yesterday she was so upset that Captain Helbert wasn't able to stay with her for very long.'

'But Julie, doesn't she, don't you realize?' I was at a loss for words, bitterly regretting that I hadn't come here three days ago as I had at first intended. Why, delaying, had I at least not brought Charlie with me? He would have come if I had asked him, but there had not seemed any reason for dragging him down here. After that one moment of insight, I had not believed that Helbert would really dare to approach the mother of the man he had murdered. Desperately trying to assume a calm which I was far from feeling, I turned to Julie.

'How long have we got before he may arrive?'

'I don't know.'

'Then will you please tell Thompson that if I am still downstairs when he does so, he is to be shown into another room.'

Julie got up to ring the bell and we sat in silence until it was answered. Thompson's face as he received Julie's instructions was impassive and his voice, as he acknowledged them, without expression; yet I knew that under that composed exterior he must be as indignant and as angry as I was myself. I wondered how he would treat Helbert when he arrived and what had passed between the two of them the day before.

While we had waited for Thompson I had had time in which to think. I must say nothing to Julie about the case, nothing that might later be passed on to Helbert. Perhaps after all it would be better not to speak at all; to go directly to Lady Guthrie. And yet I needed Julie's help. She, who was surely so much more in Lady Guthrie's confidence than I had ever been, might be able to convince her where Charlie and I had failed.

Turning back to Julie I asked if she wasn't aware of what Charlie had told Lady Guthrie.

Julie, in a low voice, said that she was. 'Edythe told me that evening when she got back to the Coburg.'

'Then how on earth, knowing that he killed her son, can she bring herself to see him, how can you as her friend allow her to do so?'

For the first time since I had come into the room Julie looked me straight in the eyes. 'You see, she doesn't believe it.'

'And you?'

'I think so, I don't know.'

'But if I promise you that it is so.'

'You can't really do that, can you? Nobody can *prove* it.'

I jumped up; began walking up and down the room. I was straining my ears for any sound that might indicate that Helbert was already here. It wasn't likely, with the double doors and the lobby between this room and the hall, that I would hear anything.

'But Julie, even if it *can't* be proved in law, there are things, some of which have only come to light in the last few days, which can leave no doubt in one's mind. He planned it, he must have done, right from the beginning, and the most dreadful part is that so much of it was done through Lady Guthrie.' I was thinking of the correspondence with Helbert which, according to the servants, had preceded the departure for America.

'Through Edythe?'

'He wrote to her, didn't he?' I was trying to make it sound as if I knew the thing for a certainty, 'telling her about the syringe which was found after Cecil was supposed to be cured. At that time the doctor had arranged for Cecil to go into a home and Cecil had agreed to go. Nothing, in order to save her distress, had been said about it to Lady Guthrie. It was going to have been kept from her which, as she never came to Paris, could have been done quite easily. But Helbert wrote and told her. He made it sound as if the arrangement about the home was a plot made between the doctor and . . . and Cecil's mistress to get Cecil out of the way—in order, perhaps, that they might get hold of his money. He also accused them of bribing Thompson in order to keep him quiet.'

As I spoke I was watching Julie closely, wondering how much of all this had in fact been in Helbert's letters.

She nodded, not contradicting anything.

I decided to go on. 'When Lady Guthrie received that letter she was quite naturally appalled. She didn't know what to do, especially as Helbert had warned her that on no account must she so much as hint to Cecil that she knew anything about what was happening. Helbert said that for Cecil to find out that his mother was receiving information about him from another person would only result in antagonizing him towards herself.'

'Yes,' Julie said, 'all that was in the letters. Captain Helbert wrote that by that time Cecil was so much under the influence of the morphia which his mistress was encouraging him to take that his mind was no longer open to reason. He said that he himself had already tried to persuade Cecil not to go into the home where he would be entirely at the mercy of the doctor. But that each time Cecil had flown into one of those rages to which addicts are susceptible. Nor would he listen to any word of warning against that dreadful woman. The letter upset Edythe terribly; as soon as she had understood everything that was implied by it, she wanted to go to Paris immediately.'

I said that it was a pity that she hadn't done so.

'Well you see she and Cecil had agreed that they were to be apart until he had finished his hook and she didn't like, I think perhaps she didn't dare, to go against the promise she had made him about that. Besides Captain Helbert was so sure that any open opposition to his going into a clinic would only make Cecil more determined to do so.'

'And it was Captain Helbert who suggested the alternative of a sea voyage?'

'No,' Julie said. 'It was Edythe herself who first hit upon the idea after reading a medical treatise on the subject. I remember how happy she was about it as providing a solution. Cecil being so fond of travel made her feel certain that it would not be difficult to persuade him to undertake it—and then as he had never been to America. . . .'

'But wasn't it Captain Helbert who was responsible for her reading the article; either sent it to her or told her where it was to be found?'

Julie, whom I had interrupted in the middle of a sentence, looked at me curiously. Evidently, it only now occurred to her that all this time she had been, not merely corroborating what I was saying, but telling me things which I had not known before.

A look of uncertainty came into her face. Hoping that this was to be attributed to doubt as to Helbert's innocence, I pointed out how unlikely it was that any qualified doctor would try and get a patient into a home in order to harm him. I told her that Cecil's mistress, far from encouraging him in his addiction, had lately been very anxious that he should give it up.

As to the truth of the last statement we did not have to rely only on Thompson's word, for more than one of Cecil's Parisian friends, including the editor who was to have published his book, later told Charlie that there was no doubt but that it was so.

As for the idea of Thompson, a devoted servant of twenty years' standing, being open to bribery, it was, as I told Julie, too ridiculous to be entertained for one moment.

How devilishly it had been contrived! Helbert, by playing on Lady Guthrie's ever-present anxiety and fears for her son's safety and her abnormal jealousy in regard to him, had manoeuvred her into providing him with the perfect setting for the intended murder. By sending her the treatise on morphinism he made it likely that the suggestion of a sea voyage would be put forward by Lady Guthrie and *not* himself. By discrediting Thompson he made it virtually certain that she would beg him, the supposedly devoted friend, to accompany Cecil—a much better plan if anything went wrong than if it had been Helbert himself who had offered to provide the adequate supervision recommended by the treatise.

'She must never know that it was her own fault.'

'But if she continues to believe in Helbert . . .' I stopped short realizing the impossibility of Lady Guthrie ever bringing herself to admit that Helbert had killed her son. If once she allowed herself to do so she had to accept as a consequence that she—by suggesting the journey and persuading the murderer to act as a travelling companion—was ultimately and tragically responsible for Cecil's death. If he had died as the result of an accident she would have nothing with which to reproach herself. But in that circumstance it would be natural for her to feel bitterly against Helbert who might so easily have prevented it. Clearly we had asked too much in asking her to believe in a murder: placed her in a position where for her own sake she was forced to cling to the chimera of Helbert's innocence.

Moving towards the door I told Julie that I was going upstairs to see Lady Guthrie.

'But won't you . . .' Julie was looking frightened, still shocked by her own acceptance of Helbert's guilt.

Before she had time to say anything further I was out of the room. I had traversed the lobby and was well into the hall when the door at the opposite end of it opened. Looking up, I saw Captain Helbert coming towards me. I had forgotten that he might already be in the house and from his look of surprise I knew that Thompson had not told him that I was here. We stood looking at each other for what seemed a long time.

'Lady Anne!' A greeting or a challenge? The words were accompanied by a sickly smile. If he had been struck down at that moment I could have crushed him under my foot. A thing which I have never been able to bring myself to do to any insect.

I passed him without a word. As I reached the door which led to the staircase I turned back. He stood staring after me, the smile had not left his face.

'If you ever dare to come to this house again. . . .'

The smile became a sneer. He started to speak, saying something about an invitation from Lady Guthrie.

'She has changed her mind, she never wishes to see you again. Thompson,' for thankfully I heard his footsteps approaching, 'will show you out.'

As I finished the sentence Thompson was beside me. We exchanged a glance and he moved towards Captain Helbert, his shoulders under the black coat looked very broad. He advanced on Helbert. The effect was that of a large dog who at last finds himself free to engage in a fight from which he has been long restrained. For a moment Frederic Helbert hesitated but after what I had said there was nothing really that he could do. Meekly he accepted the hat which Thompson, who had snatched it up from the table on which it had previously been placed, now presented to him.

'If you please, sir.' Thompson was standing very close to Helbert but otherwise there was nothing that would have indicated to an onlooker that anything unusual was going on: a manservant performing his normal duties in speeding a departing guest.

As the front door opened I turned away and continued my interrupted course towards the staircase.

I entered Lady Guthrie's bedroom to find her lying on the chaise-longue. It was in its usual position close to the fireplace but for once there was no fire. She looked frail and rather unexpectedly beautiful. Her black negligée all filmy batiste and Valenciennes lace, materials which the present stage of her mourning would not have permitted in the greater formality of a tea-gown, made her look almost youthful. The lines of deep sorrow at the corners of the mouth, the creases between the eyes which had been so noticeable when she came to Berkeley Square no longer presented themselves for attention.

'My dear how good of you to come.' She held out a hand to me, the other, holding a book, trailed near the ground. 'Forgive me for not getting up.'

I took the outstretched hand, bent down in a movement which brought my cheek momentarily close to hers and was briefly enveloped in the almost visible cloud of scent that hung about her. She waved me towards a chair.

'Tea will be here in a moment.'

I waited for her to explain her reasons for making such an arrangement, for the mention of Helbert's name, but she said nothing further. I might have known; anything disagreeable must be kept at a distance; be dealt with by other people; never allowed to touch her directly.

Louise came in, preparing the way for the tea-tray which was placed on a table beside me. She remained in the room to carry Lady Guthrie's cup to her after I had filled it; to fuss with the plate of bread and butter; the sandwiches; the inevitable little cakes. It gave me a respite but Lady Guthrie would not be able to keep Louise in the room for ever. The moment must come when we would be alone. At last Louise withdrew. I looked at Lady Guthrie and our eyes met.

'I ran into Captain Helbert as I was coming upstairs.'

The remark called forth no response. She continued to look at me, her expression infinitely sad, her eyes beginning to fill with tears.

'Julie has told me. I thought it was so brave of you to see him when . . . when we all feel that he might have been the means of saving Cecil's life.'

I saw a change in the expression of the blue eyes; arrested, the tears failed to brim over.

I went on quickly, 'I know what you are going to say'—but that was a lie too, for any talking that was to be done would have to be done by me—'Charlie told you,' desperately I searched my memory in an effort to remember exactly what Charlie *had* said to her. 'He said—he believed then that Captain Helbert had . . .'

I realized that murder was too strong a word—'that Captain Helbert had been the cause of Cecil's death.'

Lady Guthrie's hand, again the well-remembered gesture, went to her heart. 'Please, I cannot bear.'

'Charlie, all of us, were terribly upset and there were so many circumstances . . . Now upon reflection, he believes only that he might have prevented it.'

The blue eyes looked directly into mine: the head dropped slowly forward.

'It was Captain Helbert's business to make sure that no such mistake could have been made. The two bottles, so alike, should never have been placed so near together. Anyone else would have made sure that they were not; have gone over the cabin after the steward had unpacked. Cecil after all was a sick man. One would not expect him to see to such things for himself.'

'If only Thompson had been with him,' Lady Guthrie was speaking so softly I had difficulty in catching the words, 'but when I wrote suggesting it, Cecil said that he would be like the fifth wheel of a coach; the extra fare an unnecessary expense. I think he really *preferred* the idea of being alone with Frederic. I can show you.'

She reached out to the large lacquered box placed on the table at her side. I prevented her from showing me the letter then and there; when I saw it later I was certain, from the unusual wording—'I am now convinced that Frederic is really very fond of me'—that it had been written in answer to one of hers.

One in which she had sought to persuade him—and had alas succeeded—to accept Helbert as a travelling companion.

'The very least he could have done was to go in to Cecil during the night.' There was bitter resentment in Lady Guthrie's voice. 'He told me again yesterday that when they went to bed Cecil was not at all well. Does not Charlie think it was the least he could have done?'

'It is for that reason that he feels, most strongly, that none of us should see Helbert again or give him any kind of countenance.'

We had come to the crucial point. With all my strength I willed her to do what I wanted; to decide, if only for the reason that he might have saved Cecil's life, that Captain Helbert had been responsible for his death.

'He was very anxious to come here again. I have been very unhappy about it all night and all of today. I suppose when you saw him just now he was on his way to the drawing-room to have tea with Julie?'

I said nothing and she went on.

'I do not believe, not having slept and having heard Charlie's opinion from you, that I am up to seeing him; to come to a decision about it all at the moment. After all there is nothing more he can tell me about my darling. It was all told yesterday, those last dreadful hours . . .' The tears had run over now and were coursing down her cheeks. 'Please tell them that I am not well enough to receive Captain Helbert. Later, if my feelings are still the same, we can send word to the hotel, can't we, telling him not to call again.' She looked at me pathetically. 'Charlie doesn't think that I ought to see him, does he, he doesn't want me to?'

It was the nearest she would come to a capitulation but it was enough to make me certain that all danger of her 'going over to Helbert's side' was averted. The sad victory was mine.

Lady Guthrie's tears were now accompanied by sobs and knowing my strength to be unequal to bearing any further emotion I said that I would send Julie to her.

'Louise, tell Louise to come to me.'

The words came chokingly as I reached the door. I shut it behind me and set off in search of the maid.

## Chapter Seventeen

Having promised Lady Guthrie that I would remain at The Manor for at least three days I felt constrained, although the danger of her consorting with Helbert had been removed within a few hours of my being there, to keep my promise. At the time I was of course very worried as to the outcome of the case that Sir Terrence was preparing against Helbert. As Charlie had explained it to me there were a great many difficulties to be got over. The greatest, now fortunately behind us, was that Lady Guthrie, in order to disclaim her own responsibility in having arranged for the fateful voyage, might have gone over to Helbert's side. If he had managed to bring her to the point where she would have been willing to give evidence of her own faith in his disinterested devotion to her son, there would have been little point in seeking to show that he had in fact used undue influence with regard to the will.

All the same I would have been glad to have had everything to do with the case behind us. I wished I was back in London with Charlie to reassure me; and to prevent me from continuously brooding on the subject. The gloom which descended on me was, I think, fairly unreasonable but being at The Manor between Lady Guthrie and Julie was not, to say the least, conducive to cheerfulness. There was a great deal too that I did not understand and which made me uneasy. Lady Guthrie seemed to have withdrawn into herself. She never came downstairs although both Thompson and Julie told me that up until the day I arrived she had been in the habit of doing so. Been better in herself, as Thompson put it, than he'd ever seen her.

'You'd have thought, wouldn't you, that Mr Cecil's death would have thrown her completely? But you see it didn't because she was able to travel up to Paris and then come over to England without hardly turning a hair. I don't mean that she wasn't upset. It was only natural that she should be, but she never took to her bed which is what would have been natural for her, for it's what she's always done.'

I said something about people sometimes feeling things more, at any rate being more affected by them, after the first shock had passed off. Probably, the news of Mr Cecil's death being so terrible, it took her a little while to realize fully what had happened.'

Thompson said that he supposed that must have been what it was; but I don't think that he was convinced.

Another aspect of Lady Guthrie's behaviour that now began to perplex me was her attitude towards Julie. When I had last seen them together at the Villa Victoria they had obviously been on terms of intimate friendship. Clearly, this was no longer the case and everything that Lady Guthrie said to me about the girl tended to disparage her. I was given to understand that Julie was a particularly tiresome hanger-on whom she had originally—I reckoned it must have been at least two years ago—taken into her home in charity and of whom she would now be very glad to be rid. 'She treats the house quite as if it belongs to her and is officious in every respect.'

Juke, on her side, seemed to be utterly bewildered by her sudden and totally unexpected fall from favour. She put it down, after much heart-searching, conducted aloud and for my benefit, to Lady Guthrie's mind having perhaps been turned by the tremendous shock of Cecil's death. 'It does sometimes happen, I believe.' She was begging me to agree with her. 'People do become temporarily unbalanced and turn against those who love them, those to whom, perhaps, most is owed?'

'You think she really is less affectionate towards you than formerly?'

Julie, with tears in her eyes, told me that during the last few weeks Lady Guthrie's manner towards her had completely changed. She said that she had begun to notice it about five days after they received the cable announcing Cecil's death. 'And it has got worse and worse until now, as you see, she hardly speaks to me and is always sending messages by Louise that I am not to go to her room: whenever I do she is unkind.'

I was as sympathetic as I could be. I realized that it would be a serious thing for the girl if Lady Guthrie, who to all intents and purposes had adopted her, were to turn against her permanently.

I believed that it was a considerable time since Julie had last seen her parents, from whom she was now estranged, so if Lady Guthrie turned her out she would have nowhere to go and probably, as the Wrottesleys were extremely poor, no money. I thought, not for the first time, what a pity it was that Julie had never married. It is of course sometimes the prettiest girls who somehow contrive, owing usually to aiming too high, to miss their opportunities. Julie, in the first year or two after she came out, had spent her time, in flitting unproductively from one eldest son to another. There had followed the short mysterious engagement to Cecil which had ended, according to my daughter, owing to an entanglement which Julie had allowed herself to get into with another man. Since then, living exclusively with Lady Guthrie in the semi-retirement of the Villa Victoria, she had had few opportunities of meeting anyone suitable.

'She was so wonderfully kind and understanding,' Julie said, 'when Cecil and I . . . were . . . were no longer to be married and when I had no one to whom I could turn. My own parents, perhaps Sybil told you, have never been very generous. My brother and I always had to fend for ourselves. When I became engaged to Cecil—not that I ever told them that it was a positive engagement—and went to France to stay with Edythe they were really angry. The Guthries didn't know and thought everything was all right. But in fact my parents had forbidden me to go. When I returned home and they thought I was going to marry that Frenchman things were better for a while, but when that came to nothing my father said that he wanted to have nothing more to do with me and I was sent to those cousins in Ireland. It was just after that that my parents gave up the last house they ever lived in together. My mother went to live with a cousin and has been there ever since. My father went to Canada and I hear that he is still roaming about somewhere in the West trying to make a fortune. During the whole of my childhood he was always going backwards and forwards to Canada and the United States and each time he was going to make a fortune but of course he never did.'

There was a note of bitterness in the girl's voice. I was sorry to hear it.

Easy enough for me, whose ways—apart from one great sorrow which came upon us later—have always been set in pleasant places, to sound censorious. It is for that reason that I am anxious to make it plain that I have never felt anything but sympathy for Julie's resentment against the circumstances of her life. Hers was the old problem—taking the thing back to her father's generation—of the younger son of a rich man condemned by his place in the family to live and bring up his children in comparative poverty. There is something about it that is all wrong and one day I hope that something will be done so that it may be resolved.

'Edythe has always said that when, that if, I marry she will do everything she can to help me and that if not I shall not be left without support.'

I found this confession of Julie's financial dependence on Lady Guthrie, and it evidently embarrassed her to make it, extremely painful. I gave what comfort I could by saying that I thought she was being precipitate; making more of the situation than was warranted by the facts. Lady Guthrie had not, so far at least, retracted any of the promises made to Julie in the past or said anything to her about living elsewhere. 'We may quite likely find that in a short while she will again have changed completely, be fond of you and as anxious to have you near her as ever.'

Julie begged that if I had an opportunity of speaking to Lady Guthrie on the subject I would do so.

I promised that I would do anything that lay in my power to bring about a *rapprochement*. 'But there is a good deal to be said you know for letting sleeping dogs lie, in this case, by not interfering, to allow her to come round by herself.'

Julie agreed that I was probably right but I noticed, despite the smile with which the remarks were accompanied, that she still looked frightened.

It was with the idea of discussing Julie's situation and if possible putting in some kind of a word for her, that later on the same afternoon I went up to Lady Guthrie's room.

As usual she was lying on the chaise-longue, the box containing the precious letters by her side; everything about her and about the room the same as it had been three days before. I sat down on the chair that was always assigned to me. She seemed disinclined to talk but when I suggested that she might like to be left alone and continue to rest she was insistent that I should not leave her.

I looked round the beautiful room with its familiar air of luxury and fussy furnishings. Nothing about it ever changed and yet the whole always gave one the feeling that it had been assembled, only a moment ago, to provide a background for the present. Suddenly, almost forcibly, I was reminded of the day when I sat in front of the dressing-table taking down my hair, worrying, just a little, as to how it was going to look when I had finished arranging it. Cecil and Charlie were downstairs, Lydia Marsden and her mother still being shown over the attics by the housekeeper or perhaps already by then on the staircase. I could imagine Cecil, although this was a scene which I had never actually witnessed, standing at the foot of the stairs, I saw the glances exchanged between him and Lydia, the look of happiness on the faces of both. It was all so vivid, and unbearably painful. I closed my eyes for a moment in an effort to shut out the memory, but it was not to be cheated in that way. The pain, the intolerable contrast between now and then, was as bad as ever. In a moment I would hear the echo of their voices; Lydia's light laugh responding to Cecil's, both of them laughing for no very sensible reason. I opened my eyes; was almost surprised to find myself sitting not at the dressing-table but in a low chair on the other side of the room. I looked across at Lady Guthrie and found myself wondering how she came to be there. Nothing had changed except . . . I was looking at the wall above the fire-place, pleated hangings of a patterned silk! One of the silks, hadn't I been told about them often enough, which Sir David had brought back from Persia. But it shouldn't be there, should it? There should be a portrait of Lady Guthrie hanging just in that place, a copy of the one in Sir David's sitting-room in Cannes. Hadn't I seen it reflected in the glass while I was doing my hair, just as I was finishing my hair, and the housekeeper had come into the room and I had gone downstairs?

'What happened to the picture?'

My remark, coming after so long a silence, seemed to startle Lady Guthrie. I had to explain what I meant: 'The picture of you that used to be there,' I pointed to the wall, 'I think it was copied from the one at the Villa Victoria.'

'No copy was ever made. I never had any picture of myself hanging in this room.'

There was no doubt but that she was certain of what she said. I felt a contraction of my heart; a feeling of intense cold came at the back of my neck. But for what reason? What could there be at all frightening in making a mistake about a picture? I had thought that nine years ago a portrait of Lady Guthrie had hung above the fireplace, now I was told that it hadn't. My memory as to something quite unimportant had been at fault. And yet, I had been so sure of the thing, had thought so often since of the strange way the eyes, reflected in the looking-glass, had seemed to rest, almost malevolently, on the place where Lydia had stood only a few minutes before.

'The face reflected in the glass!'

Interrupted by the abrupt entrance of the housekeeper I had never turned to compare the mirrored face, a picture of a picture, with the portrait itself.

I believe luncheon is ready, and, because I had been talking to myself, Mrs Pomfret had looked at me oddly. To cover my embarrassment I had hurried from the room. And afterwards? We had not come back in here, our mantles and outdoor things had been taken down to the Prior's lodging. I had never in fact seen the picture at all!

I realized that my knees were trembling and that my heart had begun to beat much faster than usual. Lady Guthrie, who had noticed nothing of my agitated state, was still talking about the various portraits which had been made of herself and her family.

The one of Sir David, painted when he was an old man and for which he had worn the court uniform of an ambassador, was very like him. She regretted that the only painting of Cecil had been executed when he was six years old.

'I have very many photographs of course.' Her eyes, travelling round the room, came to rest on the one placed with her Bible and prayer book on a table beside the bed. It showed Cecil to great advantage, undeniably handsome, the face somewhat thinner than I remembered.

Lady Guthrie explained that it was the last one ever to be taken. 'Only a few days, I am told, before he left Paris. He himself never saw it and I did so only after his death. When it arrived in the odd manner it did I had the feeling that it had been sent to me from beyond the grave.'

I waited for her to say something more about the photograph but instead she began to speak in quite a practical manner about her own plans for the future.

'The Villa Victoria is as you know already sold. My darling and I were to have lived in this house or at any rate made it our head-quarters. He was so pleased with the idea. His last letters were filled with plans for it and for all the good and charitable things he meant to do . . . and such beautiful descriptions of the voyages we were to make in *Thalassa*. There were so many places which I had never seen and which he longed to show me; so many others which we would have explored together. Now of course those things will never be and it can be of little importance to me where I live or for that matter die, but worldly arrangements have always to be made.'

Remembering what Nealie had said as to Lady Guthrie eventually deciding to settle in Paris I waited with some interest for what was to come.

'Bereft of the two beloved beings who made up my entire world, I have to find some corner in which to be while I wait to rejoin them. I pray to God in his mercy that I will not need it for very long. It was in the course of nature that my dearest husband should be called to his rest before myself. But that a mother should have to live on after her child!'

'It is as you say very hard.' I hesitated but for a grief such as hers there are after all no easy words of comfort. To speak to her of the consolations of religion would I felt be presumptuous.

'My first thought when I knew I had been left utterly alone was to come to The Manor. I thought that in this house, which we built for him when he was a little boy and where every room, every piece of furniture, every ornament even, recalls his presence I would feel closer to my darling than would be possible anywhere else. I thought it was what he himself would have wished; that it would be the best place in which to remember him.'

Lady Guthrie was looking at me intently and I nodded encouragement.

'I know now that I was mistaken. Cecil doesn't want me to live here by myself. It would make him extremely unhappy. His will for me is quite otherwise.'

Again I nodded but this time less certainly. Was she reverting to her former belief—at the time it had never seemed to be more than a half-belief—in spiritualist doctrine? I knew that Sir David, stigmatizing all forms of spiritualism as so much table-rapping, had, as soon as he had become aware of what was going on, persuaded her to have nothing more to do with it. But with Cecil's death it seemed only too likely that she would be tempted to turn to it again for the sake of the comfort it pretended to give.

'Just as unhappy,' Lady Guthrie, still speaking of Cecil, continued firmly, 'as he used to be, while still of this world, whenever circumstances for a time compelled him to leave me alone. I have therefore given up the idea of leading the cloistered existence which I had mapped out for myself.'

Feeling unequal to enter into a theological argument, I said that I thought it would probably be a mistake for her to live altogether in solitude. 'And then you have been out of England for so many years and are so unused to its dreadful winters!'

'It is not a question of my own inclination.'

The remark was clearly a reproof; having made it she fell silent and, judging this to be an unpropitious moment to introduce the subject of Julie, I rose to go.

Returning to the drawing-room I found it empty and was just settling myself at a writing-table when Thompson came into the room. Glad, after my uncomfortable interlude with Lady Guthrie, to have someone to talk to, I detained him by some casual remark. Within a few minutes we were talking about the subject which was uppermost in both our minds.

'. . . and even up to the last I was hoping that Mr Cecil would take me with him to America. Or at least to England so that I could have seen him on to the boat. But it wasn't to be. The two of them went off alone and I went down to Cannes to be with her ladyship.'

After once again going over all the circumstances which had preceded the tragic voyage we passed on to what Thompson considered to be Lady Guthrie's unaccountable behaviour.

'It would have been more natural if she'd taken to her bed, but she didn't and within a few days we were off to Paris. When Louise first told me we were to go I couldn't believe it but it turned out to be true enough. We spent two nights there and then came on to England. And I suppose now that we shan't be going back to the Villa at all, because all the furniture has to be out of it by the end of July so the coming and going wouldn't be worth her ladyship's while?'

This was a leading question; to avoid answering it I said that I had just been looking at Cecil's photograph, adding that Lady Guthrie seemed very glad that one had been taken so recently.

'She told you about that, did she?'

'That . . . that she saw it for the first time only after Mr Cecil's death?'

Thompson hesitated. 'I don't know if I'm doing right to speak of it at all because when it first arrived in Cannes, without a message or anything with it, she was very upset. And it did seem strange too—a photograph which nobody knew had been taken—coming out of the blue, just like that, after he was dead.'

'And what was the explanation . . . or,' for Thompson hadn't answered immediately, 'wasn't there one?'

'I thought from what you said that her ladyship had told you about it herself.' Again Thompson hesitated and then, evidently deciding that he had now said too much not to go on, told me that the photograph had been sent to Lady Guthrie by 'the lady' . . . Mademoiselle Laurent.

I agreed with Thompson that he had acted correctly.

'But what I wasn't prepared for was her calling at the hotel. How she'd found out that her ladyship was in Paris I couldn't think; for you see it didn't occur to me that letters might have passed between the two of them.'

'Did Lady Guthrie see her?'

'Indeed she did and didn't turn a hair about it either. It so happened that I was in the sitting-room with her when Mademoiselle's card was brought in. When I took it from the page and saw the name on it I didn't know what to do. Well, there wasn't anything—except to give it to her ladyship which is what I did, and she said that Mademoiselle was to be shown up to the suite. I did just ask if she knew who Mademoiselle was and she said, "Yes, Thompson, perfectly well," and didn't sound too pleased about it either—too pleased with me for having asked, I mean. What she was thinking about Mademoiselle being there I couldn't say. Then she told me to go and said I was to let Miss Wrottesley know not to disturb her; and I went out into the corridor. After a minute or two I saw Mademoiselle coming towards me. She was dressed all in black and if she'd been in England you might have taken her for a widow, but the French, as I expect you know, have different customs as to mourning and so on than ourselves. I suppose in a manner of speaking my still being in the corridor might have been called hanging about, and I know that none of it was any of my business.'

The meeting between Mademoiselle Laurent and Lady Guthrie was not any of my business either but I was far too interested in it to make any attempt at silencing Thompson.

He told me that on catching sight of him Mademoiselle Laurent had stopped and they had exchanged a few words '. . . and she said something rude about Captain Helbert because you see she never liked him and she knew, for we'd talked about it more than once, that I was of the same way of thinking. I told her that Captain Helbert was on his way back from America and with that she sailed into her ladyship's room and didn't stir out of it again until eleven o'clock at night. So altogether she was there for more than five hours. Her ladyship had dinner sent up to the suite just for the two of them and Miss Wrottesley had hers downstairs by herself. I wasn't sent for to serve it either because everything was done by the hotel waiters. Louise did just go in for a moment but her ladyship sent her away before she was hardly into the room.'

The servants' curiosity with regard to this meeting between Lady Guthrie and the Parisian *cocotte* who had been her son's mistress was hardly surprising. Twenty years ago, and I imagine it would be much the same today, such an encounter was unheard of and consequently unthinkable. I could imagine all the same how Lady Guthrie's longing to talk to anyone who had seen her son more recently than herself had overcome her sense of conventional propriety.

'When one thinks how unhappy she is one can perhaps understand it.'

Thompson with whom compassion, as I had noticed in all his dealings with Cecil, was never very far away, said something which indicated agreement.

'Miss Wrottesley, you understand my lady, knows nothing about it; nor about Mademoiselle coming again the next day and staying with her ladyship almost up to the time of our leaving for the station. On that occasion she asked for me before going upstairs. She seemed very pleased about her ladyship having, as she said, taken to her. She said some more very hard things about Captain Helbert too. Not, mind you, that I didn't agree with them. Indeed I even went so far as to say that to my way of thinking there was a lot more to the way in which Mr Cecil died than we knew anything about. For that was in my mind you know even before Mr Guthrie had met Captain Helbert and heard what he had to say. Of course I warned Mademoiselle not to hint at anything of the kind to her ladyship. That, I said, would have to be done, if it ever came to the point, by a member of the family; it wouldn't be for us to take the responsibility of it.'

This conversation with Thompson was the last one of any import that I had with anyone at The Manor. The following day I returned home, but before I left I did try once more to talk to Lady Guthrie about Julie. I thought it was only right, if the girl was going to be dropped, that she should be told of it as soon as possible. I hoped, too, if that was to be the way of it, that I might be able to persuade Lady Guthrie, if that was not already her intention, to do something for her protégée in regard to finances. My attempt at interference met, however, with no success whatsoever for Lady Guthrie utterly refused to discuss the subject.

Arrived in London I found Charlie very pleased because he had just heard from Sir Terrence that he had subpoenaed both General Cameron and the British Naval Attaché in Paris to give evidence against Helbert.

'The case is to be sent to the fellow's solicitors today so now we have only to wait and see what kind of an answer they and he manage to make to it. Sir Terrence's opinion is that they'll be hard put to it to find one and it won't surprise him if it ends in their never going into court at all.'

## Chapter Eighteen

'But, my dear, you actually *met* the creature. Edythe dared present her to you?'

The Madeira chair creaked protestingly as Nealie, charmingly mixing extreme disapproval with delighted curiosity, leant towards me.

She and I were sitting in the large elaborately furnished winter garden which she had caused to be attached to her latest house—at Englefield Green, Surrey. More than four months had elapsed since my last visit to The Manor which had since been sold. Charlie and I had just returned from France where, on our way through Paris, we had visited Lady Guthrie now installed—according to herself at Cecil's request—in an apartment on the Boulevard Haussman. Julie Wrottesley, having been dismissed only a week after I left The Manor, was no longer with her. Through Nealie's good offices, and otherwise I really do not know what would have happened to the girl, she was now in America; acting as a kind of lady-in-waiting and general arbiter on English taste to a rich family from Chicago.

'Tell,' Nealie commanded, 'everything that happened. One wouldn't have thought that even Edythe . . . I'm surprised that Charlie didn't march you out of the house before you'd had time to find out anything interesting.'

'Then you can't have been listening because I've already told you that when Charlie and I called on Lady Guthrie together there was no one with her. It was the second time when I went alone that I found her with Mademoiselle Laurent.'

'You call her by her name!' Nealie sounding seriously shocked was no longer smiling. 'My dear, do think what you're saying—that abandoned woman can't possibly *have* a name, as far anyhow as we are concerned . . . Oh bother!' and with every appearance of pleasure she turned to welcome Charlie and Willie who had just appeared through one of the doors leading into the house.

Unaware that his presence was at the moment unwelcome Willie, drawing up a chair, came and sat down by Nealie who told him that she thought he had decided to spend the afternoon writing letters to the people who had been sending him such lovely presents.

The presents referred to were the usual silver candlesticks and cigar-cutters considered to be suitable offerings to prospective bride-grooms, for at long last Willie, entirely at Nealie's instigation, had made up his mind to get married. Whether he would ever do so and whether he would ever succeed in persuading Nealie herself to become his wife were questions which had occupied all Nealie's friends for a number of years. She on her part had always protested that she was much too old for him and that the thing was ridiculous. He must, so she had been saying almost since the beginning of their friendship, find some nice girl who would help him on in the world and produce some children. This, by interpretation, meant that Willie, the son of a modest Scottish attorney, was to marry into a great family. I am quite sure that left to himself he would never have done any such thing. In the end Nealie, taking a more than usually strong line, introduced him to the fifth daughter of a duke and then gave neither of them any peace until she had got them engaged and the notice of their forthcoming marriage inserted in the *Morning Post*. The girl selected was, to our secret amusement, by no means good looking. She has, however, made Willie an excellent wife while he on his side has remained as devoted to Nealie as ever before.

'We were talking,' Nealie, patting Willie's hand turned from him to Charlie, 'about your interesting visit to Paris.'

'Ah yes,' Charlie, wandering about the winter garden, stopped in front of a low growing plant which he appeared to be examining with particular interest. Our visit to Lady Guthrie, upon which Nealie had already and with small success tried to draw him out at luncheon, was clearly not a subject which he wished to pursue.

Nealie, subtly changing her ground, said what a great relief it was to know that that disgusting Helbert was not going to inherit the money. 'But I'm sure the expenses involved in having the case prepared must have cost you a great deal more than poor little Cecil ever had to leave. And I'm perfectly sure too that it is you and not Edythe who is going to pay for everything.'

This as a matter of fact was perfectly true but Charlie did not care to enlighten Nealie either on that point or several others concerning the complicities of the case.

'Anyhow,' Nealie, having waited in vain for Charlie to reply to her question, went on, 'the important thing is that Helbert has taken fright and isn't going to defend it.'

'He isn't,' Willie corrected, 'going to put in an answer to the plea.'

'It's the same thing,' Nealie said, 'and it means that in spite of the way he blustered in the beginning that we've won.'

Willie cautiously agreed that in essence that was so.

Nealie, unaware of the disgraceful circumstances which had resulted in the traitor Helbert's dismissal from his diplomatic post, said that she didn't see that he had had anything to lose by appearing in court. 'After all he is no longer in the army and almost certainly penniless. I therefore presume that he received at least something for so conveniently deciding to abandon his claim to Cecil's fifteen thousand pounds.'

As she spoke I wondered if there might not perhaps be something in what she said; on the other hand it was perfectly possible that when it came to the point Helbert hadn't been prepared to face the scandal which would undoubtedly have ensued from General Cameron's evidence. To lay himself open to being publicly branded as a traitor was after all a very different matter from having his guilt known to only a handful of embassy officials. There was another thing too which may well have weighed with Helbert and his advisers. This was the near impossibility of their having been able to find any doctor or chemist prepared to say that the small quantity of photographic mixture which Cecil—according to Helbert himself—had taken would have been likely to prove fatal even to a sick man. Cecil's symptoms at the end however—and they could be vouched for by the ship's surgeon—were perfectly consistent with the criminal administration of strychnine.

Impossible to prove, either that strychnine poisoning had indeed been the cause of death, or, that if it had, Helbert's had been the hand to administer it. Even so Counsel would certainly have contrived to draw attention to the possibility in open court and, if allowed by the judge, called medical evidence in support of his statement. Knowing this, a much braver, or perhaps a more innocent man than Helbert might well have hesitated. As it was Helbert decided not to risk going into court and the case, officially one alleging undue influence with regard to a will, was never heard.

This was exactly the result that Sir Terrence Lucas had been aiming for and confidently expecting, and he succeeded in what he set out to do. If there are those who think that the way in which he handled the situation came very near to blackmail I do not believe there can be anyone who would not say that if that were so he was entirely justified.

'Well,' Nealie looked impatiently from Charlie to Willie, 'Isn't anybody going to tell me anything?'

Willie, after first glancing at Charlie—still engaged in admiring the vegetation of the winter garden—said that the less discussion there was about any of it, now that it was all happily over, the better.

Nealie immediately complained that it was all very well for Willie, who as a member of Sir Terrence's firm must know everything there was to know, to talk like that. 'But it's really too bad,' the appeal was made to Charlie's crouched back, 'if you're going to keep me in the dark about all the interesting part. I do think it's very hard, especially when one considers that I am one of the very few people who has ever known that there was a will in existence.'

Charlie, slowly straightening himself, reminded Nealie that that was something that must now be forgotten.

'If Helbert had decided to fight the case there could have been no secret about it.'

'Now, Nealie, you must stop being cross.' Charlie, giving up all pretence of a new-found fascination for potted palms, came over and joined us. 'The point is that, very fortunately, Helbert has decided not to pursue his claim and in consequence we have been able to decide not to take any official notice of the will Cecil signed just before he left Paris. If we were to do so it would lead to a whole new lot of quite unnecessary legal complications. Is that much at any rate clear?'

Nealie said it was.

'And I would rather that you didn't go on saying that I don't tell you things. I am indeed just about to tell you what is going to happen next, which is that in a year's time our family lawyer, who has not been concerned with this case, will apply with me and possibly Anne's brother, all of us acting on my stepmother's behalf, for letters of administration so that Cecil's estate can be dealt with as an intestacy.'

'As by now the estate has undoubtedly been reduced to *less* than nothing I suppose it is unimportant that such a proceeding will be quite illegal. The risk Sir Terrence is taking in allowing the French will to be suppressed is of course enormous. Either he is being unbelievably chivalrous or has received an unbelievable amount for agreeing to hold his tongue.'

As often before I was struck by Nealie's instinctive shrewdness.

Charlie, obviously somewhat taken aback, said that for an American farm girl her knowledge of English law was truly remarkable and that he supposed he must congratulate her.

Nealie, uncertain I think as to whether or not she was being teased, said that that wasn't a very nice way of putting it.

'I'm sorry,' Charlie started to get up, 'it was meant as a compliment. And now, in what remains of the light I am going for a walk.'

'In that case,' Nealie said, 'you might as well take Willie with you, unless,' she looked at Willie, 'you really feel you should get on with those letters?'

Willie, taking his dismissal gracefully, said something about needing some exercise and keeping Charlie company.

As soon as we were alone Nealie ordered me to hurry up and tell her a great deal more about the abandoned woman, because if I didn't Charlie and Willie would be back before I had finished.

'And so far you know you haven't made it interesting at all. If I didn't dislike Edythe so very whole-heartedly I would go over to Paris next week and see for myself. My sister Nannie did go, as I told you, on her way from Pau but all she seems to have noticed in any detail was a particular kind of cake, hitherto unknown to her, that was on the tea-table. But then Nannie was always a very dull woman. You haven't the same excuse.'

'Very well then, I, like Nannie, was invited to tea and when I got there Thompson showed me into the *salon* where Lady

Guthrie was sitting on a sofa with the abandoned woman close by her on a small chair covered in red damask.'

'Thompson should have warned you not to go in or at least, if he didn't like to do that, said that Edythe was after all not at home.'

'But he did warn me and I must say it was done most discreetly.'

'Oh well,' Nealie having made her protest was anxious to get on with the story, 'what happened and what was she like and did she *look* like an abandoned woman? I'm told that they very often turn into little govemessy people, all rusty black and with tiny gold crosses round their necks.'

'She was wearing black but it wasn't rusty and I didn't notice a cross.'

Pressed for a fuller description I said that the abandoned woman appeared to be in her early thirties, was possessed of what is usually called a handsome figure and had fair hair bordering on auburn. 'If one hadn't known what she was I doubt whether one would have guessed it. On the other hand I do not think, although with the French one is less able to judge by the voice, one would have mistaken her for a lady. There was, too, something about her manner which, although it is difficult to describe it exactly, was not pleasing.'

'She sounds very much as I imagined.'

'Then I'm afraid I haven't given you a very good description of her because I'm sure that you must have expected her to be extremely feminine and she wasn't so in the very least.'

Nealie said that didn't surprise her at all because Cecil had always needed a great deal of bolstering up and support of the kind which he wouldn't have been likely to get from a little namby pamby, clinging vine, sort of woman. 'That's what happens when mothers make their sons dependent on them; for the rest of their lives the poor things are doomed to go round choosing domineering women.'

'But poor little Lydia Marsden wasn't in the least domineering *or* masculine.'

'Which is probably why the engagement never came to anything. As to what happened over Julie, I consider that to have been a trick, quite a clever one in fact. One has to admit that whatever else she is, Edythe is *thorough*.'

'When I first got there the main topic of conversation—we had only heard the day before about the captain having climbed down—was the case.'

'I should have thought that would have been a forbidden subject. Edythe really had no qualms about discussing it in front of that woman?'

'We didn't go into it in any great detail but that I think was because Lady Guthrie wasn't particularly interested as to how exactly it had been managed. She was pleased with the result and said so. After that it was mostly vituperation of Helbert whom she now regards as the arch villain who failed to take proper care of her invalid son.'

'She still doesn't believe that he killed him?'

'She does not say so openly and when Mademoiselle Laurent was, I think, about to do so I saw a look pass between them and she was instantly silent.'

'I wonder,' Nealie hesitated, 'but now that everything has been settled there can be no harm in saying it, at least to you, if he really *did* kill him?'

'Of course he did—there was never any doubt of it.'

'All the same, that time when Cecil stayed with you, just after his engagement to Lydia was broken off. He had tried to commit suicide then, hadn't he?'

'I didn't realize that you ever knew that.'

Nealie shrugged her shoulders.

'In any case Cecil never admitted to it. It was never more than a supposition.'

'Like almost everything else that concerns his life and the manner of his death. And if Edythe had only died when he was born, as she has so often told us that she nearly did, he might have grown up to be a fine man. As things were he never had a chance.'

'I suppose he didn't.' I drew a long breath, thinking sadly of the young man whom over the years I had come to love. His death, conventionally considered as being a tragedy, seemed ordinary, almost unimportant, when set against the far greater tragedy of his wasted life.

I looked at Nealie wondering if I might not at last share with another human being the burden laid on me by Cecil's confession during his delirium. But there are loyalties owed to the dead as well as to the living. For his sake I must, as long as his mother lived, remain silent. No one must know of the terrible accusation made against her when he said that, in order to prevent his marriage, she had let it be known—falsely for the thing was not true—that he was suffering from a shameful disease. He had accused and later he had retracted but which of the two statements was a lie—I would never know.

'I was thinking,' Nealie was saying, 'about Julie. I suppose that when Edythe got rid of her in the sudden unkind way she did, she had already decided that that horrible woman was to go and live with her?'

I said that I really had no idea, but I believed that Mademoiselle Laurent had joined Lady Guthrie in Paris as soon as she moved there from The Manor. 'At first they stayed together at the hotel and then, as soon as it was ready, went to the apartment.'

'But how can Edythe stand having a woman of that kind constantly with her?' Nealie wrinkled her nose in distaste. 'And when Cecil was still alive she couldn't bear even the idea of her!'

As Nealie spoke I was reminded of the time at Cannes, more than a year ago now. Lady Guthrie had just finished telling me how Cecil had got himself entangled with a woman of bad character. A horrible woman who—but that information I now realized, with something of a shock, had come to her from Helbert—had introduced him to the habit of taking drugs. 'The creature must be absolutely abandoned. If I could only get near her I would strangle her with my naked hands.' And now the so-called 'creature' was her dearest friend!

'And you say, and so does Nannie, for that much I did get out of her, that Edythe treats the woman absolutely as an equal. And there they are, cooped up in that apartment day in and day out with only each other for company. What on earth do they find to talk about and think how dull it must be for the woman herself.'

'I think, that is I gathered, that most of their conversation is concerned with Cecil. They believe you know that they are in communication with his spirit.'

'It's really too disgusting,' Nealie tapped her foot angrily, 'so disgusting that it doesn't bear thinking about. And I suppose the creature is making a very good thing out of it.'

'Thompson, who used rather to like her, is quite certain, so he told Charlie, that she is, as he said, feathering her nest.'

'Of course she is; a French woman of the lower classes is bound to be shrewd enough for that. Nor,' and Nealie, looking very fierce, glared challengingly at the palms growing against the wall on the far side of the winter garden, 'can one altogether blame the creature. Edythe has absolutely laid herself open to being exploited by her and any unscrupulous person who didn't take advantage of it would be a fool.'

'We don't know that Mademoiselle Laurent *is* taking advantage, it is only Thompson's opinion.'

Nealie, becoming increasingly vehement, said that the thing was obvious. Edythe had never had any judgment whatsoever. She was a vain stupid woman susceptible in an inordinate degree to flattery. Look how she had been taken in by Helbert merely because he had, to use a vulgar expression, buttered her up; although everyone else had seen at a first glance that he was an arch adventurer.

I started to say that Charlie and I, alas, had not done so; that when we did come to distrust him it was too late, for by that time Lady Guthrie would hear no word against him.

Nealie, disregarding the interruption, swept on under full sail. The whole situation with regard to the abandoned woman was deplorable but, given Edythe's character, in no way surprising.

'And you said,' the question came unexpectedly, 'that there was something in the woman's manner that you didn't like but couldn't explain?'

'That's just it; there was something . . . something in the whole atmosphere that I found profoundly disturbing.'

'Try,' Nealie said, 'to be sensible. *What* was disturbing and what was it you didn't like?'

Speaking slowly, searching for words with which to give a form to something which in fact was formless, I said that I was sure that my feeling as to something being wrong had very little to do with the spiritualism. 'Although I do feel that there is something somewhat repugnant about that also. I keep thinking, you see, of Cecil as he was when he was happiest—and away from Lady Guthrie—sailing his boat perhaps or playing croquet on the lawn at Kildonan—and then I see those two women huddled together over a table trying to shut his spirit into that dark room.'

As I finished speaking it seemed as if the cheerful scent of Messrs Floris's rose geranium which had previously filled the winter garden was being gradually replaced by a more exotic and much heavier odour.

'She only liked them,' Nealie said, 'after Cecil had done with them. It was the same with Julie and now with this other.'

She paused and I waited for her to say something more, something which might somehow explain a situation which to me was so nearly incomprehensible. I thought of the dim *salon*, of the secret looks exchanged between the two women who sat there together; looks which had reminded me, although at the time I hadn't been able to think why, of others which I had once seen pass between Lady Guthrie and Cecil.

'There is something horrible about it,' Nealie said, 'something that I think we would rather not understand even if we could.'

Lady Guthrie, surviving Cecil by ten years, did not die until 1906. But after the meeting in Paris we did not see her again. This drawing apart was mutual for there was nothing left to hold us together. We heard rumours of her movements from time to time from mutual acquaintances of which, for she and Sir David had lived so long abroad, there were surprisingly few. At one time I was told that she intended to found a house in the South of France in memory of Cecil for French writers and artists who might be in need of a rest or a place to work, but I do not think that the idea was ever carried into effect. Mademoiselle Laurent remained with her, I believe, for several years, but at the time of Lady Guthrie's death she was no longer with her and there was no mention of her in the will.

One curious fact emerging from a story so much of which will always remain conjecture: Lady Guthrie stated in *The Life* that the novel which Cecil had completed during those last months in Paris had unaccountably disappeared. No trace of it, so she wrote, was ever found amongst his papers and manuscripts. One is left in doubt as to whether Cecil ever did, in fact, write the book of which he spoke so often in his letters to his mother or whether she, finding it not to her liking, caused it to be destroyed.

The wretched Helbert continued for several years to drag out his existence in Paris—the city in which, as he had once told us sitting on the terrace at Kildonan, he most wanted to live. I last heard of him through a strange coincidence from a hospital nurse who was with us for a short while just before the war. Talking of her professional life which had been largely passed, for she was bilingual, in nursing the British colony in Paris she told me that one of her patients had been a certain Captain Helbert. After we had elucidated the fact that 'her' Helbert and mine was the same man I was naturally anxious to hear anything she could tell me about him, but, disappointingly she could remember very little, only that in delirium he had raved on and on about women. And she had heard, but only in the vaguest manner, that at the time she was nursing him he had been connected with some trouble to do with a diamond ring. Either he had stolen it or perhaps, she thought on the whole that was more likely, he had had it on approval from a shop and then pawned it.

My own last encounter, although really that is not I think the right word, with Helbert was in the autumn of 1902. We were up at Kildonan and had a large party of young people, including our younger son, Ian, by then grown into a schoolboy, staying in the house. The children, having decided that 'polo on bicycles' would be a pleasant way of spending the afternoon, wanted to know where they could find some extra mallets. I suggested that there were probably some old ones in one of the cupboards in the gun room. Ian, accompanied by several of his friends, immediately rushed off to look and I, I do not quite know why, followed them. With regard to the mallets I proved to be right. Ian found several which, although somewhat cracked and generally the worse for wear, were declared to be 'quite good enough for polo'.

'And this,' emerging tousle-headed from the cupboard, Ian held up a cap, 'must have been here for donkey's years. It's gone all green round the edges.'

The thing he held up for inspection was an ordinary tweed cap but something about it had stirred a memory. Before Ian, who had been about to do so, had time to put it on his head I snatched it away from him. It fell on the floor, lining side upwards, and there in the centre in black marking ink was the name of the owner: F. Helbert.

Without a word I turned, picked the thing up with the tongs and then—either to the children's astonishment, or not, for the young, after all, are not much concerned with the vagaries of the middle aged—marched out of the room. I went down to the shore and dropped the cap into the loch.

THE END

# FURROWED MIDDLEBROW

FM1. *A Footman for the Peacock* (1940) . . . . . . . Rachel Ferguson
FM2. *Evenfield* (1942) . . . . . . . . . . . . . . . . . . . . . . Rachel Ferguson
FM3. *A Harp in Lowndes Square* (1936) . . . . . . . Rachel Ferguson
FM4. *A Chelsea Concerto* (1959) . . . . . . . . . . . . . . . Frances Faviell
FM5. *The Dancing Bear* (1954) . . . . . . . . . . . . . . . . Frances Faviell
FM6. *A House on the Rhine* (1955) . . . . . . . . . . . . . Frances Faviell
FM7. *Thalia* (1957) . . . . . . . . . . . . . . . . . . . . . . . . . Frances Faviell
FM8. *The Fledgeling* (1958) . . . . . . . . . . . . . . . . . . . Frances Faviell
FM9. *Bewildering Cares* (1940) . . . . . . . . . . . . . . . . . Winifred Peck
FM10. *Tom Tiddler's Ground* (1941) . . . . . . . . . . . . . Ursula Orange
FM11. *Begin Again* (1936) . . . . . . . . . . . . . . . . . . . . . Ursula Orange
FM12. *Company in the Evening* (1944) . . . . . . . . . . Ursula Orange
FM13. *The Late Mrs. Prioleau* (1946) . . . . . . . . . . . Monica Tindall
FM14. *Bramton Wick* (1952) . . . . . . . . . . . . . . . . . . . . Elizabeth Fair
FM15. *Landscape in Sunlight* (1953) . . . . . . . . . . . . . Elizabeth Fair
FM16. *The Native Heath* (1954) . . . . . . . . . . . . . . . . . Elizabeth Fair
FM17. *Seaview House* (1955) . . . . . . . . . . . . . . . . . . . Elizabeth Fair
FM18. *A Winter Away* (1957) . . . . . . . . . . . . . . . . . . . Elizabeth Fair
FM19. *The Mingham Air* (1960) . . . . . . . . . . . . . . . . . Elizabeth Fair
FM20. *The Lark* (1922) . . . . . . . . . . . . . . . . . . . . . . . . . . . . . E. Nesbit
FM21. *Smouldering Fire* (1935) . . . . . . . . . . . . . . . . . D.E. Stevenson
FM22. *Spring Magic* (1942) . . . . . . . . . . . . . . . . . . . . D.E. Stevenson
FM23. *Mrs. Tim Carries On* (1941) . . . . . . . . . . . . . . D.E. Stevenson
FM24. *Mrs. Tim Gets a Job* (1947) . . . . . . . . . . . . . . D.E. Stevenson
FM25. *Mrs. Tim Flies Home* (1952) . . . . . . . . . . . . . D.E. Stevenson
FM26. *Alice* (1949) . . . . . . . . . . . . . . . . . . . . . . . . . . Elizabeth Eliot
FM27. *Henry* (1950) . . . . . . . . . . . . . . . . . . . . . . . . . Elizabeth Eliot
FM28. *Mrs. Martell* (1953) . . . . . . . . . . . . . . . . . . . . Elizabeth Eliot
FM29. *Cecil* (1962) . . . . . . . . . . . . . . . . . . . . . . . . . . Elizabeth Eliot

Printed in Great Britain
by Amazon